With Open Arms

BOOK YOUR PLACE ON OUR WEBSITE AND MAKE THE ARABESQUE ROMANCE CONNECTION!

We've created a customized website just for our very special Arabesque readers, where you can get the inside scoop on everything that's going on with Arabesque romance novels.

When you come online, you'll have the exciting opportunity to:

- View covers of upcoming books

- Learn about our future publishing schedule (listed by publication month and author)

- Find out when your favorite authors will be visiting a city near you

- Search for and order backlist books

- Check out author bios and background information

- Send e-mail to your favorite authors

- Join us in weekly chats with authors, readers and other guests

- Get writing guidelines

- AND MUCH MORE!

Visit our website at
http://www.arabesquebooks.com

With Open Arms

Kim Louise

ARABESQUE

BET☆ BOOKS

BET Publications, LLC
http://www.bet.com
http://www.arabesquebooks.com

ARABESQUE BOOKS are published by

BET Publications, LLC
c/o BET BOOKS
One BET Plaza
1900 W Place NE
Washington, DC 20018-1211

All Kensington Titles, Imprints, and Distributed Lines are available at special quantity discounts for bulk purchases for sales promotions, premiums, fund-raising, and educational or institutional use. Special book excerpts or customized printings can also be created to fit specific needs. For details, write or phone the office of the Kensington special sales manager: Kensington Publishing Corp., 850 Third Avenue, New York, NY 10022, attn: Special Sales Department, Phone: 1-800-221-2647.

First Printing: July 2005

10 9 8 7 6 5 4 3 2 1

Printed in the United States of America

For Ms. Lola

Acknowledgments

They say, "You can't do it alone." That sentiment is true for me in the writing of this book. I would like to thank meteorologists Jim Flowers, Ryan McPike, and Bill Ranby for answering all of my crazy questions on storm chasing. You guys are the best! Special thanks to Sandra Smith who talked me through the process of making a wedding dress. You awe me with your talent! Thanks to Misherald Brown, Betty Dowdell, and Regina Hightower for being the kind of readers that every writer dreams of having. Your encouragement is a blessing! Thank you Niobia Bryant and Melanie Shuster. Your friendship over the past year has been wonderful! Thanks to Claudia Menza. I appreciate your wisdom and patience more than I can accurately express. As always, thanks to He who created me. I live to serve.

Chapter One

Thirty years ago

Donovan McNeil couldn't breathe. The grown-ups had made him squeeze into a shirt and pants that were too small for him, and who knew how long it would be before he could change back to his play clothes. They said they were waiting for a girl to arrive so they could start shooting. *She better hurry up and come on,* he thought.

All Donovan wanted was to get this silly stuff over with. He hated commercials. Even the ones he was in. He'd started hating them when he discovered how fake they were. Sets instead of real places. Clay models instead of real food.

And all those people who claimed, "This soup is the best. Get this juice. Eat this cookie," had never even tasted the stuff they were talking about.

It was all phony.

"You look so cute, Don!" his mother said. She always said that. On every set. On every shoot. Whether he had food smeared all over his mouth or like today, when he knew that at any minute his clothes might rip apart and he would have to go through wardrobe all over again.

"Uu-uah," he groaned. He was tired and hungry and wished the girl would just get here already!

There were three other kids on the set with him—they were playing on the other side of the room. Somebody's mother probably brought in some toys, or maybe the business people did. Making commercials was like that. They always had food and toys. Sometimes, there were animals like puppies and rabbits, but today just toys.

Donovan never played with the other kids. They always ended up being just like the kids at his school, teasing him or calling him names like Big Boy or Fat Albert. So, he would stay close to his mother until the red lights of the cameras blinked on. Then he would say his lines (if he had any), finish the commercial, and head home with his mom. The sooner he got out of there, the sooner he could get to his short-wave radio and listen for aliens and other weird stuff in the sky.

Donovan sighed again. He couldn't wait until he was a grown-up. The first thing he would do was change his name to something cool like Douglas or William or William Douglas, like one of the older kids in his school. Then he would stop doing all the things he hated doing like the running, jumping, and climbing he had to do in most of these commercials. Even today, he and the other kids were climbing up and down a ladder to a tree house. Then at the end he had to try to catch up with all the kids who'd climbed down and run away. He was supposed to say, "Hey, wait for me!"

His mother was happy. She liked it when he said stuff. Donovan just thought it was more stupid stuff for him to do.

And another thing, when he grew up, he would stop eating so much. His mother was always feeding him. Snacks, snacks, and more snacks. He was tired of that, too!

Donovan looked at the ladder he had to climb. After climbing up and down that thing, he'd be too tired to say his line! Maybe he would ask his mother if he could stop making commercials. Yes! That's what he would do. He knew they made her happy. But maybe she would understand and say he didn't have to anymore. That would be great.

"Where have you been?" one of the grown-ups asked.

Just then a woman came through the doorway. She looked like she should be in charge instead of the people that were. The way she walked and the way she dressed made Donovan think she must be real smart and rich. She was with a girl. This must be the one they'd been waiting for, Donovan thought.

"Look, you all phoned us an hour ago. We got here as soon as we could, and under the circumstances, I'd say that was pretty darn good."

Sherri Raye, the girl who had been there at first, had thrown up when the cameras started rolling earlier that day. This girl must have been there to take her place.

The two came closer and Donovan forgot how tight his clothes were and that for the past two hours he'd been struggling to breathe. All he could think about was the girl coming in the room with her mother.

Was anybody else in the room? Donovan didn't think so. Just him and the girl he couldn't keep his eyes off. She looked like someone really, really smart had made her. She was so pretty, the only reason Donovan knew she was alive—and not a doll or a picture of a doll—was that he could see her walking and breathing and blinking. He didn't think he would ever be able to look at anything else for the rest of his life.

From head to toe, she was dressed in all white— white bonnet, white ruffle dress, white gloves, white stockings, and white patent leather shoes. Now Donovan understood what made his grandmother cry, "Good

God in heaven!" or, "Thank you, Jesus!" at the strangest times. Those were the only words that came to his mind and he'd never been exactly sure what they meant.

Until now.

"Don, are you ready, honey?"

Donovan didn't know if he nodded or spoke. He just knew that finally there was a kid here he wouldn't mind playing with.

"Kids! Come over here," the director said.

"Everybody, this is Morgan Allgood. Morgan, this is Olivette, Gary, René, and Donovan."

"*Dino*van," he heard Gary snicker.

Donovan gritted his teeth and told his anger to go away. But it didn't, and if that kid kept making fun of him, especially in front of the new girl, he would punch him in the mouth.

Morgan's "Hi, hi, hi, and nice to meet you!" made Donovan's heart thump louder than he'd ever heard it.

She said "Nice to meet me," he thought. *She said, "Nice to meet me."*

"Okay, since Morgan is taking Sherri's place, let's rehearse with her a couple of times and then we'll make it happen," the director said, then clapped his hands as if cheering for himself. If there was one thing Donovan hated more than commercials, it was rehearsing commercials.

"Come on, Don," Gary whispered. "Move your dinosaur butt."

That's it, Donovan thought. Before the kid could turn and walk away, Donovan balled up his fist and punched him dead in the mouth.

It didn't happen like it did in the movies, though. Gary didn't fall down or fall out. His head just snapped backward from the blow, and Donovan yowled in pain. Hitting someone in the mouth hurt. Donovan grabbed his hand and rubbed it where it already seemed to be swelling up.

"Hey! Hey!" the director cried. "Break that up!"

"Donovan!" his mother shrieked. "What's gotten into you!"

"Ted, get on the horn again," the director said. "We need another fat kid." Then he looked at Donovan. "Sorry, kid. No fighting on the set."

While Gary and his mother hugged each other and watched with really big eyes, Donovan and his mom slowly walked off the set.

"Do we get a check for today?" his mother asked.

Donovan didn't hear the answer. He only stared at the girl in all white, silently begging her to understand. She frowned as he walked past. But it wasn't a bad frown—he was used to those. It was more like a question. That was good. He couldn't stand to have her look at him like all the other kids did, especially if they were going to get married one day.

Chapter Two

Present day

Van McNeil kept his eyes closed, believing that if he didn't see the woman go, then she really wasn't leaving. But who was he kidding? They all left sooner or later. Pam, Elaine, Marie, Clorissa, and the rest. They all left him when they figured out that he wasn't playing when he told them, "I'm not, nor will I ever be, a one-woman man."

In the past, he'd often wondered how many times a brother had to be out with his latest hottie before all the others wised up and realized that *no, she is not my sister. No, she's not a cousin, or a good friend.*

He fought the urge to turn over and assure the woman putting on her black lace thong that she didn't have to go. To make her know that she need not concern herself with any other honey who might turn his eye, because as soon as he got out of bed, he was determined to rip up his player card, pour acid on the shards, and set fire to whatever was left. But of course a brother like him couldn't go out like that. Van refused to let her know his nose was that far open. And just when he'd convinced himself that it wasn't his heart talking, but the sex they'd had last night, he heard himself say in a voice that was just too high to be manly, "Morgan, don't go."

He was begging, and he didn't like it. After all, what was so big and bad about this woman that had him acting like Mars Blackmon in *She's Gotta Have It?* *Please, baby, please. Baby, baby, please.* But it wasn't just him. Last night Morgan was in the movie, too, and *she* had to have it. Van saw it as his duty to give it to her. And if Morgan's reaction was any indication of how successful he was, she—to coin a phrase—"definitely wasn't mad."

So if Morgan was the one who got all bent outta shape last night—over the top, take it to the max, never had loving like this before—then why was he the one trippin' he wondered, as she zipped up her skirt and buttoned her blouse. Amazing. It was almost as sexy to watch her putting on her clothes as it was helping her take them off.

"You didn't answer me," he said.

She looked up without looking at him. "I know. I'm sorry, Van. Last night was great and all—"

"Great?" he asked, offended. That sat him up. "It had to be more than great. I mean, you were si—"

"Yes." She combed her fingers through her hair. "Look, I've got five go-sees today and in case you don't know what they are . . ."

She had tried to change the subject, but he knew . . . he had made her sing. Really sing. At first it sounded like some Catholic priest kinda stuff. *Aah-aah, aah-aah.* Then it had turned into some Minnie Riperton, *"Lovin' You"* stuff—*la la, la, la, la!* And he hadn't even hit her spot yet. When he did, he could swear he'd heard her softly crooning *"I'm Every Woman."* Both versions. The craziest thing of all was that he'd liked it.

"I know what they are," he said. And he did. He'd been on enough of them; five in one day was pushing it. She'd be pressed for every second and have barely enough time to breathe between appointments. He wondered why Morgan would do that to herself. She didn't look, or act, like someone desperate for a modeling job. As a matter of fact, she seemed to be the exact opposite.

He got up, not bothering to cover himself. She'd seen all of him, *had* all of him. What else was there? For whatever reason, it didn't feel wrong to stand in front of Morgan naked. It felt . . . kinda good, actually. Right.

"What about dinner?" he asked. Inside he was slapping himself upside the head. *Shut up, fool! Shut up! She'll think you don't have any play.* And he had more play than he knew what to do with sometimes. But all of that was out the door, just like Morgan was about to be.

"Sorry, Van," she said. Finally she turned and looked at him. He didn't see her clothes. Too bad, too, because they were nice clothes from what he could remember. All he saw were his arms around her and hers around him. They made a good team last night. Better than . . . Suddenly he didn't want to think about what last night had been better than. It would put him in a mood he didn't want to be in. Worse than the begging mood he was already in.

"I have dinner plans."

He wouldn't allow himself to be jealous. Not this soon. "I want to see you again. Here in Chicago or when we get back."

"Maybe," her mouth said. Her eyes told a different story. A story he was not willing to accept.

Van nodded. He'd punked himself out enough for one night. Time to stop acting like he'd been whipped. God knows that wasn't true.

She opened the door. The light from the hotel hallway spilled into his dark room. It bathed her in its cold, hard light and cast a shadow between them. Van stepped back a bit so that anyone walking by didn't get a full frontal.

Before she left, he had to touch her again. Just one more time. And, if he could help it, not for the last time either. Van reached out and cupped the back of her neck. She didn't keep walking or resist. Instead she responded ever so slightly, her head curving back just a bit. But that was all he needed. He pulled her back toward him and kissed her. Kissed her like he meant it. Kissed her like a strong footnote stating that the door to Van McNeil was open for her for anything, anytime.

He thought she got the message. She moaned softly for a moment, then pulled away. Her eyes stared into his dazed and pleading eyes.

"Do you remember what I told you?"

"Yes," she said. "And thank you. But I'm going to fly back to Atlanta." She pulled away even more. He let her go. "Thanks for the offer, though."

Van stared at her mouth for a moment and spoke his thoughts. "Anytime."

She opened the door all the way, then, and he didn't care who saw him *or* the effect Morgan had on him. She stepped away without another word and headed down the long hallway. Van moved back and closed the door, thinking how good they were last night.

He could get used to that easily, he thought. He didn't want to commit to her and he definitely didn't want to marry her, but to have a woman like that in his hip pocket was not a bad thought.

He lay back on the bed and rested his hands behind his head. He'd done it. He'd finally done it. After all these years, Van had had a megadose of Morgan Allgood. And one thing was certain, he'd have her again.

Chapter Three

"Girrrrrl, I can't believe you left that man standin' there like that."

Morgan smiled while her good friend and famed clothing designer, Connie LaPris—pronounced L'pree—fanned himself vigorously. Morgan and Connie went back almost twenty years. When they first met, Connie LaPris had been Conway Prince. And back then, he'd done everything big. Big Jheri Curl, big gestures, and big dreams. While Morgan and her friends were busy talking about life after college, Connie was already living it.

He'd started by doing everyone in the neighborhood's make up and hair—that included his own. Then he graduated to making clothes, and the next thing you know, he was sewing for everybody. If you lived on the south side of Atlanta in the eighties and didn't have an outfit made by LaPris, you were talked about.

One day Calvin Lockhart, the actor, was in town for a charity fund-raiser and decided to make a few stops in the hood before the event. He saw a young man sporting a LaPris suit and asked him where he got it. The rest was hometown history.

The papers read *Local boy makes good*. Morgan didn't know about the "boy" part, but Connie sure had done allright for himself. For years she did fitting work for him pro bono. But now they had a business relationship. Connie made so much money, he could afford to pay top dollar to fit his clothes. And he did. Morgan flew to Chicago four times a year and also on special occasions, like now.

"Enough about my sex life, Connie. Let's get back to the benefit. Are you sure you want to go with your new stuff?"

"Stuff? Are you calling my designs stuff?"

"Yeah."

"Don't make me cut you!"

"I'd like to see you try."

Connie was a big teddy bear, and the nicest man she'd ever known. Morgan knew he was all talk, and usually backed down without a fight.

"Okay, then, yes, I want to show the new stuff. I want to get it out there. Plus, if it's leaked to the press that it's a new line, people will beat the doors down to get into this thing. The World AIDS Foundation could end up with half a mil."

"And just who would leak the information?"

"Mind your business and try on something else," Connie said, showing Morgan out of the room.

She strolled into the area of Connie's studio she felt most comfortable in—the dressing area. It was massive, just like the rest of the warehouse, with fifteen-foot ceilings, exposed pipes, and brick walls. The warehouse was really one large room, all ten thousand square feet, with equipment, clothing racks, and furniture serving as room dividers.

When Morgan returned, Dol, Connie's assistant, had brought him a carafe of coffee and three newspapers on a tray.

"Did you fall asleep without your **eye** patch on or what?" Connie said, not even looking at the dress that he had pinned on her. Morgan thought she looked good in it.

"What are you talking about?"

"This," Connie said, holding up the *Inquirer.* Four news stories were pictured: Madonna, who reportedly plagiarized her new book; Michael Jordan, threatening to come out of retirement again; a miracle fat-eating pill for dieters; and rap's latest bad boy, Murder One, suspected of stabbing his baby's momma. Whom no one besides Connie would recognize as the woman in the largest picture, holding Murder One's hand, was Morgan.

"So my eyes look puffy. I can't do the cover-girl gig all the time."

"You're a model, sweet thing. You *must* be beautiful—even in your sleep. Now turn around and let me see how this dress looks on someone with a big butt."

"My butt is not . . . that big," she protested, turning around.

"It's big enough. What are you going to do if Mr. Murder, with his *fine* behind—I mean, talk about a big ass— finds out about the weatherman?"

Clyde Turner. Morgan had met him on the shoot of his video for his rap rendition of "Me and Mrs. Jones." They had wanted a woman much older than the rapper's twenty-six years, and she'd been selected. For professionals in her business, music videos could be quite lucrative if you got enough gigs. That, however, was her first and only video.

The song went on to be number one, and Morgan got lots of calls from other producers and directors who wanted to see her again. But after the antics of Clyde's posse—clique, crew, entourage, or whatever the rappers called all the others who hung around them—Morgan felt she'd had enough of that world to last a lifetime.

Little did she know that she and Clyde would hit it off . . . big time. Away from his entourage or the media, he was polite, well mannered, respectful, and walked with his pants pulled up. They became fast friends. And they were still friends to this day, although the media and everyone else claimed they were dating.

And that was fine with both of them.

Being with him had helped her career. Suddenly everybody wanted to know who that older woman with Murder One was. She couldn't count the number of interviews she'd declined. She had no desire to become a tabloid princess.

She came out again, another chiffon dress taped together against her body. Dol fussed over her like an overprotective mother, pulling and tugging at the fabric.

Connie had already downed a cup of coffee. It was his obsession. He cared as much for his fresh-brewed Kenyan beans as he did about fashion. There were two ways to Connie's heart—through his coffee grinder or his sewing machine.

"Well?" Morgan said, posing. It truly was a beautiful gown. Morgan knew it would bring in a huge donation for the World AIDS Foundation. "What do you think?" Morgan asked. She walked and spun as if she were on a runway instead of in Connie's warehouse.

"I think you need to get your groove on more often. You're glowing like a pregnant woman." Then his eyes grew large. "You're not pregnant, are you?"

"Hell, no!" Morgan responded. She realized that this had been her automatic response when people mentioned children, that she'd never taken the time to think about whether she might actually want children someday. And if so, she'd better get busy. She'd be forty soon.

"Ooh, I guess *some*body's got a little nurture nature.

Well, you'd better get a move on sister before your biological clock ticks for the last time."

Morgan laughed, but only half-heartedly. Being childless was slowly losing its appeal.

"Turn around, sweetheart. Connie can't stand to see you that sad."

Morgan did as she was instructed and knew instinctively what to do with her hips, thighs, and legs to make the dress look good—better than it actually did.

"Yes," Connie said. "Those waves of fabric were a marvelous choice. I'm too brilliant for my own mind!"

Connie got up from his throne, tugged the fabric here and there, pulled the shining pink collar away from Morgan's neck. Finally, he tore the collar off. "I like it better with more skin. Of course, your skin, sweetheart, is exquisite. It's not going to look nearly this good on anyone who buys it."

Morgan let the compliment fade into the background against the thoughts suddenly raging loudly in her head. Connie's words were an echo. A husband, children . . . a family. She hadn't exactly lived the kind of life that led to those things. And she knew her fast-paced world wasn't the kind that children could thrive in or a relationship with a husband could readily withstand. So, she'd put those things on hold, and on hold, and on hold again. Eventually, a life like her older sister Yolanda and her youngest sister Marti had seemed more like a dream in someone else's head than her own.

"Ooh, child, you look like a live turkey on Thanksgiving. Whatever it is, let it go, please! You're ruining my design."

Connie threw his hands in the air and made mad, flamboyant circles as if conducting a hip-hop orchestra. That made her laugh.

"Look, sweetheart, your mind is obviously on other

things. I'll call one of the other girls, somebody less hippy. . . ."

Morgan popped Connie upside the head—lightly enough so it wouldn't hurt, but hard enough to make a sound. "That's for threatening to bring some other woman in on my territory. Now tape something else on me or I'll break one of your sewing machines."

Connie plopped back onto his big, gaudy chair. "You are lucky I like you. You know most models aren't allowed to speak during a fitting!"

A sad fact, but often true, Morgan thought. Her friendship with Connie was good that way. She wasn't just a mannequin that moved and breathed. She was a real person who just might have something to say about fashion, and her opinion was valued.

But today she didn't much feel like talking about fashion, which was strange in and of itself. Fashion was something she always loved talking about. But today was not a usual day. Today had started off in the arms of a man she still wasn't sure if she even liked. And though she and Connie had already talked about Van McNeil, she wanted to talk about him again. She was having a hard time keeping her lips from forming his name and describing all the ways in which he'd pleased her, ways she'd thought people made up in fantastic stories of all-nighters with men who had the stamina of horses. But what she'd shared with Van had been the truth. They'd spent hours forgetting the first time they met, the second time they met, and the fact that the only thing they probably had in common was an attraction that neither of them could fathom.

Her pulse raced. It was a good thing she'd left when she did. If she hadn't, she'd still be in his arms, surrendering, coming, and moaning in the strangest most beautiful way.

She would probably be his for a long, long time.

"Now, I get it," Connie said. "You never got up this morning."

"What?"

"*You* are still in bed. The fitting's over. Get dressed, sweetheart. I'll meet you on the roof."

Morgan followed Dol back to the changing area. By the time she put on her own clothes and joined Connie on the roof garden of his warehouse, she'd relived in her mind the entire night with Van.

She'd been pumped. After years of being what was known in the industry as a belly broad, she'd finally auditioned for something that might make her enough money to retire. If her family knew she was interviewing for a job at ESPN, they would probably think she'd gone crazy. Her oldest sister Yolanda would probably recommend a good shrink.

But Morgan needed a change. A crazy, drastic, unexpected change that would transition her from her past-her-prime-supermodel status and still allow her to capitalize on her face for a job.

Part of her had been a little sad though. She regretted all the years she'd spent making money with her looks instead of her mind. When she got a steady job in the cosmetics industry and had been the face on the package of every hair-care product from Soft Sheen to TCB, she'd dropped out of college, favoring photo shoots over final exams. Aside from sewing—which she only did for herself and her family—modeling was all she knew.

Her family had expected to see her on magazine covers and walking down runways. Morgan hadn't done much of that. But she had been able to keep a more-than-decent roof over her head posing for stock photography shoots, corporate videos, and catalog modeling. Recently, however, her cash cow had been her midriff. Morgan was probably the highest-paid African-American midriff model in the business. Her belly button had been a featured part of movie posters, book covers, commercials, and magazine ads. She'd even been a stomach double, if anyone could imagine that, for a couple of actresses.

So even though she'd never been a Cover Girl spokesmodel, a Victoria's Secret model, or in the swimsuit edition of *Sports Illustrated*, she'd done all right for herself in the industry.

But her life of flying from shoot to shoot had gotten old.

Very old.

Morgan had come to Chicago to make a change.

She'd gotten the idea for her next career move while she'd been in the middle of three go-sees in L.A. Some big-time director was shooting a rock-umentary on six-pack abs. He wanted to shoot a montage of generic abs to intersperse with those of celebs. Morgan's agent called to let her know she'd been requested.

Her reputation was getting around.

After spending the day in a room full of folks all half her age, Morgan stiffly realized that her spotlight was fading. She was being—as were most other models her age—replaced by young girls, some of them not even in high school. To them, she was practically a grandma by industry standards.

To unwind, Morgan had holed up in her hotel room with a bag of Reese's Pieces and a game between the Minnesota Vikings and the Seattle Seahawks. She settled in for her favorite pastime . . . watching football. She ate the pieces one by one and cheered as her favorite quarterback, Daunte Culpepper, threw a bullet into the end zone for a touchdown. When the sidelines reporter flubbed her lines and the announcer, Al Michaels, teasingly asked, "How'd you get this job, anyway?" Morgan had started to wonder. How *did* those women get those sportscaster jobs? All at once, her mind started racing and suddenly she wasn't in her hotel room anymore, she was on the sidelines, reporting the action, interviewing players, and best of all spending time with a whole bunch of sweaty, well-muscled men.

She loved the idea.

Morgan knew she would have to do something soon. She'd long since entered the stage when models start branching into other industries to make money. They created perfumes, clothing lines, opened restaurants. But Morgan didn't have the kind of following that would allow her to have the success she would need to make it outside modeling. But talk about football— that's something she could do in a coma, knocked out cold, or under anesthesia.

The combination of large men and physical activity intoxicated her. At first she'd just watched football to see what tight uniforms did to accentuate a man's butt. In time, she'd come to appreciate the sport and all that came with it. Unfortunately, in the world of glamour, not many shared the same affinity for the game as she did. Not the men and not the women. She couldn't even get her family jazzed about a good game. Her brother, maybe, but he was always on tour performing, which was part of his singing career. Her four sisters were busy with their families and not much interested in the grid-iron. So Morgan had spent many an evening with a box of Peanut Butter Crunch and her flat-screen television, yelling and screaming at the players as though they could hear her. She often wished they could. They'd play a lot better and would win a lot more games.

After that evening in the hotel room, Morgan did some research on the Internet and found out about try-out information for a sideline commentator. She kept everything to herself and didn't tell her family anything; she knew what their reaction would be. If she got the job, she would have an announcement to make. If she didn't get the job, she didn't have to tell them a thing.

Morgan finished changing and joined her designer friend on the roof of his warehouse. From the top of the building, where Connie had created a combination mini spa and lounge area, they could see for miles into the next state.

Connie was almost as bad as Morgan's sisters. Almost. He always wanted the details of her love life and generously supplied her with the details of his. The difference was, Connie never told her what to do or insisted she take a particular action. Sometimes he joked around, but mostly he simply listened. And he was a great ear.

Morgan strolled over to the bar, glanced at the bright sun, mixed herself an orange juice and Sprite, and prepared to tell Connie the blow-by-blow details of her encounter with Van.

Morgan had come out of the ESPN office pumped. More pumped than any shoot she'd done in a long time. The thrill of being in the midst of top-notch sportscasters and being on national television in front of millions of people excited her. Covering the games instead of watching them from her living room would be a great thing. And her audition had been impressive, if she did say so herself. As good as Bonnie Bernstein and Suzy Kolber, the current divas of the sports world. The local network affiliate said they would be making a decision very quickly, possibly within the week. Morgan closed her eyes and said a silent prayer as she walked out of the building. Little did she know that the world was a lot smaller than she had imagined.

She didn't have a problem with people patting themselves on the back. Actually, she thought it was unhealthy if you couldn't celebrate your own success. Morgan was headed out of the ESPN office like a new woman. She felt *good*. Immediately she started thinking of all the ways she could celebrate. But first, she would call Clyde and tell him the news.

She put her sunglasses on as soon as she stepped outside. Then she put her earpiece in, said, "Murder," and waited for the call to connect. She was disappointed when the answering machine picked up. "Clyde," she said, turning away from a couple that was arguing just a few feet away. They were so loud, she could barely hear herself. "Clyde, the interview went well, I think. He didn't come out and tell me that I had the job, but—"

Now the couple was getting on her nerves. She turned back around to see a beautiful woman all up in this man's face. She was reading him his rights three ways from Sunday. Then a sliver of recognition slid through her.

The man was Van McNeil.

She had to admit, Van had been difficult to shake off. He was disarmingly handsome, the kind of handsome that was hard to look at or look away from. More than once she caught herself turning to Fox5 to watch him deliver the weather forecast for the week. Always dressed in the most impeccable suits, he was the kind of television personality that probably got shiploads of fan mail. Literally running into him, in Chicago, was a shock—like bringing a character to life.

Darn if he didn't look fine. Dark wavy hair cut short, but still long enough to run your hands through. An olive-brown complexion that made him look East Indian, although her sister Ashley said both of his parents were African-American. He was tall and thick-muscled, just the way she liked a man. For a minute, she couldn't take her eyes off him and would have sworn on a stack of Bibles that she was having a hot flash. Morgan couldn't stop the corners of her mouth from turning up—a good-looking man always made her smile.

Van's expression was not so pleasant. The look of

frustration on his face was unmistakable. Morgan's first thought had been "serves you right!" For the way he had drop-kicked Morgan to the curb a year ago, he deserved some woman to break him down a little bit.

Van tried to usher the woman into a building. Sister wasn't having any of that. People stared and frowned as they walked by. Suddenly, and surprisingly, Morgan felt sorry for the guy. And she resented the woman. If anyone deserved to give Van McNeil a verbal beat-down, it was her.

"Clyde, I'll call you back."

Morgan turned off her phone, stuck the earpiece in her purse, and walked up to the feuding lovers with a plan already formed in her mind.

"There you are!" Morgan said as she approached.

She walked up to Van, pulled him toward her, and placed a big, fat, juicy kiss on his mouth. Not bad, she thought, for a little playacting.

"Van, baby, where have you been? I had to send the kids off with my sister. We didn't think you were coming."

Van's eyes were as big as two moons on his face. "Morgan?" he said slowly. Inside, Morgan laughed herself silly. This was too good.

"Where are my manners?" she said, extending her hand to the woman whose face looked like she'd belched up bad pizza. "I'm Mrs. McNeil."

The shock spread to Van and his friend instantaneously. The expressions on their faces were priceless.

"You're married? And you have kids?"

Morgan played along into her reaction. "My husband is so modest. Now, I'm sure you two have important business, but I really must steal him away. I'm starving and need to get some lunch." She rubbed her stomach then and looked lovingly at Van. "You know how the baby kicks when I don't eat regularly."

The woman spewed a line of filth a mile long at Van,

then stormed off down the street so fast Morgan didn't know a sister could move that quickly in six-inch heels.

As soon as the woman turned the corner, Morgan let out the laugh she'd been holding. "Are you all right?" she managed to say between chuckles.

"I am now. Thanks. I think."

Um, that voice. She thought it sounded like a combination of dark coffee and good sex. Whether on television or in person, it still had the power to make her shiver with delight.

"Don't mention it. I couldn't let that woman just beat up on you like that." *Not when I deserve that honor,* she wanted to add. "What did you do to her?"

"She was getting too serious. I told her to lighten up."

Traffic on the sidewalk increased. Lunchtime. People dashing quickly, gulping down coffee to-go and sandwiches on the run. Didn't anybody just take it easy anymore? Cars honked and voices floated past them as they stood in front of each other for a moment. Morgan guessed that neither one of them knew what to say next. And, frankly, she was quite content to soak up the sensual aura of Mr. Van McNeil up close. Nearly a year had gone by since their disastrous date, but the memory of it was still fresh and moist like wet paint.

The man was handsome in every way possible. Some guys had nice eyes, some soft hair, others perfect teeth, a great body, or a nice voice. When it came to men, a woman was lucky to get one of those things. Sometimes, if she was really lucky, she got two. But Van had the whole package. Even in her world of beautiful people, that was a rarity. Some of the male models she'd met were really good-looking, but they were short. Or they were gorgeous from afar and in photos, but face-to-face they had a lazy eye or Quasimodo teeth. She'd seen men whose upper body looked great, but they stood on chicken legs. There was almost always something. But when it came to the total package, Van was doin' the dang thing!

"Where're you headed?" he asked.

"I'm on my way to my hotel." She motioned down the street.

"Mind if I walk with you?"

Yes, her mind shouted. *You're the guy who walked out on me during our first date. I haven't forgiven you for that, you turd!* Her mouth said, "No, I don't mind."

They walked in typical Midwest late summer weather—slightly overcast, an undertone of coolness in the wind. One never knew whether to carry an umbrella or wear a light jacket. Morgan had neither. Van, on the other hand, looked like he was ready for anything.

She had grown accustomed to deflecting men's leering and appraising glances like Jackie Chan blocking punches. Van was a whole 'nother story. He absorbed all the slow once-overs and flirtatious looks from women passing by like the bloodstream absorbing a potent drug: the more he got, the more handsome he became. His smile broadened. He even nodded to a couple of women as they walked. He loved the attention, and he got as good as he craved.

"So what are you doing in Chicago?" he asked.

That was a good sign. It meant that her sister hadn't told her man and her man hadn't told his best friend Van.

"I'm on a few go-sees," she said vaguely. She didn't believe in telling all her business so she kept the ESPN interview to herself.

"Still modeling?" he asked.

"It pays the bills," she said.

They were getting close to her hotel. She was eager to get her feet out of her three-inch Blahniks and say good-bye to Van; he was making her forget that for the past several months, she'd sworn off men in general—dating and sex in particular. Every step they took together made that promise to herself harder to keep.

"So what are *you* doing in Chicago?" she asked, hoping to detour her mind from the direction in which it was moving.

"Conference," he said. "Three hundred and fifty meteorologists all in one hotel."

Morgan frowned. "Sounds, uh, exciting."

"Actually, it can be. Some of the speakers talk about the times when they've had to report weather from the middle of a storm. They've got pictures, video. Better than *Storm Stories* on the Weather Channel because it's not staged, it's the real thing."

It was all coming back to her now. Before he had skipped out on their date, he had talked on and on about weather. She had no idea clouds could be so interesting . . . to anyone. Maybe he wasn't perfect after all.

"Well, this is me," she said as they reached the front of the Westin Hotel where she was staying. The Jacuzzi in her room was calling to her loud and clear. Looking into Van's handsome-times-ten face, something else called to her, too—the desire to be held in his strong arms. In the interest of her time-out from the fast life, she decided not to listen.

"Listen, Morgan, let me take you to dinner. I want to thank you for getting that woman out of my face. Besides, I owe you a proper dinner anyway."

She gnashed her teeth at that statement. Should she let this trifling yet gorgeous man try to make it up to her? Not if she wanted to keep her temperature down and her panties up. She decided to pass.

"Thanks for the offer, Van, but it's not necessary. Let's just call it even, okay?"

His eyes molested her sweetly. She felt as though her clothes had just melted off her body at his will; She imagined that she was standing naked on a downtown sidewalk during the Chicago lunchtime rush. Thankfully, her stomach growled and broke her daydream.

"If you're sure I can't persuade you . . ."

Damn, why did God make men with voices that made you want to find the nearest bed and fall back on it? Despite the fact that her mind was already imagining the end of a night on the town with Van, Morgan couldn't compromise her goal. She was just starting to enjoy her much-needed year off from men.

She couldn't resist. She had to cop a little feel, so she touched him on the shoulder. The fabric of his suit was soft to the touch, but there was no mistaking the hard muscle beneath. She sighed inside.

"You take care, Van. It was good to see you." She used her runway strut to walk away—she couldn't resist that either. She wanted to give Van a little somethin'-somethin' as a forget-me-not. She tossed her head and let wavy, no-weave hair whip slowly around. He was watching. "Enjoy the conference," she said, and entered the hotel.

Morgan entered the building and took a right toward the elevator, thoughts of her interview lost to questions. What were the chances of her bumping into him again before she left? And what on earth was that wonderful cologne he was wearing?

Chapter Four

Morgan got the answers to all her questions less than twenty-four hours later. Bored in her room, she decided to see if there was a sports bar within walking distance. The television in her room wasn't large enough for her to really enjoy the game the way she liked. There had to be someplace in the neighborhood that had big screens and cold beer. She didn't regularly drink beer—or anything she knew would immediately turn to sugar in her system—but something in her soul wanted to break the rules tonight, do something exciting.

Maybe she'd order light beer.

Ten minutes and three swigs later, Morgan sat at the bar. The screen she watched looked as tall as her five-ten-in-flats body. She picked up the bottle and, drinking straight from the neck, coaxed the cold, hard, tart beer down her throat. Her team was winning, but just barely. Normally she'd be shouting game plays to the quarter-back by now, but since she was in a public place, she reined in her exuberance, until . . .

The play of the game. After a kickoff, Tony Fisher ran the ball back for a ninety-six-yard touchdown. "Yes!" she exclaimed, pumping a fist in the air. Her shouts of encouragement had followed him all the way down the field and into the end zone. The bar erupted. Some for, and some disappointed by the fantastic play.

Morgan settled back into her seat, feeling that all was right with the world. She was about to take a celebratory swig of light beer when she noticed a man out of the corner of her eye. She didn't get a good look at his face. He came up beside her, leaning against the bar. She didn't turn around. It was best not to encourage strangers, but it felt like he was taking his time checking her out.

"You're cheering for the wrong team," he said.

Morgan stiffened. She knew that voice. It was the voice that told everyone in Atlanta their weekend weather outlook. Suddenly her weekend outlook wasn't so good. She tore herself from the game long enough to stare up at him.

"Please. Ahman Green couldn't beat eleven old ladies in rusty wheelchairs."

"You're crazy! Green is the best running back in the league."

"I doubt that, but even so, he coughs up the ball way too much."

That shut him up. Morgan smiled and took another sip of beer.

Van signaled for the bartender to bring him a beer and angled toward her.

The place was upscale as far as sports bars went, and huge, living up to its name, Big Bar. The windows were so large they were more like walls and the television over the lobby was the size of a dinosaur.

"I'll bet they win this game."

"How many of those have you had?" she asked. She wanted to say, "Go away, Van. Leave me alone. Let's let bygones be bygones."

"This is my first," he said, holding up the bottle of

light beer, same as her own. "And if my team wins, I'd like to have another drink, maybe wine. With you."

Despite her initial reaction, the pit of her stomach felt golden and warm at the thought of having a glass of wine with Van.

"Besides," he continued, "it would give me a chance to redeem myself for my behavior on our first date."

"And if I win?" she asked, noting disappointedly that her team had just fumbled the ball.

"Name it," he said, looking sexy and devourable. He turned up the beer, emptying out in one drink what it would have taken her three to do. *Men*, she thought, *so amazingly different from women.*

"Do I have to name it now?" she said, wanting to mull over her choices.

"No. There are three more quarters to go." He signaled the bartender and ordered a Cosmopolitan and another beer. When they came, he paid.

"Enjoy the game," he said, heading toward a table near the corner of the room where a woman watched with a stare hot enough to burn through steel.

Ain't that just like a dog, Morgan thought. *He's over here flirting with me while he's on a date. Unbelievable.* But that thought didn't stop her from watching him walk away.

She didn't just watch him walk away, she indulged herself—something she hadn't allowed herself to do recently. Morgan had put herself on fast-life "time-out." Even though she was a low-key model who kept her gigs under the radar, she'd still found out quickly what it was like to live the life of the glitz and glamour. Parties, celebs, jetting whenever, wherever. She'd done that for the first three years she got regular jobs and steady work. She saw more fast, flashy flesh than she cared to remember. Money, drugs, and skin were the name of the game. And she played it well for a few years before she got burned out. And the men! They weren't slaves, but almost, except for the ones who were supa-fine or had so much money, that models drooled over them.

It's usually the other way around, though.

She'd certainly had her share of supa-fine men. For a while, that was all she dated. Morgan didn't think she planned it that way, it had just happened. Unfortunately, most of them had their heads in the clouds, in her pocket, up their behinds, or between another woman's legs. So they never lasted long.

The longest relationship she'd had had been with Clyde "Murder One" Turner. Over the past two years, he had come into her life and made it better—crazier— but better. Now she felt like she could live the fast life on her own terms. She was not attending some function to be a decoration for a man, She was hanging with a good friend. That took a lot of "the hectic" out of her hectic life. That's when she decided that there was no looking back. No more returning to that crazy world of the rich and fabulous. Morgan wanted something a little more boring. And she found it.

She decided that if she really wanted to make changes in her life, she had to remove the thing that made her most susceptible to it in the first place—men. And, more specifically, sex.

Sex, more importantly good sex, was Morgan's weakness. If a man could bring her to the big O on a consistent, regular, creative, prolific, inventive basis, she was hard to get rid of—for a while anyway. And Van had a walk that said, without doubt or hesitation, "I'm very good with my body."

Sometimes a woman could tell which men had a way with their sexuality by their walk, the way they moved. And that if the two of you ever wound up in bed together . . . call the fire department.

She wondered if Van studied women in the same way. Paid attention to them. Learned them. He seemed self-centered, yet at the same time, he seemed the kind of man who could lie next to a woman for days without her ever getting tired of him—ever.

Several words jumped into her head the first time Morgan saw Van: Playa-playa, Mack-a-Don, Cool Nasty, and Pimp2K. Since her sister Ashley had introduced them, Morgan figured he couldn't be that bad. But when he left before dinner came on their first and only date, just one word entered her head.

Dog.

You'd think she would get the hint. A hint that big should slap a woman upside the head, right? Humph. After eight months, Morgan's brain was still playing *what if* games with her.

What if he had stayed? What if she had come back to the table before he left? What if she hadn't left the table? What if she had made it plain that he would get some that night?

Morgan kept wondering what was wrong with her. Why couldn't she shake off that make-believe date? She'd had an easier time forgetting men with whom she'd had long relationships. But Van was unforgettable. And since she'd spent the last few months not forgetting him, Morgan took her time remembering when they finally caught up with each other again.

She'd just started on her second beer, the one he bought her. Already he'd flirted with the waitress, visually checked on Morgan a few times, and caught the eye of a much older woman who was out with a man Morgan assumed was her husband, all while carrying on a conversation with the woman sitting with him at his table.

Damn, he was good . . . in a bad way, of course.

She'd all but forgotten the football game was on. It was much more interesting to see how the attraction game worked from the other side's perspective.

Morgan had to admit, being the center of attention

was like wearing a favorite pair of high-heel pumps: it fit Morgan just right and made her look good. She was so used to turning heads when she walked into a place—it was nice to see the flip side of that, and interesting to watch. Every woman in the bar had looked at Van at least three times. He soaked in the light of their interest like a sunbather at the beach. But he did it in a way that wasn't arrogant, self-centered, or pompous. It was just the way he was. A smile—however flirtatious or lascivious—was like fuel to him, like air and water. Morgan recognized it because she lived it. Then she realized the truce had been called already. In a way, they were like twin souls. She couldn't work it nearly as well as he did, though. Where she came from, a woman who worked a room like that was a slut, a whore, or worse. But in a world of double standards, a handsome man was being, well, a handsome man. Morgan chuckled out loud even though she was in a public place by herself. *Show's over,* she thought, and resumed watching the big screen.

"Care to share the joke?" a man asked. "I could use some humor." He ordered a shot of Jack Daniel's and sat down beside her.

The words *none of your freaking business* were poised at the tip of Morgan's tongue, ready to strike, but she reined them in. People could be so nosy she thought, and decided to give the man exactly what he deserved. A straight answer.

"See the brother at that table?" she asked, pointing at Van. "I'm laughing at him."

"Thanks," the guy said to the bartender and paid for his drink. "Why? Did he make a joke or are you just cruel?"

The man beside her was nice-looking. He wasn't in Van's league, but he was definitely easy on the eye. Tall, stocky, mid- to late forties. He was built more for wrangling bulls than hanging in bars. He wore a long-sleeved denim shirt, jeans, and Timberland boots. The only thing keeping the yee-haw at bay was the missing Stetson. She wished she'd seen him first instead of Van.

Van was flash and fortune in designer clothes and a million-dollar smile. He had eyes anesthesiologists would kill to get their hands on because they could definitely knock a woman out cold. Morgan told herself not to stare at them for too long or she would be down for the count.

"No, it's just funny how he's got about five or six different women on a string in this place."

"Including you?" he asked, swallowing a sip of whiskey.

"Not even," she said, noticing that her voice didn't sound convincing.

"You think it's funny to string women along?"

"Of course not. I just think it's funny that he thinks he can."

The man took another sip of whiskey and a slow glance around the bar. "You're probably right. I don't think there's a woman in here who hasn't given him the once-over a couple of times." Then he rested his dark eyes on Morgan. "That is, except for you, right?"

Morgan nodded and pulled a nice-sized gulp of beer. Best to put something into her mouth before something bad came out, like, "No, me, too!"

"I'm Brax Garrett," the man said, extending his hand. He had big, strong workman hands. The kind of man-hands Morgan rarely encountered in the world of photographers and moneymakers who have standing appointments with their own personal nail technicians.

The bartender must have overheard. "Brax? Is that short for Braxton?"

"Not unless you want a black eye," he said without looking up.

"Wow," Morgan said, wondering if the man was just rude or, well, just rude.

"I've had a hard day," he responded.

"Want to talk about it?" Morgan asked, wondering why she asked that question of a total stranger.

He grunted and kept his eye on his drink. "Not in this lifetime."

"I'm Morgan," she said, and shook the hand that swallowed hers. It felt strong and thick and calloused, but not neglected.

"You look familiar, Morgan. Where've I seen you before?"

Morgan doubted this man had many encounters with the world of glitz and glamour. The only thing she could think of was a bad choice she made more than ten years ago.

"Unless you've got a *PlayaBoy* calendar from a long, long time ago, probably nowhere."

His glaze was hot, sizzling. It raked over her body quickly, thoroughly. Then a flare of recognition ignited in Brax's eyes. "I remember," he said, then finished his whiskey.

"You're kidding," Morgan said, refusing to believe that this stranger could recall a shoot she did so long ago.

Brax sat back, looked toward the ceiling, and squinted his eyes. "August . . . nineteen . . . ninety-five."

"Wow. That's good." She eyed his disappearing glass of whiskey. "Let me get the next one."

His eyes flashed appreciatively, then rehardened with seriousness. "Deal," he said.

"So, Brax"—she said his name with brass, stretched it out—"what do you do?"

"I'm in transportation," he responded. Then he gave her an inoffensive once over. "You?"

"I'm still modeling. These days my gigs are much more respectable."

"Such as?"

Here we go, she thought. Guys—no, make that people

in general—always wanted a rundown of all the places they might have seen her. Sometimes she was thorough, if it was someone she wanted to impress.

"Hair products, skin-care products, stuff like that."

He nodded. "I thought all the model types lived in New York."

"I do, for part of the year. I have an apartment in Manhattan. I also have a place in Atlanta. My family's there. I like to be near them when I can."

"Small world. I've got people in Savannah. I'm actually headed back down there in a few days."

"I love Savannah. I thought about moving there once."

"Sixty-five, twenty-four, seventy-five," Brax said, rolling his glass between his fingers absentmindedly.

"I beg your pardon?" Morgan said, hoping those weren't measurements he was quoting.

"The interstate. I drive it all the time. It's the quickest way home. I've got to stop for a day or two in Indianapolis, but after that, it's straight to Savannah."

"So where's home, Mr. Garrett?"

He stared into the bottom of his glass and then said, "Where my heart is,"

This man is far more interesting than Van, she thought. Morgan had already turned from the pimp spectacle in the outer bar, and even from the game. The man brooding over the drink beside her looked like someone who knew how to handle a temporary love thang. Keep it short and sweet, the way it's supposed to be. And when it's over, no regrets. Van, on the other hand—with his flash and feng-shui hair—would always try to get the upper hand. Brax would be content to let her have the upper hand if she wanted it for as long as she wanted it. That was as appealing as—

"Let me get you another drink," Van said, bumping into her thoughts. He stepped heavily between she and Brax and then turned in her direction. They stared at each other for a moment too long to count. He didn't say it, but the admonition in his eyes said, "Don't even think about it."

Men, Morgan thought, again. She loved them. They were so predictable. Always up for a challenge. One always trying to outdo the other. "I think you should concentrate on your team. If they lose, you lose." She crossed one of her long, stocking-free legs over the other. Strangely, his stare was not diverted. It held fast on her eyes.

"You let me know if you need . . . anything," he said, turned just enough to brush his thigh against hers, and returned to his seat.

Brax stared straight ahead, away from her, Van, and the big-screen TV. "Husband, boyfriend, or toy?" he asked, not blinking, not moving.

She noticed that his whiskey glass was empty. She signaled the bartender for another. "None of the above," she said.

"Take my advice," Brax said. "You'd be better off with a vibrator. It'll do what you want, when you want, for as long as you want. And you don't have to listen to BS or tell it how good it looks. Now," he continued and threw back the fresh shot of Jack, "if you want some real company . . ." He let his words trail off.

A proposition. Morgan sighed. They came so frequently, the thrill was almost gone. For Brax to be as interesting as she found him, his proposition fell flat on her ears. In her mind, she'd made it tempting. In reality, it was just another invitation to sleep with a stranger. She reminded herself that she'd just spent the last six months trying to dry out from that.

I'm definitely off the wagon, Morgan thought. *I'm not going to make it through the night.* Between Brax's rough handsomeness and Van's eye-blinking beauty, she'd go crazy. But as much as the essence of a rugged man pulled at her, what she felt was what any woman feels when she's in the company of an attractive man. Van was another story altogether. Considering everything—the botched first date, the months of not seeing him, the fact that he'd flirted with every beautiful woman in the bar— a deeper connection wouldn't let her look away from him for too long. Wouldn't keep him out of her thoughts for more than a moment. There was an emotional tether she found fascinating and wanted to explore.

Brax turned to her for an answer. His eyes burned intensely. There was lust there, sure. There was also something else simmering just beneath the surface. Sadness, maybe. She couldn't quite make it out.

"Brax," she said, and touched the back of his hand. She couldn't resist. His hand was warm, hard, rough. He looked away slowly, but his expression never changed.

"I hope he's worth it," he said, reaching into his pocket. He pulled out a twenty, slid it onto the counter, and stepped off the bar stool.

Hmm, did I make a mistake? she wondered as soon as he stood. He was solid from head to toe, body-builder thick and packed into his denim. She ordered a Sprite and hoped that Van was worth it, too.

"Well, Ms. August, thanks for the company."

"You're welcome, Mr. Garrett." Morgan gave him a real smile, not the one that was practiced and automatic.

"If you ever have a need," he said, leaving a business card on the bar, "I'll be in the area for a few days."

She kept her eyes on him as he swaggered out the door. If he had gotten on a horse and rode off into the sunset, she wouldn't have been surprised.

Nice butt, she thought, sliding the card into her purse and turning just in time to see the game score. Twenty-seven-six. That's okay, she thought, then took a sip of Sprite. Win or lose, if it got her some time with Van, she'd won.

By the time the last quarter rolled around, she was bored and disappointed. Her team was losing and the men were leaving. Some of the women went with them. All except Miss Giggles over there with Van. The woman had the craziest laugh Morgan had ever heard. She sounded like she was laughing and burping at the same time. Morgan didn't know how Van, or anyone else in the bar for that matter, could stand it. Miss Giggles had a round head, round eyes, round everything. Morgan could see how Van found her attractive. She was wide-eyed and cute, in a doting-puppy sort of way. A couple of times Morgan had to choke back the urge to walk over and pat her on the head. "Good girl," she wanted to say. Or, better yet, "Fetch. Fetch me my man."

The last quarter of the game was a snoozer. Morgan couldn't believe that Van was actually waiting until the end to gloat. She also couldn't believe how much time he spent glancing at her, checking her out from the corner of his eye, like he wanted to make sure she was still at the bar and hadn't snuck out.

At this point, her team had lost and she wasn't going on any wine date with Van, tonight or maybe ever. As a matter of fact, she'd had enough of the sports-bar scene for one evening. She drained the last of her drink and rose to leave.

Before she could walk out of the bar, the woman from Van's table stormed past her. Van was on her heels, but he didn't try to stop the woman. Instead, he watched her walk for a bit, then turned to Morgan. "I didn't mean to make you jealous back there," he said.

Morgan crossed her arms, cocked her hip to the side, and looked at him like he was crazy. "Don't worry, you didn't."

His eyes rose in surprise.

"I know a performance when I see one," she said.

He smiled but didn't admit whether she'd pegged his actions correctly. "What about the game?" he asked.

"Bump the game. I'm out of here."

"Well, if not the game, then . . . what about us?" he

asked. His eyes bore hotly into hers. His invitation stoked the embers of a fire that had been burning softly for eight months.

Something told her Van was still trifling. But she had been a good girl for nearly a year. Maybe it was time to have some fun.

And the rest was sexual history.

Alone in his hotel room, Van forced his mind to remember why he was in Chicago. For some people it was coffee, for some alcohol, sex, shoe fetishes. For some women, it was shopping, for some men gambling. For him, it was stormy weather. Dark clouds. Unsettled skies. He believed Mother Nature was a beautiful woman with untamable mood swings and a brilliant, yet sometimes cruel sense of humor.

He loved every season-changing aspect of her—especially when she got mad or started crying or both.

To keep his mind off the turbulent woman who had left his hotel room in the middle of the night, Van focused on the turbulent woman he understood better than he understood himself. He switched on his laptop and accessed the National Weather Service Web site. If Morgan wouldn't cooperate, maybe the jet stream would.

He zoomed in on a radar map of the country. If his hunch was correct, he would be leaving Chicago just in time to intercept a severe storm. After investing eight thousand dollars in new equipment—laptop, scanner, digital camera, digital video, even a new PDA cell phone, he was ready to chase the fiercest storm.

Fiercest storm? That would be Morgan Allgood. She had been a fierce storm last night. He stopped watching the time-lapse of the approaching front and turned to stare at the bed, replaying in his mind what had happened there, and then on the floor, then the chair, and then the bed again. He'd had a better workout with

Morgan than he got with his Bowflex. He'd like to think that they worked each other, but the truth was, she'd worked him. He didn't know a woman could be so intense. He was good at predicting storms, but he never could have predicted the tempest in his hotel room last night, even with the best equipment and all the fantasies he'd had about Morgan over the years.

Truth really was stranger than fiction. And the truth was, he knew that even after just one night with Morgan, his membership in the player's club hall of fame was in jeopardy. His fascination with Morgan Allgood had paid off, big time. He'd done the thing he'd wanted to do for years: kiss her, hold her, pleasure her, bury himself inside her tender, moist, and accommodating flesh. Now it was time to get back to what he did best: study the sky to keep people informed and safe. He would concentrate on the weather conference he'd driven all the way to Chicago to attend and once and for all put Morgan Allgood out of his mind. Maybe he would find the woman he'd met in the hotel lobby yesterday, take her out for a drink, get the most out of the workshops, and drive back to Atlanta.

Alone.

He turned off his computer, satisfied that fate had allowed him to quench his decades-long thirst for Morgan, determined not to linger in the place in his mind that was telling him he wanted more. She was one storm he'd made up his mind not to chase.

Chapter Five

Thanks to Morgan, Van wouldn't be spending any "quality" time with Collette. Not that he was mad; Collette Jamison had become a problem. He'd met her a long time ago when he was in grad school, before he'd learned the golden rule: never get involved with a woman who can't *play*. Recently Collette had gotten way too serious about him, talking about flying to Atlanta to spend more time with him. He couldn't have that. Ms. Jamison didn't take the news that he wanted her to back off too well. But now he had some time to kill. He had thought he would spend his first day in Chi-town putting in some serious time with Collette. Instead, he had pulled an all-nighter with Morgan and now had an entire day to fill until the welcome reception for the conference started that evening.

He could stay in his room and check the Doppler radar for updates, send a few e-mails, look at a few products on eBay, or he could get out of the hotel altogether.

He decided on the latter.

On the way out, Van stopped on the conference floor. Every year he attended this conference—he liked to check out the facilities, get his bearings, and give himself a preview of events before the conference got underway.

A row of vendors' booths greeted him on the third floor. The theme of this year's conference was "Verifiable Vortexes," which was a trumped-up way of saying "Calling all storm geeks." Most of the time, the National Weather Association did well in presenting information in a professional, upstanding manner. But sometimes, like this year, when the association needed to raise some money and would do just about anything to bring in the dollars, they let their professionalism slip to a level that encouraged weirdos and oddballs. He knew he was in for an interesting week.

Van had never been afraid to show his emotions, yet he felt the disgust drawing his face into a frown as he walked past vendors only a fool would buy from. The charlatans, setting up booths, were selling storm monitors, tornado trackers, and wind watchers. They looked like contraptions a teenager put together in a basement—in the same league as divining rods, prayer cloths, and healing gloves. Unfortunately, these were the booths that would probably have the longest lines. Most people wanted quick answers and magic potions for everything. The reality—that someone else was in charge of things, weather being just one, and that even with the most sophisticated and expensive equipment on earth, storm finding, tracking, and predicting was still largely a matter of luck and instinct—fell well beyond the minds of many weather fanatics.

Van glanced around, looking for something engaging, something to let him know that the conference would be worth his time and money. First impressions were everything. So far it looked like the annual conference had a long way to go before it would be ready for this evening's opening session. Men in hotel maintenance uniforms moved like circus performers, carrying cables, putting up banners, and operating levers that turned one enormous room into eight smaller ones.

He told himself that if the first couple of days at the conference turned out to be a bust, he would scout out the cluster of hotels in the area and cajole his way into another weeklong conference that was more interesting. He'd heard the National Order of Bricklayers, the International Skeet Shooting Club, and a Mary Kay Convention were in town. One of them ought to be informative or at least interesting. His money was on Mary Kay. Van had a mind to do a walk-through anyway. It would do his mind, and hopefully his body, good to see a hotel full of beautiful women. He mentally put that on his list of things to do in Chicago.

As he got farther into the conference area, the louder his stomach growled. Food, more specifically breakfast, became his mission before he did any more looking around.

"Van!" a voice shouted. "Van McNeil!"

He looked to the right, and barreling down the hallway was a tall, thin man with a bald head and eyes that made him look like he was in a constant state of surprise. Van stuck out his hand, but prepared to be enveloped.

"Rich!" Van said, trying to match the man's enthusiasm, but it was impossible. Within seconds Van was hugged by a man known as the car salesman of weather forecasters. When it came to delivering the weather on television, Erdrich Kenison was as unique as they came. His style was flamboyant, almost manic. He talked loud, fast, and used a trunkful of props like giant sunglasses to tell the folks in Oshkosh, Wisconsin, population 60,005, that the weather outlook for the next few days would be clear skies and sunny.

Van remembered the time Rich was a keynote speaker

at the National Weather Association conference and he blew out the speaker system when he used the mike. For some reason, the speakers were on the same circuit as the lights, so one second after the speakers blew, the lights went out. But one monkey never stopped Rich's show. He kept right on talking. By the time the lights came back up, Rich was nearly finished. That was one of the best presentations Van had ever seen. It had taught him that, no matter what the constraints were and no matter what happened because of them, keep on going. The goal hadn't changed—he would keep going until he got there. From that moment on, he and Erdrich Kenison had been tight.

Van pushed away from Rich's hug of death before he suffocated.

"I didn't know you were coming! Why didn't you tell me?"

Van stood back. In addition to being loud as hell, Rich's breath was kickin'. "I didn't decide to attend until the last minute."

"Well, this is just great!" Rich shouted and slung a long arm across Van's shoulders. Good thing Rich was brilliant. Anyone else who would have tried this crazy mess with Van would have been laid out with a right cross.

"Walk with me while I check on the booths!"

"The booths" were a solid row of hucksters, charlatans, gadgets and devices Van had scanned only moments before. Everything on those tables looked like it belonged in an infomercial and should be sold for $19.95.

"They put me in charge of vendors this year, buddy! I wanted to do something more fun, so I let the fund-raising committee do what they wanted!"

Rich leaned over in a gesture that signaled he was going to attempt whispering. Van braced for an on-slaught of hollering and halitosis.

"It's a fiasco!" he whispered.

Van stepped out of his embrace. Rich was his dog, but his breath was ruining Van's appetite.

They had both been first-timers at the '95 conference in Reno. No one would think it to look at him, but despite his unusual nature, Rich was a hit with the ladies. Maybe all weathermen were. All Van knew was, Rich would give him a run for his money in the Mack of the Year contest.

"Look at this!" Rich said.

Oh, hell. He's going to talk about these people, loudly, right in their faces. Van gritted his teeth, hoping that none of the sedate-looking vendors were really a loose cannon who would take offense to Rich's words or his breath. Van did not feel like fighting today.

They stopped at the booth selling what a giant sign professed to be the world's best "Storm Stalker"—guaranteed to keep a chaser on the trail of the storm in any weather. Van would like to think that what stopped him in his tracks was the ridiculous sign and the slender piece of wood on the table that resembled an incense holder. It was partly that. But it was mostly the woman arranging brochures on the table. She looked like someone a man would want to remember for a long time. And just the type of woman that might be able to rid his mind of images of Morgan Allgood that had been flashing through his head all morning. He couldn't have produced clearer pictures if he had recorded their marathon session on a digital video camera. He hadn't. He didn't need to. His memory was more vivid than any camera. If he inhaled even slightly, he could still smell her perfume on his skin, draw in her femininity as if it were all over his body taunting him, teasing him, making him regret the fact that he didn't bolt the door last night, block the exit with his body, or kiss her into submission one more time.

The world was getting smaller by the minute, though.

He was sure he would run into her back in Atlanta one day. And when he did, he would find a better way to convince her to stay longer. He realized they had a long way to go before they would have their fill of each other. For a moment last night, he thought Morgan was going to accept his offer and drive back with him to Georgia. Her hesitation was only for a second, before her soft "No" came out of the sweetest lips he'd ever tasted.

One day, he thought, *I will taste them again.* Until that time, he had to do something or his thoughts and desires for Morgan would drive him crazy.

Van reached for one of the brochures on the table. He flipped through it, not reading, but surrendering to his impulses.

One day, Morgan Allgood, he thought to himself, again. *Until then . . . I need a companion after tonight's reception.*

"I'd like to learn all about this Storm Stalker . . . say . . . after the reception?" Van said and smiled. Women had a thing for his smile.

The woman looked up. Her brown eyes softened. She returned his smile and licked her pair of near-perfect lips.

That was easy.

Every time Morgan thought about the incident outside of ESPN with Van and that woman, she cracked up. People were staring at her like she was crazy on the elevator to her hotel room. She felt good. Her day was going well. If she could just get Van's all-too-handsome face out of her mind, it would be even better.

The suite she was staying in looked like it belonged in a magazine. With a living room, dining room, bar, and entertainment room, Morgan hoped she wouldn't get lost on the way to the bedroom that night.

Of course, if she had a man like Van in her room, it wouldn't matter where the bed was. They would find each other by instinct alone. His essence was just as potent to her now as it had been the first time they'd met. She thought if she had been blindfolded in a dark room wearing ear and nose plugs, her body would still find him.

But not today. Today she would do the second thing she came to Chicago to do: start making her sister's wedding dress.

Morgan's sister Ashley was getting married to her best friend, Gordon Steele. They had wanted a fall wedding, but Ashley's schedule as a *Cirque du Soleil* singer meant they had to plan their union around her performances. With her being new and having to perform two shows a day, it didn't give them much leeway to plan. When a brief window opened in Ashley's performance schedule in August, the happy couple decided to jump at the chance. Everyone in the family had been scrambling to put everything together ever since.

Morgan was the official wedding dressmaker in the family. She'd made dresses for her oldest sister Yolanda and her niece Amara. Even when her next-oldest sister Roxy eloped with her now-husband, Haughton, Roxy wore an evening gown Morgan had made her years ago.

But Morgan was behind. If her sister knew how far behind she was—as in not even started—Ashley would panic. Her wedding was in two weeks. And until this point, Morgan had had her using a stand-in gown for measurements and ideas.

Ashley didn't know that Morgan had been planning her gown for longer than her sister had been engaged. Ashley was so unique, the chance to make a gown equally unique frequently occupied Morgan's mind. She'd collected scraps of fabric from clothing she'd made for her sisters and brother over the years. She'd saved buttons from the shirts and blouses of her parents—God rest them—and her Uncle Sammy. Connie agreed to give her as much fabric as she needed, free of charge. And Ashley, bless her heart, gave her a general idea of the type of gown she wanted, but was willing to let Morgan have free rein with the dress after that. All that had been in place for months. But when it came time to actually make the dress, Morgan hadn't been able to make her hands touch the sewing machine.

The truth was, she was sulking over the fact that all her siblings had found their "someone special," and she hadn't. She—who was supposed to be the beautiful one—couldn't find a man to settle down with. Even her niece, who was sixteen years younger than Morgan, had found the man of her dreams.

Since Morgan was a girl, all the older women she'd known had told her two things: "You sure are a beautiful child," and, "You'll have to beat the men off with a stick." Well, she had made a living from her looks and it hadn't made a bit of difference. She was still manless, childless, loveless. Of course, her family and friends loved her. But she didn't know what it was like to feel like she'd met her soul mate or have the love of the person she believed with all her heart had been created to love her.

Her self-pity kept her inspiration and desire to make Ashley's wedding dress at bay. Now she'd wasted so much time, she might never get the dress made on time.

Morgan blew a hot breath between her lips. She'd made her bed and now she had to lie in it . . . alone. The best thing she could do at this point was push those pitiful thoughts away and get on with the sewing. She just prayed she finished in time.

Morgan eyed all the fabric in Connie's warehouse as if it were a line of Chippendale men. She couldn't help it. Her mind buzzed with all the pantsuits, sexy blouses, and hip-loving skirts she could make with all that material. She ran her hands lovingly across silk, chiffon, taffeta. The fabric felt like a gentle whisper across her skin. Before she could stop it, a soft moan escaped her lips.

"I can see you and my sewing machine want to be left alone."

"Yes, thanks, Connie," she said. Morgan had brought all her sewing supplies with her. Connie let her pick out a beautiful bolt of silk and use his top-of-the-line sewing machine with a built-in microprocessor to make the dress.

She brought tuna sandwiches and fruit—lots of fruit for her meals. She was on a six-day mission and needed as much energy as she could get.

Morgan worked in Connie's private shop, the part of his warehouse that was his own personal domain. The other open areas of the large building were crowded with tables, sewing machines, fabric, needles, thread, stools, ironing boards, and people sewing dresses and other garments by the hundreds. That part of the warehouse never seemed to be neat or tidy. Thimbles, thread, and swatches of fabric covered the floor like a patchy carpet. But here, in this small room accessed from Connie's office, was the epitome of neatness. The floor was spotless. The table was well organized with drawers, containers, and slots for everything. Morgan envied Connie's work space and his ability to create a place in his life for his passion. He'd found what he loved and thrown his entire being into it.

She emptied her box of sewing supplies on a giant-sized table, wondering why she hadn't been able to find anything in her life that she felt passionate about in that way.

She walked around the table, her footsteps on the hardwood floor echoing off the high walls. Morgan pulled her fingers along the smooth, cool surface of the metal table, trying to absorb the love and commitment that had created this room in the first place. She wanted to take it in like fuel to help her get the dress done in a week. That was why she wanted to come to Connie's—to be surrounded by the inspiration that led to Connie becoming designer of the year. She also wanted to get far enough away from her home and her family so that she could think with a clearer head and conscience.

It wasn't working.

Somehow she had to make her desire to create the perfect dress for her sister more powerful than her need to wallow in her own self pity and her deep longing to feel Van McNeil's hot, hard body against hers.

She touched the fabric she had chosen. It was an orange silk. Orange represented one of the charkas Ashley was always talking about. Morgan thought about that for a moment, and then . . . she did it. She gritted her teeth and put her all into making her sister's wedding gown.

The process started slowly as she got her bearings in Connie's private room and laid out all her materials and tools. Soon she'd cut out the fabric from a pattern she saw in her mind and had the sewing machine humming in no time. She didn't know if Connie or other designers felt completely absorbed by a project, but she felt on the brink of it.

Everything in her soul told her this was right, even though she'd waited until the last minute to start. Her sister's heirloom dress would be every bit as special as Morgan imagined—strapless on top, tapered at the waist, and form-fitting at the bottom, the skirt would have a sheer and flowing overlay. The conversation piece of the dress would be the handstitched neckline decorated with their grandmother's pearls, as well as diamonds, jewels, and beads from every immediate family member. She would finish the dress with real gold trim so Ashley would look like the princess she was.

Morgan moved automatically and quickly, cutting, pinning, hemming, ironing. Soon the dress seemed to be making itself and her mind cleared of all the self-absorbed thoughts she'd had before. It was all about her sister, her special day, and the dress that would cover her with elements from their family and the future she had in store. Morgan felt possessed by love and an over-whelming spirit of joy. She felt like her mom and dad, who'd died years ago, were there with her as she added buttons from their old clothing to the new gown. To create an accent track that twisted down the front of the dress, she sewed in scraps of fabric, earrings, cuff links, and scarf pieces from other members of her family. She said prayers over each stitch asking God to bless her sister and her new husband with a life full of love and bliss.

Several days later, when she realized she was creating as much for herself as she was for her sister, she started to cry. Soon her tears became another contribution to the dress she was making. She couldn't stop them from flowing and she couldn't stop sewing until the dress was finished.

The tears she cried were not sad, resentful, or jealous. They were the opposite, because, magically, sewing the essence of her family's soul into her sister's gown renewed her faith in the kind of love she'd had all her life.

The dress was saving her. It was saving her from becoming bitter, resentful, and believing that she had missed out on her chance for love.

Love was out there. *He* was out there. Her turn was coming. The dress was a testament to that truth.

Morgan wiped away the tears, believing that just like her sisters and brother, she would find her true love, a man who would respect her from the inside out and deserve all the love she could give him. And if she didn't find him, she'd have to go to Ashley's closet and destroy the dress for not working the right mojo. She laughed to herself.

"You all right, sweetheart?"

So far, she'd been left alone. But she knew Connie would visit her eventually. He was much too nosy to leave someone, even a good friend like her, alone in his private room for too many days.

She made sure her remaining tears were wiped away before she turned toward him.

"Yeah, I'm cool."

Connie raised a beautifully arched eyebrow. "Let me see," he said.

Morgan turned all the way around.

"Not you, the dress!"

She blew out a chuckle and held up her creation, nearly finished after only five days.

Connie's eyes widened, his mouth dropped, and his right hand flew to his chest.

"Magnificent!" he said, his pet word for everything he liked. Morgan was flattered.

He circled around the dress, touching, lifting, examining the design.

"Little Miss Thing, you are baaad. I asked you once before if you wanted to join forces. With your designs and my vision, we would bury Dolce and Gabbana in a pile of couture so fierce every celebrity in the world would pay *us* to wear our clothes. We could be the fashion world's new Bonnie and . . . well . . . Bonnie. But you know what I'm saying."

Morgan took a good look at her handiwork. She had not only wiped away tears a few moments ago, but sweat as well. She really had given herself over. The dress looked better than the picture she had in her mind. And Ashley would be a beautiful bride in it. She couldn't wait for her to try it on. Morgan had the wildest urge to forgo her go-sees for tomorrow, take the next plane back to Atlanta, and show it to Ashley.

"Are you going to give me an answer?"

"Connie," she said, "my answer hasn't changed. I do this because it's a way that allows me to show my family how much I love them. The moment sewing starts to feel like a job or a requirement, I don't know if I could do it anymore. It just wouldn't be special to me anymore. Besides, the thought of a stranger wearing something I made just doesn't sit right with me."

"Well, I tell you what, sweetheart, if you ever get tired of modeling or you need something to fall back on, you are only ten digits away from a new career."

"Thank you, Connie. I'll keep that in mind."

And she would. The future of her modeling career was narrowing by the day. Women over thirty-five were not nearly as marketable as their younger counterparts. Morgan was so busy talking to God about her love life, she'd forgotten about her livelihood.

She started the finishing stitches on her sister's dress, hoping that one of them—her career or her love life—would change for the better . . . soon.

Van couldn't believe the room temperature. The conference floor of the hotel was so cold, he wouldn't have been surprised if the words of the presenters came out frozen like ice cubes. He'd just gotten downstairs and was picking through the fresh fruit and muffins in the continental breakfast line, hoping that the hot coffee was extra hot. Whatever happened to "real" breakfast? he wondered, sorting through mango and papaya. Sausage, bacon, ham, grits, hash? A Southern boy like him was accustomed to a different kind of morning fuel. He only wanted bananas if they were stuffed into banana-maple pancakes, and he only wanted strawberries if he was in a room where there were two glasses of champagne and a beautiful woman to feed the strawberries to. For the rest of the week, room service would be his breakfast buddy.

Van held up a strawberry and stared at it. *Morgan,*

Morgan, Morgan. You left too early the other morning. I was just getting started.

After Morgan left, he'd stayed up for a while—in more ways than one. He should have been celebrating, jumping up and down, carving a notch in his belt, and knocking a few back. He'd done it. Since he was eight years old, he'd thought that one day the angel that walked into the commercial that day would be in his arms. Even at eight, he knew what he wanted to do to her, with her . . . for her.

He added a muffin and butter to his plate and headed for the coffee, thinking that a great deal of his love life had taken place in his head—him and Morgan. The fantasies of her wouldn't let him go. He'd known all his life that he would never be free of the angel's image until they were together. And now that he'd gotten his wish, he wasn't free at all. He was even more imprisoned than before.

"Pass the sugar, please," a man beside him requested.

"Sure," Van said, obliging and wishing he could do the same thing emotionally—pass the sugar right on by. But his specialty was savoring the sugar. Tasting it. Covering himself in it. Swimming in it. He'd been that way all his adult life.

He found a seat and tried to redirect his thoughts to the weather and storms, then laughed when he thought how similar women and storms were. Unpredictable, powerful . . . beautiful. He growled, noting the bulge forming in his trousers. Like a junkie trying to go cold turkey, he knew the next few days would be torture.

Morgan. Get out of my head!

The weather conference was a huge success. Van attended workshops on new forecasting research, analyses, and techniques. He attended a panel discussion on

clustered convective events, extended forecast verifica-
tion, and supercell case studies. The highlight of the
conference was a presentation by Dr. Bernard Keystone.
His topic was the 1999 tornado in Heidelberg, South
Africa, that picked up water from a dam and dropped it
on a nearby hill. Van was in his element and absorbing
everything. It was such a different experience to just be
an attendee at the conference instead of one of the presenters. He'd grown tired of being "on" each year, being
an expert, and always answering questions from people
instead of asking some of his own. This time, he took
the opportunity to just learn, and it felt good. Now if he
could just stop himself from feeling like there was
something missing, everything would be perfect.

"Van!" the booming voice called from across the
room.

Now there's a distraction. Rich would keep him occupied with all kinds of fantastic stories, and would talk so
loudly, he'd drown out any thoughts of Morgan that
were swimming in Van's head.

"Hey, Rich," Van said.

In three strides, Rich bounded over to him in a space
it would have taken the average man at least six steps to
cross. Once again, Van found himself cocooned by long
arms and a hearty greeting. He pulled back before Rich
started talking and the volume punctured his ear-drums.
"Are you enjoying the conference? We worked hard on
it, you know!"

"It's top-notch, man. Really first-rate and worth every
dime."

"Thank you, Van! Thanks!"

Van promised himself that if he spent any more time
with Rich, he would buy some earplugs.

A woman strolled up next to Rich. She was pretty,
with long, straight, jet-black hair she'd pulled into a
ponytail. Based on her eyes and skin color, Van would
bet she was half Asian and half African-American. He

folded in his bottom lip and licked it. Nice combination.

"Van, this is Fan! Hey, that rhymes! Fan . . . Van!"

"Nice to meet you," Van said, wondering how loud mouth brother al-migh-ty pulled that nice piece of flesh.

Rich leaned toward him. "She's got a sister! *Twin* sister!"

Van sized up the woman hanging on Rich's arm. Not bad, really. "Identical?"

"Yes! We're going out for drinks tonight at a place called Big Bar! Are you in?"

Big Bar, Van thought. The mention of Big Bar cooled Van's enthusiasm. He knew that if he went there, the only woman's face he would see would be Morgan's. Suddenly going out lost its appeal. The memory of the woman Van had been working hard to forget came blazing back into his mind. He still couldn't believe she'd walked out on him. And to think that Rich, as zany as he was, had absolutely no problem pulling any woman he wanted.

"Rich, man, I'm going to have to pass on tonight."

"Your loss, Van, but all right!"

Rich extended his fist. Van tapped it with his own.

"Were're out!" Rich said.

"Before you go," Van said, pulling his friend to the side, "I gotta know. What is your secret?"

Rich smiled. He knew exactly what Van was talking about. "The reason it's a secret is because I don't tell it!"

"Come on, man, every time I see you, there is some pretty young thing hanging off your arm. What's up?"

"All right," Rich said in a voice barely loud enough to hear. "The next time you go downtown, spell her name . . . you know . . . with your tongue. And take your time. They hate it when you rush. Anyway, it works like magic. Like casting some kind of spell. After that, word gets around. Well, gotta go!" he shouted, back in full voice. "I've got a spelling bee tonight."

And I've got to get my ears checked, Van thought.

Chapter Six

After her last go-see that Friday, Morgan was like Wanda—*ret-ta-go*. She had officially entered the older-woman phase of her career. Any face work she got was for products that promised to eliminate wrinkles, or a mother-daughter ad. It was enough to make a sister depressed.

But she wasn't. She had packed her bags, said a fond farewell and generous thank you to Connie, and was on her way to O'Hare. The cab ride was long and crazy. Traffic was more congested than a sinus sufferer during hay-fever season and the cab driver paid more attention to the radio than to the cars on the road.

He kept looking at the radio as if it were a television. The story of the morning was the security level in the country the past week. Several terrorist arrests had been made in the last month and one of the men arrested had died in custody. Government officials speculated that sympathizers could retaliate. There was even speculation that intelligence agencies had already discovered a revenge plan and were keeping it quiet from the public.

Morgan was so tired of terrorist stuff, and just plain

tired period. All she wanted was three hours that would get her to the airport, home, and in her bed. She'd had enough of Chicago to last a while.

Happily, she glanced at the garment bag beside her and told herself her eagerness was to get her sister's dress to her. That was true. It was also true that she couldn't wait to turn on WAGA to see if her favorite weatherman could tell her what the outlook was. And she could listen to his sexy voice and watch closely as he walked in front of the green screen, reminding her how well Van McNeil could hang a suit.

The cab screeched to a halt.

"Hey!" she protested.

"Sorry," the driver said.

Morgan closed her eyes and sent up another prayer. "Please, Lord, let me get back home in one piece."

By the time she got to the airport, she had had her fill of traffic and crazy driving. Whoever said Atlanta traffic was bad had never been to Chicago. Traffic at the airport was more backed up than she had ever seen it. She paid the driver and gave him a tip but he didn't seem too impressed with the five dollars. Instead, he gave a smirk and spat out, "Good luck!"

Morgan had planned to check her pulley bag, but not her masterpiece—the wedding dress was going with her on the plane. She headed toward curbside check-in, discovering it had to be the longest line in the history of airport check-ins. She decided on taking her chances with the line inside; at least she would be out of the heat.

Eight steps later, and she realized that coming inside wasn't going to be any better. The line was just as long and there were many more people milling around than usual—some standing against walls, some seated on the floor, even a man lying down with a newspaper covering his face.

Not good. Not good.

A woman in line looked just as disgusted and outraged as Morgan felt. Morgan walked up to her, hoping to get some answers.

"Excuse me, do you know what's going on?"

"High alert," she said. "All flights are canceled."

"You're kidding," Morgan said, noticing the number of stranded travelers huddled around radios and cell phones. Everyone was glued to the news, wanting to know about the level of alert.

This can't be happening, she thought to herself, wondering who she had to bat her eyelashes at to find out if what she'd heard was really true. She didn't want to believe it.

Was the entire country on lockdown or just O'Hare? If it was just O'Hare, she was going to be powerful sad and plenty mad.

"Excuse me," she said as a person with one of those drab airport uniforms walked past. Dang if they didn't keep on going.

Suddenly her pulley and garment bag looked like enemies as she considered walking around to find someone who could tell her what was going on.

Another airport worker came stomping down toward ticketing. "Hey! What's going on!" Morgan said, flapping one free arm like a desperate hitchhiker.

"Threat level red!" she said and kept going.

Morgan winced inside, realizing sadly that she lived in a world where people were expected to know the meanings of the threat alert colors without explanation.

From what she could see, there was no one checking in, no one moving through the gate lines, very little movement at all. She gritted her teeth, determined not to be stuck in the airport.

A pudgy man in a tight skycap uniform came scuttling past, his too-short legs moving like thick tree trunks on high speed.

"Pardon me, sir," Morgan said, lowering her voice and stepping into his path. She licked her lips and he stopped immediately, dropping the stack of papers he was carrying.

"Yes?" he said, eyes walking all over her body.

"I need to know something. Are the planes just grounded for this airline, the entire airport, or every airport in the country?"

The man's face reddened as she shifted the weight of her garment bag and her braless breasts jostled with the movement.

"It's just O'Hare. We've been shut down for about half an hour."

"How long will the shutdown last"—Morgan glanced at his name badge—"Raymond?"

He smiled then. "They aren't saying."

She cocked her head slightly. "Are you sure they haven't told you?"

"Well . . ." He leaned over in a whispering gesture, but Morgan could tell what he really wanted was to do was get closer to "the sisters."

"The alert will probably be lifted tomorrow morning. Tomorrow night at the latest. They'll give the all-clear then."

Tomorrow night! She could drive and get there faster.

"Thanks," she said, gave Raymond her famous wink and a smile, and was off to rent a car.

Three trams, a bus, and several moving sidewalks later, she finally made it to ground transportation. Considering all that was happening, Morgan was in luck. She could see as she approached Avis, Hertz, and Budget that she had come up with the idea of renting a car before the rush. There was absolutely no one in line. When she got to the desk, she found out why. The small sign read *Out of Cars.*

She should have known. All the other rental car companies had similar signs on their counters. Her heart and some of her strength and determination faded. There had to be something she could do.

She walked up to the young man behind the counter, her hips leading the way. He was cute, even cuter the closer she got. *Maybe,* she thought, flashing her eyes, *he can help me.*

"Yes?" he said, flicking the cap of a pen faster and faster as she approached. When it finally ricocheted out of his hand, she wasn't surprised. Only amused.

"I know we're in a state of emergency. I see by your sign that there aren't any cars available. Can you tell me if there will be a car coming in anytime soon? My sister is getting married in a few days. This is her wedding dress that still needs to be fitted. Is there any way you can let me know when the next car comes in?"

He struggled to keep his eyes on hers and not some other parts of her body. "Sure!" he said with all the enthusiasm of an early twentysomething. Her hopes rose until he pulled out a legal pad and flipped through page after page of names. When he finally got to a blank space, Morgan blew out an exasperated breath.

"Never mind," she said, resigning herself to that fact that she was stuck in O'Hare for the next twenty-four hours unless she checked into a hotel and waited it out.

But Morgan wasn't good at waiting. She never had been. The thought of lugging everything back to a hotel seemed so empty and pointless. Too bad there wasn't a man in a hotel room waiting for her—that would make all this unpleasantry a bit easier to take. Instantly her mind filled with hot and tender images of Van McNeil, his olive-brown body hard and sweaty beneath hers. He'd asked her to stay with him. Maybe he would be willing to put her up for the night until the alert was over and the planes were flying again.

Her heart pumped furiously at the thought; she didn't

want to think about why. She just wanted to get out of this airport where people were packing in like sardines and get into the first cab she saw.

News of the grounding had traveled fast. There were a fleet of cabs waiting outside for frustrated and disappointed travelers, transforming curbside O'Hare into a Disney World ride. The cars only appeared to slow down while the passengers waiting hopped in, one after the other, and sped away. Morgan stood in line, waiting for her turn to get in.

Chicago traffic was Chicago traffic: coming and going. This time she had a smoother cab ride back downtown, although it took way too long. Suddenly she was in a hurry. She couldn't get back to Van fast enough.

Morgan did everything—twiddle her thumbs, flip through a magazine someone left in the car, watch the skyline rise on the horizon, listen to the radio play-by-play report of the airport shutdown. They were warning travelers away from O'Hare until the situation was resolved. In this time of turmoil, all she wanted to do was be with someone that meant something to her. Usually, that meant her sisters. She pulled her cell phone out of her purse three times to call them. Once she even thought about calling Clyde. But each time, she closed the flip before she could dial the numbers, and didn't know why.

When the cab parked in front of the Peninsula Hotel, Morgan prayed she was doing the right thing. She didn't have Van's number so she couldn't call and tell him she was coming. All she had was his room number and the name of his hotel. She could have called the hotel and asked for his room, but talking to him on the phone meant she could easily lose her nerve and he could easily turn her away. This way there was no ignoring her presence, for either of them.

She was taking a big risk. She knew what kind of man

Van was. If he was in his room at all, there was a good chance he was in there with a woman. Morgan felt crazy for going back. She also felt like she couldn't help herself. The fates had engineered it so that, against her better judgment, she was showing up at Van's hotel room like a lost puppy. The only things missing were the whimpering noises—which she was sure she would make as soon as he got her in his arms again.

Morgan kept the dress with her but left her luggage with the bell captain and headed to the twenty-fourth floor.

Please, God, don't let the man of my latest fantasies be in this room, buck naked and ass up with some woman I may not be able to stop myself from beating down.

She knocked on the door.

She knocked again. Nothing. Grateful that her sisters couldn't see her, she pressed her ear against the door, bracing herself emotionally for the sounds of copulation and Van's magnificent prowess being enjoyed by some other woman.

There was no sound. He must have gone out.

Morgan was relieved and disappointed at the same time. She decided to wait around for a few minutes to see if he would come back soon. She took the elevator back down to the lobby, shifted the dress in her arms, and headed toward the front desk. She would leave a message there to let Van know she was in the hotel to see him.

"What was the name?" the desk clerk asked.

"Van McNeil, room twenty-four twenty-three."

"Let me check again," the clerk said, tucking a stray hair behind her ear. "Here it is. Mr. McNeil checked out. Twenty minutes ago. Looks like you just missed him."

A hard stone of disappointment dropped into the pit of Morgan's stomach; it had nothing to do with the inconvenience and everything to do with her feelings.

"Thank you," she said, debating whether she should just check into a room herself. It was a nice hotel, really nice. Even on a meteorologist's salary, Van had to be taking advantage of the conference rate.

"How much is a room?" she asked.

"Single for one night?"

She nodded.

"Three twenty-five," the clerk said as calmly as if the rate she'd quoted wasn't absolutely outrageous.

Morgan was sure her face conveyed the "umph" as if she'd just been punched in the nose. She made a nice dollar herself, but three hundred and twenty-five dollars for one night? She'd go back to Connie's warehouse and sleep in one of the changing rooms first.

"Thanks anyway," she said, hitching her sister's wedding dress—which was getting heavier by the minute— smoothed the little black and white dress she wore, and headed for the bell captain's area.

Van McNeil, she said in her mind, *it just wasn't meant to be.*

Laptop. Digital camera. Digital video camera. Scanner. PDA. Cell phone. Map. Van checked his gear three times over, but he still felt like he'd forgotten something. The freeway on-ramp was coming up. Whatever it was, he would have to hit the road without it. He reached over and rooted through his briefcase for his sunglasses. His hand brushed across a small slip of paper and it came to him.

Betina.

At the next light, he made a left turn and headed back to the hotel.

Betina was one of the sweetest young women he'd ever met. She was one of the front-desk crew and she had made it her business to make sure his stay at the hotel was exceptional.

He'd written her a thank-you note and wrapped it around a fifty-dollar bill. He'd meant to give it to her before he left, but he had gotten caught up in his eagerness to get on the road and—if Mother Nature was on his side—intersect a developing storm three fourths of the way to Atlanta. The storm should be substantial enough to allow him to use his new equipment and report his findings to the National Weather Service, the Weather Channel, and his home station. This small delay wouldn't make any difference in his timetable. As a matter of fact, he had planed on playing this trip loose and free until he got to Georgia.

Van parked his SUV in the hotel unloading circle and hopped out. When he entered the lobby, he scanned the reception counter for Betina. Since he hadn't seen her at the front desk when he checked out, he hoped she didn't have the day off.

Maneuvering around an older couple making their way outside, he caught a glimpse of a beautiful backside. A woman was bending over, picking up luggage in the captain's room. The black and white dress she wore held her hips in all the right ways. He paused to admire the view, then continued to the front desk. Betina greeted him with bright eyes and a wide smile.

"Mr. McNeil. What can I do for you?"

"You can let me thank you for everything you've done already." He slid the note across the counter. "You provided great service, Betina. You really made me feel like a king here." Her smile broadened. Van could tell that in a few years she was going to be a gorgeous woman with the same kind of mesmerizing beauty Morgan had.

Damn, there I go again. Comparing anyone, and for that matter anything, beautiful to Morgan. The woman had dug into his mind like a Georgia tick. Nothing he did would make her memory let go of his mind. He would have to use brute emotional strength to break her hold. The thing was, he wasn't sure he really wanted to.

"You be good, Betina," he said, then, following an impulse, leaned over and gave her a kiss on the cheek. Her entire face lit up. Van felt good.

Before she opened the note, Van left the line and headed out of the hotel.

The open road was calling to him . . . loudly. The sounds of the city, chatter, sirens, cars honking, tires screeching were starting to sound like too much bad noise. The only loud noise he liked to hear for extended periods of time was the sound of a good storm, or the sound of a good woman in the throes of passion.

Morgan had the most unique sound he'd ever heard. She didn't just moan or scream, she sa—

"Morgan," he said, a lot more relaxed than he felt. The sight of her standing next to his car raised his body temperature by ten degrees and made his blood rush hotly through his veins. He allowed himself a slight smile. He should have recognized that behind when he walked past it the first time.

"What are you doing here?" he asked, as if he didn't know. With her luggage beside her, it was obvious. She'd come to take him up on his offer.

With Morgan by his side, that open road was looking better and better.

Morgan didn't hold herself back. She drank in the sight of Van McNeil. She gulped without coming up for air. As a result, her voice came out low and smoky.

"I came back to stay with you."

She shifted her weight and gave the handsome man standing beside her a great view of her legs. His eyes held hers for one hot moment. When the moment cooled, he reached down without a word and picked up her bags.

"Wait," she said, "where are you going?"

He looked at her and smiled. She remembered all the

ways she had fantasized about this man off and on during the eight months since their first date. She remembered all the ways he had smiled at her the other night while their bodies were joined together and aching from a pleasure so exquisite it brought tears to her eyes.

His smile broadened and, like soft butter in a hot kitchen, Morgan melted.

"You're coming with me," he said. "Back to Atlanta. It's a twelve-hour drive if we go straight through. I don't mind stopping though," he said, eyes sparkling and mischievous.

"No." She shook her head. "I just came to see if I could crash for the night. O'Hare is shut down and—"

Van opened the rear hatch and placed her suitcase inside the storage area of his SUV, then took her garment bag and laid it alongside. "Yeah, I heard."

"Hey, be careful with that!"

Van threw his keys up in the air and caught them. "Ready?"

His question implied more than just a simple road trip. He wanted to know if she was ready for them to be proximate, to bring the white-hot lust of their previous encounter into the small contained space of his car— for twelve hours. He closed the hatch and waited.

"Maybe we should have some kind of rules or come to some agreement about our . . . behavior," Morgan said.

"Mmm-hmm," he said, holding the passenger door open. "Get in."

Morgan tried to keep a smile off her face. She loved it when a man knew how to take charge. He just couldn't be *too* bossy. "Look, Van," she said, pausing a moment before she got in, "don't assume you're gonna get some just because of what happened between us the other day."

"That's funny. I was about to tell you the same thing."

She racked her brain for a good comeback and couldn't think of a thing. The best retort she could come up with was "Whatever." That was so lame she decided to just keep her mouth shut.

She knew Van wasn't the settling-down type. After making her sister's wedding dress, Morgan realized that that was exactly what she wanted—the same thing her sisters had. She glanced at the tall, well-built Adonis standing next to her, knowing that if her lust went too often to that man, her heart would go, too.

No matter what, Morgan couldn't let that happen.

She hoisted herself into Van's Ford Explorer. "Dang, dude. A sister needs a stepladder to get up in your ride."

"Or long legs," he said, closing his door.

"Those I got," she said, remembering all the jokes she'd ever heard about her legs going all the way up.

They clicked their seatbelts in unison and their eyes held for a hot moment. It was going to be one long, steamy ride back to Georgia. She would have to keep reminding herself that the love life she wanted was not here in this car. If she wanted that kind of love, her party, just-for-fun, boys-on-the-side days had to be over. And Van was definitely a boy on the side. A dessert. Something quick and sweet. Not the main course. She felt like she had been gorging herself on pretty boys and side orders her entire adult life. She'd wasted too much time already. She couldn't afford to waste another second.

He pulled away from the hotel and they were on their way.

Morgan looked around, liking what she saw. Serious interior. Midnight-black leather, room enough for five other people, and a dash that looked more than a little complicated.

"Nice car," she said. "But I thought you drove a Viper?"

"You've been inquiring about my transportation?"

"No, a little birdie named Ashley told me." Morgan couldn't stop herself from inhaling deeply. "You've got some serious new-car smell. Buy it brand-new?"

"Yeah, eight months ago."

The interior was impeccable, as if no one had ever been in it until that moment. "Do you take care of your women as good as you take care of your car?"

"How curious are you?"

Morgan licked her lips. "Mildly," she said casually. "Whatever happened to the woman who was sweatin' you that day?" She really wanted to know if he was seeing anyone, though she was usually more direct. She couldn't figure out why she was beating around the bush.

"Nothing. After she took off, she never called and I didn't either." Van merged smoothly into the main vein of traffic. "What happened with you and that old man? He call you?"

Her head snapped toward Van. "What old man?"

"Ol' boy at the bar. You two looked like you were about to get jiggy with it there for a while."

"Are you talking about Brax? That was just a case of two people enjoying drinks together."

"Mmm."

Morgan felt uncomfortable all of a sudden. "Okay, this is a strange conversation. We're quizzing each other about people we might be involved with."

"You started it."

"Then I can put a stop to it." Closing her eyes, she wished she could sleep the entire way. If she didn't have to see him, look into his sexy eyes, she wouldn't be reminded of how much she wanted to rip off his clothes and ride him into the sunset.

No doubt about it, she would have to go cold turkey

with a man like that—and any other man that threatened to distract her from her happiness.

"You're quiet, but your thoughts are loud and clear. Don't worry." He reached over and ran his finger along the line of her jaw. "I won't do anything you don't want me to do."

Morgan sighed heavily. *Like that was supposed to make me feel any better.*

Chapter Seven

"Van, I really appreciate the ride. And I realize you didn't have to."

He slid a glance her way. "Yes, I did."

Morgan laughed. "I guess you're right. The fact that my sister is dating your homeboy Gordon practically makes us relatives. You snub me, you'll never hear the end of it."

Van gulped. Family. Being part of Morgan's family. Now that was a frightening prospect.

"What did I say?" she asked. His face had gathered up as if someone had pulled it with a drawstring.

"Nothing," he said. "You wanna navigate?"

"Sure," she said, allowing him to change the subject. "Where's the map?"

"In the armrest."

Morgan unfolded the map. Van already had the route identified and highlighted. Very efficient, she thought, until she took a close look at the yellow streak running from Chicago to Atlanta.

"This doesn't look like the most direct route, Van. You've veered off the main highway."

"It's the primary route. The main highways are too congested for me to work in."

"Work? I thought you were just driving back home."

Van took a deep breath. She took one also and waited for his answer.

"I'm going back to Atlanta. According to some projections I made, we should intersect a fairly good-sized storm on the way. I'm going to track the storm, maybe chase it for a while when it forms, then report what I find to NWS and the Weather Channel. By that time we should reach Lexington, Kentucky. We can spend the night there and head out tomorrow. If we leave at seven, we could be back home be noon."

A ribbon of concern flashed within her. "Can't we drive straight through? We can take turns driving. Ashley's dress is in my garment bag. I still have to make alterations. . . ."

He looked at her and she imagined that the disappointment she saw in his eyes was because her plan didn't have them spending the night somewhere. "How about a compromise? We stop long enough for me to study the storm and report what I find. Then we continue. But I have a rule: nobody drives my car except me."

"Is that right?"

"Yeah. That's right." The quick look he gave her resembled a challenge.

"How about a compromise on the compromise? If you start to get tired or if I catch you weaving, I drive. Deal?"

"I don't weave."

"Let's hope so. Now, watch the road. The interchange for Highway Thirty should be coming up."

For a while they just rode in silence. Van focused on the road and Morgan stared at the digital compass on his dashboard. It was flat with an LCD display. The time and temperature glowed on the face as well. She'd never seen anything like it.

Morgan shifted her attention to the road and sat calmly in her seat, but inside her heart fluttered like a thousand butterflies. She'd never encountered a man quite like Van before. Self-contained sensuality. And he knew he was fine, but he didn't get on your nerves with it. Didn't pimp it like a ten-dollar player. No, Van was a man who could take as good as he gave. She knew. If the other night was any indication, Van McNeil was capable of taking everything she had to give.

She tried to check him out on the sly, but knew she was being obvious. Deep dimples, diamond studs, cleft chin, and a gold chain. It surprised her he wasn't strutting down some runway instead of relaying the daily barometric pressure.

"Can I help you?" he asked, noticing her appraisal— or was it her appreciation?

"How come you never became a model? You could have been hot."

"Hmph," he said, passing by a slow-moving station wagon packed with people and clothing. "As you very well know, I *am* hot. As for the modeling, I've got a few gigs to my credit. One of them you might be familiar with."

"Really?" she asked, ignoring his self-righteous comment.

"Yeah. Williams Brothers. Back in the day, I was the—"

"Oh, my God!" she said as the memory wheel clicked into place. "You were one of the Brothers Brothers."

He laughed. "Back then it was cool. Brothers Brothers and Brothers Sisters. It sounds so hokey when you say it now."

"I remember you! I thought there was something familiar about you. Didn't you do a cover spread with . . . oh . . . what was her name?"

"Monica. Monica Peters."

"Yeah! Monica Peters. I thought I never would forget her name. She got that cover and went on to be one of the top African-American cover models in the country. Would you believe I was up for that gig?"

"You don't say?"

"Yep. I was so disappointed when I didn't get that job, you could have pushed me over with a spider's web. I knew that cover meant big things."

Van kept his eyes on the road. "Mmm."

"Just think, if I had gotten that job, you and I would have been on the cover together."

He smiled and she liked it. He looked good. Great smile. Great mouth, period. Morgan felt herself staring at it. She wished she could see his eyes behind those shades he wore. She remembered what they looked like on the front of the Williams Brothers catalog. She'd put her missed opportunity in a folder where she kept all the cool modeling opportunities—hers as well as others. She'd studied them, believing that one day she'd have a portfolio of shoots just like the ones she was collecting.

"Why don't we listen to some music?" she asked.

"Fine by me."

She found a good R&B station and hoped it would last for an hour or two. It would give her something to concentrate on besides the unease she felt sitting so close to a man she'd promised herself she would shun for the rest of her life. And the fact that he sat there driving smugly and quiet—as if sitting next to her didn't make him feel the same restlessness—irritated the heck out of her.

She wasn't listening to the music at all.

"Okay. We need to talk," she said.

Van's eyes darted in her direction, then slid back to the road. "About what?"

"Let's see, where do I start?

"Look, if you think I'm going to suddenly veer off to the shoulder and rip your clothes off, relax. I've thought about it, but I won't. Not unless you ask me to."

His words ignited her libido. "See, that's what I'm talking about."

"Morgan, we're adults. We had sex. We'll probably do it again. No big deal."

But it was a big deal to her and that's what made her so uncomfortable. "Why are men so nonchalant about something so intimate as sharing your body with someone?"

"Why do women get so bent outta shape over something that is as natural as breathing?"

She blew out a breath. "I tell you what. You and I won't be doing any more 'breathing' together. Okay?"

"Oh, darn, whatever will I do now?" he asked, smacking the steering wheel. "Women talk about men who think about sex all the time. I'll bet that's all you've thought about since you've gotten in this car."

That was pretty much true. Somewhere in the back of her mind she wanted him to pull over and rip her clothes off. Without his arms around her, caressing her, she felt naked. Ironically, that thought made her hot and needy.

"Is that the highest setting your air conditioner can go?" she asked.

They shared a laugh; the tension broke between them.

It made Morgan realize that if she wanted to get anywhere with Van, she was going to have to be truthful and straightforward. She had a feeling he would respect that.

The two-lane highway was nearly deserted. Cars were so few and far between, she started to wonder if they'd stayed away just so she and Van could have some quiet time on the road. So far they had passed three large chunks of tires, a high-heeled pump, and a nasty mound of roadkill. Kamikaze bugs hit the windshield and Van had turned on the wipers and fluid twice already. She turned the radio down, listening to the hum of tires whirring against the pavement.

"Van, I lived a fast and furious life for a long time. I don't know who's had a worse track record with men, me or Jennifer Lopez. What I do know is that I need some 'me' time. And after that, I want some 'us' time with a man I can slow down with."

"What about you and First Degree?"

Morgan rolled her eyes. "Murder One."

Van gave her a side glance. "Is there a difference?"

"The tabloids blow my relationship with Clyde way out of proportion. We're really close friends and that's all."

"Clyde! Now I get it. If my name was Clyde, I'd change it to Murder One, too, just to keep people from beatin' me down." He laughed. "Morgan and Clyde . . . you're right. That has a terrible ring to it."

"Anyway, I was working my plan pretty well until last week. I lost it with you. And whatever it is I lost—my resolve, my determination"—my *sanity*, she wanted to say—"I want it back. It's time for this sister to get serious about life and love and you, mister, are about fun and games."

Van nodded and released a breath. She couldn't tell if it was frustration or disappointment. She would have been flattered by either.

"You know what I think? I think—"

In the middle of Van's sentence, her cell phone rang. She pulled it out of her purse and checked the screen. Roxy. She gulped. Roxy was probably calling about Ashley's dress. Morgan hadn't spoken to anyone since she'd finished it. It was definitely time for an update.

"Hey, you," Morgan said.

"Morgan, where are you? We heard about the airport shut down."

"I'm fine, sweetie. And the dress is fine, in case you were wondering. I'm driving back. We should be there by late tonight."

"We? Who are you driving with?"

Uh-oh. Here we go, Morgan thought. "Van McNeil."

Roxanne fell silent, and then, "The weatherman?"

.Morgan smiled over at Van, who glanced at her period-ically from the corner of his eye. "Yes."

"You go, girl. Is he as good as he looks . . . you know?"

Her face felt hot. If she had been any lighter-complexioned, she would have been blushing a warm red. "Roxy, I can't talk now. I'll see you when I get in town tomorrow."

"All right, now. Have a good time!"

"Bye, Roxy." Morgan closed her phone and hid a sly smile. Her sister was a year older and as feisty as they came. It was amazing to see the transformation that mentioning a handsome man caused in her. Suddenly a gray realization darkened her thoughts. In a matter of minutes, all her sisters and maybe even her brother would know she was with Van. The last thing she needed was for Ashley to—

Her phone rang again. She checked the caller ID. *That was quick.*

"Hey," she said.

"Roxy said you're with Van!" Ashley said so loudly, Van heard her.

"Word travels fast," Van said.

"Not so loud, Ash. I can hear you," Morgan said.

"I knew you two should be together. The fates haven't let me down. Maybe we should have a double wedding."

"Now you're talkin' crazy."

"It's in the stars, my sister. The Goddess has spoken. I hope you have enough thread left over to sew your own dress!"

"Good-bye, Ashley! And good-bye, Roxy. I know you're listening."

"Bye!" her sisters sang in unison.

Morgan snapped her phone closed and turned it off. No more calls for a while.

"So what was all that about?" Van asked. "I heard my name more than once."

"My sisters being my sisters. That's all."

"Hmph," Van mumbled.

"My sisters are concerned," she said honestly. "They just want to make sure I get home all right." Although Morgan had the distinct impression that she and her sisters had very different ideas about what it meant to be "all right" in Van's company.

Van blew out a breath and rolled his eyes. "A serial-killing meteorologist, huh? It figures!"

When Morgan didn't respond, he adjusted the air-conditioning and maneuvered the SUV smoothly around a trash can lid sitting in the middle of the lane without altering his speed or causing him or Morgan to sway sharply with the movement.

"You can tell a lot about a person—about a man—from the way he cares for his car," Van said.

Morgan turned toward him. "I know."

"Yeah, most people know on a superficial level. But if you take a close look, I mean really examine, the man's psyche and deep personality are revealed by the way he handles an instrument of his freedom."

"I don't think it's that deep," she said.

Van winked. "You've been watching me out of the corner of your eye. What have I been doing since I started driving? Describe it."

"You've been steering the car, holding the wheel," she responded. But had he been doing that? Her mind remembered vividly the feeling that Van was too close, her feelings for him too raw and sensual. And why had she felt that way? Because he handled the car with a finesse. A flare. A turn here, a light touch there. He had a quiet confidence. Master executioner with perfect timing, as though he and the car had an understanding, and when coaxed, asked, directed, and executed properly, the car would do anything he asked. As if the car was not just an inanimate object, but a thing alive, and with just the right amount of insistence it would do whatever Van asked.

"Well?"

She decided to be honest. After all, what did she have to lose? "You treat the car like you would treat a woman."

"Not just any woman, Morgan."

Morgan's breath caught. She managed to speak anyway. "You're right. It's more like the way you treated me. We had some tender explosions going on, Mr. McNeil."

"Mmm-hmm," he said. "Anytime you want that again, you let me know. You can also tell a lot about a man by the way he drives his car."

"You think?"

"I *know*," he said. "What does my driving style tell you?"

She didn't have to think about that question at all. "Cool. Smooth. You want to make an impression. You slow down before bumps in the road, but not too much. You like being shaken up sometimes. You're ready for anything, a blocked street, a detour, a holdup. You'll take it as it comes, because for you it's not about the imposition, it's about the adventure of something new."

That made him smile.

"And there's something else. I get the feeling that if you saw an interesting road, one that looked different somehow and led to someplace you'd never been, nine times out of ten you'd take it. Just because."

"Damn. You *have* been paying attention. You sound like a profiler."

"Was any of that right?" Morgan asked.

He nodded, nearly imperceptibly. "All of it."

Thank God for quiet. Women, Van thought. No, not women—Morgan. If it wasn't for the fact that her voice was as sultry as a caress, he would have told her to shut up for the duration of the trip.

Like that would have gone over.

He took a deep breath, released it slowly. Van first

thought that being this close to Morgan would be a good thing. But by good thing, he had to admit he'd thought good for his body. But all she'd done in the short time they'd been riding together was irritate him.

He tried to catch a glimpse of her eyes, hidden behind dark sunglasses. From what he could tell, they were closed. She'd leaned her head back against the headrest. Maybe Morgan would go to sleep and he could have some peace.

Who was he kidding? There would be no peace for him. He had closed down all possibilities of peace the moment he extended the invitation for Morgan to join him. The fact that she accepted meant that he would fixate on quenching his thirst for her *or* need consoling because he couldn't. Either way, Van was in hell.

She was everywhere. The air conditioner circulated her perfume. Inhaling was both a delight and a disturbance. Her legs were stretched out and were so long it was a wonder they didn't protrude through the floorboard. Deep waves of her hair splayed around her neck. He fought to keep his hands on the steering wheel and out of their strands. And her essence: it had taken over the vehicle. It was as if the Explorer were hers instead of his and she was only allowing him to chauffer her back home.

Van had to get his mind off Morgan or he would go ape giddy before they even got one hundred miles outside Chicago.

The sooner they got back to Atlanta, the better.

"What's in the cooler?" Morgan suddenly asked.

So she wasn't sleeping after all. "POWERade and some jerky."

"Cold jerky, huh?"

"Don't knock it."

She twisted around and probed through the cooler behind them. "No water?"

"I don't drink much water. Too bland."

She checked her watch. "Is it okay if we stop somewhere? I like to keep hydrated with the pure stuff."

"No problem," he said, checking the signs for a rest area or food stop and hoping that this pause in the schedule didn't turn into a long delay. Morgan seemed like the kind of woman who could turn a trip to the convenient store into an all-afternoon shopping spree, even in rural-town Illinois.

Van continued watching the road. His stomach growled thinking about food. He'd grabbed a bagel and banana from the hotel's continental breakfast bar before he got on the road—he'd been too eager to leave to order room service. Although it wasn't quite lunchtime, he suddenly craved a cheeseburger, fries, and a soda—the all-American lunch.

Thankfully the sign up ahead boasted of gas, lodging, and food at the next exit. His stomach growled again. The jerky wasn't going to cut it.

"Are you hungry?" she asked.

He took the exit and glanced at Morgan. She looked good in black and white. He knew from years of following her career that white and black were her signature colors. Today she wore a top with sleeves that came down just below her elbow and gathered just beneath her breasts. The wraparound skirt that rode low on her hips fell open just often enough to expose a tempting portion of long, dark legs. Every time he saw her, she was exposing the precise amount of skin to make a man desperately want what was beneath the rest of her clothes.

He didn't verbally respond to her question. Only offered a nod and thought, *Hungry? You have no idea.*

Van pulled up at a Casey's; even though they hadn't been driving that long, stretching his legs felt good.

"Might as well grab lunch while we're here. That way we won't have to stop again."

Morgan nodded and smiled. "Sounds good to me."

He followed her inside and enjoyed the view. *My, my, my. A runway sway even in a Casey's General Store.* Part of his mind wandered and wanted her to be moving those hips for his benefit. He licked his lips thinking about all the fun they could have. They didn't have to get serious. If last week was any indication of their chemistry, they wouldn't have to.

When Van heard the crash, he turned around to see a man at the counter. His eyes were on Morgan, but Van's landed on the mess of groceries at his feet.

"Do you always have that effect on people?" Van asked.

"Yes," she said, smiling and leaving Van standing in front of the sandwich aisle as she scanned the long wall refrigerator for water. Maybe women were right about men—their thoughts were primarily occupied by sex or something so close to it, they frequently had to sit down and cover up the evidence.

One more growl from Van's stomach got him back on task. He headed to the snack aisle to find some chips or pretzels. By the time he settled on a pickle, chips, and a microwave charburger, Morgan had paid for her purchases and was waiting for him outside. Van paid too, and went outside with a mission: he and Morgan had been dancing around each other like leery strangers since they started the trip. They would advance and retreat. That had to stop.

"Morgan," he said, walking up to her. He got close. Couldn't help himself. But what did it matter? After all, they'd already seen each other naked. He felt entitled to above-average familiarity. "Let's back this thing up."

Her eyes blinked behind the sunglasses. "What do you mean?"

"I mean us. Let's rewind everything before my hotel room, even before our date last year at Jonesy's. Let's start from a position of clear skies and get rid of these dark clouds that have been hovering over us threatening rain. And I love rain, but if we're going to have a comfortable ride back home, something between us has got to change."

She pulled off the glasses then and the sweetness in her eyes blew his mind. She had the most beautiful eyes he'd ever seen. In that moment, his brain surprised him by conjuring images of sunsets, hand-holding, and quiet days. He liked seeing her eyes and the honesty of her answer, free and unencumbered without the dark barrier of tinted plastic.

"Let's do it," she said.

He stared down into those eyes and couldn't look away, wondering if all his thoughts were pouring out of his eyes and into hers. He hoped not. He'd had some fairly explicit thoughts recently. Naked, sweaty, sated thoughts, the intensity of which might cause her to slap his face and hop the next Greyhound back to Atlanta.

He placed the glasses gently back on her face, stepped aside, and opened the car door for her. She got in with a demure "Thank you." He had to admit, he liked the sound of it. Soft and accepting, just the way Van liked his women. Yep, this trip was going to be interesting . . . real interesting.

He got in quickly, suddenly eager to be next to her again, and they were off.

"So," he said, catching a quick glance at her bag, "what'd you get besides Aquafina?"

Morgan pulled out the largest bottle of water Van had ever seen and said, "Peanut butter."

"Peanut butter crackers?" he asked, not understanding.

"No, just peanut butter . . . and a spoon."

Van couldn't believe his ears. "You're kidding?"

"It's my favorite food," she said and flashed a quick smile.

That remark got his attention. He took his eyes off

the road for a second longer than was safe while he gave her a quick but thorough once-over.

"If that's your favorite food, you wear it well."

She laughed and he enjoyed the sound. He could do worse in life than to keep her laughing.

"I don't eat it all the time. Just on special occasions."

"Is this a special occasion?" he asked, liking that idea.

"Maybe," she said.

"So what do you normally eat? You got some hips on you, so I know you're not tragically starving yourself like some models. But are you on, like, some special diet to keep your figure?"

"No. No special diet. I just watch my portions and eat whatever I want." She unscrewed the cap on a medium-sized jar of Peter Pan. "I work out, though. Ab exercises. Gotta keep my baby six-pack," she said, then slid a spoonful of peanut butter in her mouth.

"Is that what you call it, a baby six?"

"Yep. That's my bread and butter."

"Really?" he asked, as if he didn't know what she meant by that. Morgan was one of the most sought-after midriff models in the country. Her abs had seen more flash photography than most models' faces.

He wondered how she would react if she knew he had checked in on her career from time to time over the years. Definitely a fan. And he had enough Morgan-abilia to build a tiny but elaborate shrine. Hmph. She'd either freak or slap the handsome off his face. Van decided to keep his excursions into the world of her career to himself.

Morgan moaned. "This is so good."

His body temperature rose in response to her verbal appreciation of her treat. "Careful, woman. You might give a brother the impression that something else is going on over there."

Either she didn't hear him or she didn't care about

what he said. She simply dug in the jar for another spoonful, slid it into her mouth, and . . .

"Ummmm."

"Shoot," he said, just a little disturbed. "You didn't sound that delighted when you were in my hotel room the other night."

"You didn't taste like this," she said, smiling.

"What!" he shouted, indignation igniting inside him like a flare. "I taste good!"

"How would you know? Have you ever tasted yourself?"

Van remained quiet in embarrassed silence.

"Oh, my God! Tell me you have *not* tasted yourself!"

"Well, once, but it was your sister's fault. She and Gordon were at my place once and before she left she gave this metaphysical sermon about getting to know yourself. So when they left I—"

"You're sick!" she said, laughing.

He blew out a breath. "*I'm* sick? I'm not the one moaning and gyrating in my seat over, of all things, peanut butter!"

She took another taste of her treat and smacked her lips appreciatively.

"Ooh, smooth," Morgan said.

"I'm smooth!"

"Nutty," she crooned.

"Don't even try it. You know I got that covered!"

She sighed. "Creamy."

"Hey! Two out of three are good odds."

She cleaned off the white plastic spoon with a napkin, screwed the lid back on the jar, and placed them both back in her sack. "Too funny! You know you sound jealous of Peter Pan." She laughed.

He threw her a quick, sharp glance. "I'm jealous of anything that can make you moan like that. Ow!" he said, pretending to wince from her light jab in the arm.

"Oh, didn't I tell you? I work my arms, too."

They both laughed for a minute, allowing themselves to enjoy how absurd, how familiar they'd become in such a short time. Maybe it wouldn't be such a long trip after all.

Chapter Eight

Morgan stretched her legs and was pleasantly surprised to find that she could do so quite comfortably. Van's SUV was roomy. She had never wanted one herself, but she liked the feel of sitting up high and being able to see around her. A sweet combination of power and practicality, like a muscle car that had been finessed into something more elegant. She checked the speedometer. They were going sixty miles per hour, but it felt like seventy or maybe eighty. They would be there in no time. She pulled out the map to pinpoint their position.

They were just coming up on Lafayette, Indiana. She followed the route Van had highlighted: they had to drive the length of Indiana to get to Kentucky, Tennessee, and then finally Georgia. After studying the map, Morgan didn't feel as though they were making progress after all.

"Did you know that Interstate Sixty-Five goes straight through to Kentucky? If we went that way, I bet it would take some minutes off our time."

"Maybe," he said.

"So should we go that way?"

"I don't know. Let's see when we get there."

"Shouldn't we decide beforehand?"

"Relax. Let's just see where the road and circumstances take us."

A small ribbon of concern pulsed inside her. "Don't you care about the wedding?"

"Of course I care. Gordon's my dog. Besides, against my better judgment, I am the best man. What's that got to do with anything?"

"So isn't it important for you to get back in time for rehearsal and last-minute details? I mean, we could get in tonight and, knowing Ash, some things about the wedding could be different, very different."

"Then we roll with it," he said, changing lanes to pass a truck.

Morgan folded up the map. "Well, I like to be prepared," she said.

"And I like to be prepared," Van said, glancing toward her, "for anything." He winked.

Despite her frustration with a man who seemed bent on playing life by ear, his wink made her smile. Her insides felt all fluttery, schoolgirlish, like a teenager who'd managed to snag a ride with the coolest boy in school. She imagined that this was the way her sister Marti probably felt all the time. She was so youthful, energetic, and spontaneous. She looked at everything from a child's eyes. Since Morgan had been in the modeling business, she tended to look at everything from a jaded perspective. Always leery. Always wondering what the other person wanted. Suspicious. She'd made her living in a world that taught people to use or be used. For a second, she allowed herself to believe that maybe, in this car, it didn't have to be that way.

She turned and stared out the window. Van had a way with a car. It had been smooth sailing since they left Chicago. No tailgating, no unnecessary breaking, no weaving. He was master and commander of the road. They were coming up on a couple of semis; if it weren't so God-awful hot, Morgan would have rolled down her window and stuck her hand out. Let the force of the air hit it, push it back, as an homage to her sister and the changes Morgan wanted to make in her life.

As they approached the first semi, she remembered something silly from her childhood. When her family would take the station wagon and go on vacation, they used to get a kick out of motioning for truck drivers to pull the cords that would honk their horns. She didn't know what made her do it, but as soon as they caught up to the semi, she made a fist and pulled it down twice. The guy stared straight ahead, ignoring her. Not to be deterred, Morgan waited until they caught up to the second semi. When they got close enough, she pumped her fist again. The driver looked at her, smiled, and honked his horn.

"Oh, my gosh!" she said, remembering the man's face.

"What?" Van asked.

"That's Brax! I wonder where he's going?" she said as they merged from the passing lane back over to the right.

"Why?" Van asked.

"Well, at the bar, he said he was in transportation. I'm just curious now. What is he transporting and where?"

"Hmm," Van responded.

Morgan opened her water and drank in large, thirst-quenching gulps. The water hit the spot. She felt it travel to her muscles, cooling and replenishing them.

"Okay, I've never seen a woman drink quite like that. You've put some of my beer buddies to shame."

She covered her mouth, choked back a laugh, and finished swallowing. "Thanks, I think."

"So, what? Are you a water junkie?"

"Yes. I mean, it's part of my work. Water is the most important element in maintaining healthy skin. I keep my skin hydrated by drinking fifty ounces of water per day. That keeps away zits, moles, and other skin imperfections."

"Fifty? Bet you don't get out much . . . of the bathroom, that is."

"I'm used to it. Or, rather, my body is. Most of the time I can hold it pretty well."

Van looked like he was checking the level of water left in her bottle. "No wonder you wanted to shave some time off the trip. You're going to add about three hours to our time with all this stopping, so you figure that by takin' a faster route, it would compensate."

"Not hardly. I just want to get home, that's all. It doesn't matter how much water I drink. I won't make us stop unnecessarily or excessively."

"Are you kidding? Look at the size of that bottle. And you've already downed half of it. We'll have to make at least three stops with what you've had so far. You finish that puppy and we might as well plan on being at least an hour behind. Now, don't get me wrong. I'm not complaining. I'm kinda enjoying your company. Kinda. But you're the one advocating for a quick return. Well, if that's what you want, you're not going to get it by drinking all that water."

"You'll see," she said. "My bladder is well trained."

A devilish spark ignited behind Van's sunglasses. "And if it's not?"

"What do you mean?" she asked, a little hesitant.

"I mean, let's make it interesting. If you finish that and we end up stopping a bunch of times, you owe me."

"Owe you what?"

"I don't know yet. My choice, though."

Images of their night together flashed in her mind. Instinctively Morgan crossed and uncrossed her legs, feeling the tingly sensations waking up inside her. "Puhleeze. Knowing you, you'll come up with something sexual."

"Wow! You *do* know me. But so what? You think you're right, right? You're certain we won't have to make numerous stops."

"And if *I* win?"

"Whatever. Same deal. You get to choose."

Her mind flew back to Van's hotel room. The image came back much stronger now. Clearer. Maybe her wish would be one more night together, with no strings. The stipulation could be that they never do it again.

Morgan sighed. She and Van really did fit together well. Their bodies functioned so well as one. As though they were conceived and born to complement the other.

What exactly would this man want if he won? she wondered. What would any man want? she asked herself. A downtown job, probably. She had to admit, he almost got one last week, but she promised herself never to do that on a first date. Always make a man earn that kind of intimacy. If she won, she wanted something similar. The downtown express. Only, she wanted the express to slow down, take its time, be lazy getting to its destination. Morgan could almost feel it, him, approaching her—

"What are you thinking?"

"I'm thinking we've got a deal. Just don't be too shocked when I win."

"Don't worry."

Grass, grass, and more grass. Occasionally there were groves of trees, houses in the distance, a lone business or two. But mostly there was grass. And the signal for the R&B station she'd found earlier was beginning to fade. High-pitched feedback and scratchy static in stereo cut into songs just when they were getting good. When Angie Stone sang, "Black brotha, I love ya," Morgan sang along until the static made Angie's voice sound like it was being electrocuted.

"Funny," Van said as they came over a hill. "When I

was younger I used to sit for hours with this cheap transistor radio my dad bought me and listen to the feedback. I always thought that if you listened close enough, you could hear the sky talking."

Morgan smiled. Leave it to a weatherman to look to the sky for conversation. Van was becoming more interesting by the minute and she wanted to know more.

"We didn't get much chance to talk the other day," she said.

"I think our bodies talk to each other quite well, don't you?"

She warmed and licked her lips. He was right, of course. "You know what I mean."

"Yeah," he said, and looked as though he were intently concentrating on the road.

"Tell me what it's like to be a weatherman."

"It's a career that works for me. It suits my personality. It's always changing, hardly ever the same. And no matter what you hear meteorologists say about forecasting, weather is unpredictable, even with the most sophisticated, most expensive equipment. At times it seems no more scientific than licking my finger and holding it up in the wind. It's base, almost primal. Weather . . . Mother Nature . . . she's impulsive. That's why I love her."

"Hmm. I've heard people joke about wanting a career where you can be incorrect fifty percent of the time and still keep your job, along with the nice salary."

Van chuckled. "Truth be told, I'm about forty-five percent accurate."

Morgan chuckled this time, as her mind considered that fact. "I guess that makes you Mr. Wrong," she said, and burst out laughing.

Van frowned. "Too bad that's not funny."

"Sure it is!" she said. "But what do you care? For what it's worth, I hear you guys make pretty good money."

"We do all right," he said, stealing a quick glance that made her nerve endings burn with its intensity. "Why does it seem like **no m**atter how much money you make, you always want more?"

"I don't know. I'm pretty content with what I make. If something comes up—a trip I want to take or a large purchase I want to make—I just take more jobs to earn what I need. After that, I settle back into my routine."

"Must be nice."

She smiled, thinking how fortunate she was. "It is, trust me."

"I hear a 'but.'"

"It's not really a 'but.' Just the fact that all these years, everyone has expected me to be a supermodel. Walking Paris runways and smiling on magazine covers."

"Who is everyone?"

Morgan studied the water mirage on the horizon. The day was heating up. "My family, mostly. They all seem disappointed that I'm not Tyra Banks or Naomi Campbell. And they treat me as if I'm disappointed about it."

"Are you?"

She didn't even have to think about that one. "No. I'm not."

"Sounds like you've got your modeling gig on lock." Van paused to finish off the chips he'd been eating. "So, do you have a specialty?"

Morgan rubbed her midsection, caressing it with pride. "My mini six. When I said it was my bread and butter, I meant it. I do other stuff, from hair-relaxer boxes to QVC makeup guinea pig to romance-novel covers. Once I was the 'this way' escort on the BET awards show. But what pays the rent is my torso. You'd be surprised how many times you'll see the face of a model in a commercial or an actress in a movie. If they ever show the midriff without the face, it's usually because there's a stand-in. And if it's a woman of color, it's usually me."

"Really? Any woman of color or just African-American women?"

"It hasn't happened a lot, but sometimes I'll come in and they will put a special lighter makeup on my stomach to get the WIR effect."

"What's WIR?"

"Women of indeterminate race. They are popular now. The advertisers cover their diversity bases by hiring mixed-race models. Viewers don't know if the model is African-American, Latina, or, in some cases, Native American. But instead of sending a call out to find a Latina with a six-pack, they'll hire someone familiar and doctor her up with makeup. It's sad. I told my agent I didn't want any more gigs like that."

"Sounds like I'm not the only one bringin' home the Benjamins, huh?"

"I do all right," she said. Morgan was definitely more relaxed and feeling more comfortable by the minute. "So, how was your conference?"

"Not bad. They hold it in late August so all the chasers and spotters will have pictures and video from the storm season."

"Did you have any?"

"Not this time. I had an early midlife crisis last year and traded the SUV I had for the Viper. I kept the Dodge for a while, but I missed the storms too much. The last thing a man like me needs is hail damage on my sports car. So I bought this Explorer. I couldn't get chasing out of my blood."

"In more ways than one, I'll bet."

"What's that supposed to mean?"

"It means that you are a ladies' man, that's all."

"Does that bother you?"

"It doesn't bother me, but what about all the women you get involved with? I'll bet it bothers them," she said, reminding herself what kind of man she was sitting next to.

"Life is too short, Morgan."

"You got that right. It's too short to spend with someone who treats the word 'commitment' like a bad stepchild."

"There's nothing wrong with the word 'commitment' . . . as long as other people use it." He took a deep breath and rubbed a hand across his short, wavy hair. "Look, not that I owe you any explanation, but the women in my life know what's up. I only get involved with women who want the same thing I do: to have a good time. Women who can't play stay away."

"And what about me?" Morgan asked before she could stop herself.

"You fit the profile, baby. With the lifestyle you lead, we could really have some fun."

Just her luck, she thought. When she's trying to stay on the sexual-reform wagon, along comes Van. She felt like an overweight person saying, "I'm going to go on a diet as soon as I finish this big bowl of chocolate mousse."

"Look, I'm not out here deceiving women. I'm not sneaky, underhanded, or conniving. I don't lie, and since I don't have a serious relationship with any of the women I see, I don't cheat either. And I'll tell you this, I make sure my women have a *good* time."

"What about ol' girl on the street? She didn't seem like she was having a good time."

Van released a heavy breath. "That was something I let get out of hand. Collette and I had a standing engagement whenever I was in Chicago. Usually I know better than to go to the well too many times. Women are a trip. They all start to get attached if I see them more than five or six times. I just figured that since she was in another state, things would be different."

Morgan was listening to Van and trying not to be insulted by his player's code of conduct, when she felt a tiny twinge in her bladder. When was the last time she went to the bathroom? She racked her brain and realized it was more than five hours ago when she left the hotel on the way to O'Hare. Darn! She should have thought of that before taking that bet.

In the last five minutes, she must have polished off another sixteen ounces of water. She would have to concentrate hard on something else if she wanted to win. Plus, she needed to change the subject. Morgan was starting to get tired of hearing about Van and other women.

She glanced reflexively behind them, curious about Brax.

"Don't worry. He's still there," Van assured her, cold irritation lacing his words like ice.

The sting of embarrassment heated her cheeks. "I'm not worried, just curious."

"About a truck driver?"

"About a man who is obviously hurting about something, and is in need of some compassion."

"Sounds to me like a man who needs to live a little."

"Like you?"

"He could do worse."

But Morgan couldn't. The more she wanted to pass off Van as some fly-by-night Casanova, the more fascinated by him she became. She needed a distraction and reached for her cell phone. Five missed calls flashed on the LCD screen, all of them from her sisters. The biggest surprise was that her oldest sister, Yolanda, called. She hardly ever called. Without even listening to her messages, Morgan selected Yolanda's number and pushed TALK.

"Yo, what's up?" Morgan said.

"Roxanne?" Yolanda asked. She never could tell her sisters' voices apart.

"No. It's Morgan. When are you going to get caller ID?"

"The day you all stop calling me 'Yo.' You know I hate that."

"I love you, too, sweetie. Now, what's up?"

"I was calling to ask *you* that. Are you hitching home? I heard you accepted a ride from a man you don't know."

"See how stories get twisted? I know the guy I'm riding with. We'll be there by midnight."

"You got the dress?"

So much for her concern about her well-being. "I've got the dress, sister dear." Morgan took a glance at the backseat, where the dress lay safely in the garment bag. "It will be in at midnight, too."

"Good, because Ashley has called me every day for a week, worrying me. Can you calm her down?"

"Yo, I'm fifteen hundred miles away. You're fifteen minutes away. *You* calm her down."

"Just because I'm the oldest doesn't mean I have to fix everything."

"Okay, gotta go."

"All right. Don't call me when you get in. I'll be asleep at that time of night. Call me tomorrow."

"Will do."

Morgan released an exasperated breath and hung up the phone. The usual fare when she talked to Yolanda. She was the most frustrating, exasperating woman Morgan ever had to deal with. She was her sister and she loved her, but dang, she didn't know what cabbage patch her parents—God rest them—found her in.

"Another sister?" Van asked, but the tone in his voice was unmistakable. He didn't approve.

"You have family, Mr. Wrong?"

"Yes. My mother and father live in Athens, Utah."

"Utah, huh? That's different. But maybe it explains why you're so . . . unique. What about brothers and sisters?"

"No. When my parents had me, they decided life couldn't get any better," he said with a smile.

"Whatever!"

"Actually, that's pretty close to the truth. When they

got married, they knew they only wanted one child. I was born three years after they got married. They've never said, but I got the impression that my mom must have elected to have surgical birth control."

Morgan shuddered. She couldn't imagine doing something so permanent to her body. She'd been careful not to get pregnant over the years, but to cut off her ability to create life, to do that intentionally, seemed unnatural and somehow against God.

Glancing at rolling farmlands, Morgan appreciated the openness of the area. Seeing all that space made her want to stretch, take deep breaths, and breathe deeply. The scenery was certainly more relaxing than that of the concrete jungle she was used to.

"What's it like to grow up in a household where it's just you?" she asked.

He smiled. It was the first time she'd seen him do that without something mischievous behind it. "Since it's the only thing I know, the only answer I have is: normal. And it was never just me. My parents were there. I have aunts, uncles, cousins, friends. I was never alone."

Morgan tried to imagine life without her sisters and brother. The silence was awful. "I'll bet you were the center of attention, though."

"What's wrong with that?"

"Nothing, as long as you don't get used to it."

Silence.

A light of realization dawned in Morgan's mind. "But you have, haven't you? To see you on television, giving the weather. It's like a performance with you. You look good, you sound good. You've got this kind of pizzazz thing that's inexplicable."

"I take it you've seen me a time or two."

She smiled at her admission.

"I see. Well, I've seen you, or rather your mini six, a couple of times, too."

"Really? Where?" she asked.

"The Nivea ad when you were lying on that table. Your dark skin against that stark white. Mmm. Delicious! I saw that ad in *People* magazine and bought a jar of Nivea body cream. I have no idea why. I finally ended up giving it to a co-worker at the station. The other time was in the movie *Nora's Game.* You were the body double for Angel Harris in the shower scene. Whew! You got skills!"

Van's knowledge impressed her. She doubted whether her sisters would have recognized her if she hadn't told them about the movie role. Knowing that he'd noticed her and paid that much attention made her proud. Her whole body thrummed sweetly from it.

"How did you know it was me?"

He shrugged. "Just a feeling."

Now it was her turn to be quiet. How could a womanizer be annoying and endearing at the same time?

The moment brought them closer. Morgan could feel it in the air. Their emotions were touching more intimately than if they had reached over and held hands. She wondered if he was as nervous about that as she was.

"Funny," he said. "Our conversations seem to be a lot more lively when we're disagreeing about something."

She laughed at the truth in his statement. "You may have a point. What should we do about that?"

"Well, let's see if we can find something we disagree on."

"Go for it!" she said, grateful for anything that would take her mind off the growing heaviness in her bladder.

"All right," he said. "Favorite music?"

That was easy. "Salsa, Latin jazz," she said.

He frowned.

"What's the matter?"

"I like Latin jazz, too. It's classy and sexy at the same time. It creates and it breaks all the rules."

"Good point. What about food? You already know mine."

"I don't really have a favorite. Just whatever tastes good to me at the time. That's my favorite."

"Kinda like women?"

"Kinda," he admitted. "Okay, what about place? Where's your favorite place to be?"

"Vegas," Morgan said. "I love how alive it is, how electric and . . . and . . . "

"Liberating," he finished. "Anything goes in the desert. Sin City, baby! I've done some things there that will go to my grave with me."

She laughed. "I'll bet you have. So is that a unanimous on Vegas?"

"Sounds like it."

"This is terrible," she said, still laughing. "There's got to be something we can disagree on. How about books, movies?"

"I don't read. Too boring. I'd rather live an adventure than read about one."

"I hear that. But don't tell Yolanda that I don't make reading a daily habit. Ms. Schoolteacher would kill me. Now, let's see. My favorite movie . . . there's this indie film probably no one has ever heard of. Oh, this is awful. I can't think of the name of it. It's about a model who has a torrid affair with a cabdriver and—"

"*Fall.* I know that one. It's a great movie. But you've got it wrong. The movie is about a cabdriver who falls for the wrong woman."

"Guess it depends on how you look at it."

"Hmm, is that a disagreement?"

She smiled. "Yeah! Now we're talkin'. Let's find something else."

"What's your favorite scene in that movie?" he asked.

Her mind didn't have to work too hard to recall it. "I love the ending, when he flies all the way to Paris to bring her back, but she can't leave. The movie comes full circle, then. She told him in the beginning not to fall in love with her." The movie ended tragically but logically, Morgan thought. Sometimes there wasn't a happy ending. "What was your favorite scene?"

Van tapped the brake to interrupt the cruise control. There were several cars ahead of them slowing the flow of traffic. "My favorite scene was when he makes her come by whispering in her ear. When I saw that, I was like, 'My Man!'"

"Typical. That was the only part of the movie I thought was fantastical. The rest of it was pretty realistic."

"So you don't think it's possible?"

"Don't tell me you do."

"That obviously means it's never been done to you."

"If you whispered in a woman's ear and she came, you better believe she's got some serious *When Harry Met Sally*, 'I'll have what she's having,' faking-it vibe going on."

Van huffed his disagreement. "I've never seen the movie, but I've heard enough about it."

"You've never seen *When Harry Met Sally*?"

"Is that a crime?"

"For a man like you, I suppose not."

He glanced over. His eyes raked over her flesh like hot coals. She took in a sharp breath. "What's that look for?"

He returned his attention to the road. "My favorite scene. For some reason, I can't get it out of my head."

Morgan swallowed hard. If he could increase her body temperature with just a look, maybe he *could* talk her into an orgasm. Nah—she'd just been celibate for so long before last week, it had got her to thinking crazy.

"Hey, what about sports? You like football?"

"Woman, I'm the football king, baby. Ask me anything."

"I don't have to ask you anything. You might want to ask me a few questions, though. I've been hooked on football since I was in high school. My sister used to drag me to games to watch her boyfriend play. After a while, hanging around big, muscular guys was just . . . um . . . well, let's just say I liked it. I haven't missed a Super Bowl in fifteen years."

"Please. Try twenty-two years. Five years ago, I even *went* to the Super Bowl. St. Louis versus Tennessee. I'll admit, we sat in the nosebleed section, but I tell you what, it was one of the best times I've ever had."

He glanced at her. His eyes smoldered with dark desire and she knew he was remembering last week.

"If you're thinking about getting to another first down with me, you've got another thing coming. You are third and nineteen, dude."

He laughed and she liked the sound of it.

"We'll see," he said.

Van finally finished the bag of chips, crumpled the empty bag, and placed it back in the grocery sack.

"May I change the station?" Morgan asked. The R&B station was long gone, along with the static. What was left were soft echoes and an occasional crackle of sound. She wanted to find some fast music, music she could tap her feet to without giving away the fact that she had to use the bathroom so badly. If she even thought about water for too long, Van would have a drenched passenger seat on his hands.

There was no luck with the stations. They were far and few between and the ones she found either had infomercials, some guy spouting off about the political state of the country, or slow-moving country-western. Finally she found a station that was playing what sounded like hoe-down music. She imagined people do-si-doing with overalls and flared ruffled dresses—both of which she wouldn't be caught dead wearing. She sighed. The station would have to do.

Van's face drew up tight. "You're kidding, right?"

She tapped her feet to the rhythm. "Don't you like country music?"

"No, and you don't either."

"How would you know?" she asked. Yet ever since she'd gotten into Van's car, she'd felt as though he knew her—well. It was like they were in perfect harmony, even when they disagreed about something. With each passing moment, she was getting closer and closer to saying to hell with her promise to lay off the players.

"There's got to be something else we can find to listen to," he said, reaching for the radio dial.

"No!" she shouted, blocking his hand with her own and patting both feet so fast and furious she could have worn a hole in the floorboard.

Van eyed her suspiciously for a second, glanced at her neurotic feet, and smiled. The sun glinted knowingly off a set of perfect white teeth. "If I stuck your hand in a bowl of warm water right now, what would happen?"

A country group called the Red Belles sang the words "Already found me some love" in four-part harmony. "I'm fine," she assured him. Her feet tap-tapped quicker now. Much quicker than the Red Belles were singing. Van was the model of relaxation and calm behind the wheel of his SUV. Morgan, on the other hand, felt a tidal wave building in her bladder. Any moment now it was going to come crashing onto shore.

She kept quiet, but read the highway signs with acute interest. Gas next exit. Lodging next exit. Food three-fourths of a mile. Rest area thirty-five miles.

She had to go!

"Okay, stop!"

She was shaking by then. She didn't know why she wanted to win the stupid bet so badly, other than the fact that she and her sister Roxy were just alike: they both liked to be in control, especially when it came to men.

At that point, she didn't care what Van would ask for or what she would have asked for had she won. She just needed to feel the merciful release of her bladder emptying itself into a restroom toilet.

Now she was hopping in her seat.

Van took the exit and pulled into the parking lot of a restaurant. They knew it was a restaurant because of the four-foot letters painted red on the tin roof of the place that said Restaurant. Before he put the SUV in park Morgan was out of the car and sprinting inside. Van's full laughter trailed behind her.

She dashed past the entrance/gift shop, darted through clothes for sale, and followed the signs to the ladies' restroom. As she bounded around the corner, a woman was just coming out and another woman approached from the left. She picked up the pace, cut off the woman on the left, and bolted into a room a half size larger than a small closet. She didn't even bother to lock the door.

Morgan could still hear Van's laugher vibrating right through the thin plaster walls. She didn't care. When she finished, she let go one of the longest sighs in her life, washed her hands, and prepared herself to hear his request.

"Where are we?" she asked, stalling and walking slowly toward him where he stood in the gift shop.

"We're in Spencer, Indiana, and I want to whisper in your ear."

Heat rose from all the lower parts of her body, throbbed around her breasts, settled at her neck, then exploded onto her face. He'd done it; he'd put a small crack in her resolve. But she didn't want him to know it.

"Oh, is that all?" she asked, proceeding to meander around as if looking for souvenirs. She tried to ignore Van, but found it impossible to keep her eyes off him for too long. He looked so out of place in a roadside joint like the one they were in. His domain was high-class hotels, fine dining, and sunsets on a beach in Morocco. His exotic features belonged in a place where English was the second language and making love was a national pastime.

His gaze held hers, wild, brash, searing. He didn't approach her, he hunted her—always allowing something to come between them and periodically obstruct their view of each other—a rack of clothes, shot glass display, rows of magnets that read *I've been to Indiana*—a visual predator and prey. But his gaze never faltered. Always hot, always there. Waiting.

"All right," she said, giving in the way she'd known she would the moment she first buckled her seatbelt in his Explorer. She'd felt, like faint tremors before an earthquake, that before their road trip was over, she and Van McNeil would be exploring each other . . . again.

Chapter Nine

There were four words Van wanted to shout as he all but stalked Morgan in the roadside restaurant: *What am I doing!* His mind told him he shouldn't get involved with Morgan Allgood. Not even a little bit. She was just like her sister Ashley, who had snagged his best friend, Gordon, and the next thing you knew, Van was promising to stand up for him at a wedding. No, no, no! Van could not be seen waiting at the end of anybody's aisle for a woman in a white dress. Nuh-uh! But ever since Morgan had left his hotel room, he had been craving her, jonesing for her body like a junkie six days from his last fix.

Van had to admit, they went well together. Like wine and caviar. Thunder and lightning. Their sex was on! Like it was preordained that he and Morgan should take lovemaking to a whole 'nother level. And that's what he wanted. With what they had, they could go to a sexual stratosphere no one had gone to before. Until that point, he had prided himself on being the player with the most self-control on the planet. When it came to Morgan Allgood, all that self-control nonsense went down the chute right with yesterday's garbage.

"Let me whisper in your ear," he had said. And he

meant it. He wanted to murmur words in Morgan's ear, all the things he knew in his soul she wanted to hear. He'd spent too much time over the years checking in on Morgan, keeping up with her career and catching the periodic personal write-ups about her in *People* magazine and *Ebony*. Her likes, dislikes, her loves and lovers, her whereabouts and frequents. He knew more about her than her own sisters probably did. And etched in the front of his mind was everything a man needed to know to make her come with only the sound of his voice.

He couldn't wait.

Morgan continued her leisurely look around the oversize gift shop. Van kept himself close to her, his mind ablaze with visions of what he wanted to do.

He would do it on his terms. When she'd forgotten about their agreement and was just focusing on getting home, he would pull her close, kiss her the way she liked to be kissed, and speak her orgasm into existence. He would do it or his name wasn't Donovan Isaiah McNeil.

"Hey," he said, needing a distraction from the urgent tightening already occurring just below his abdomen. "Let's grab a *real* lunch rather than those snacks we bought."

"Where?" she asked, checking her makeup in a mirror.

"Here."

She frowned and looked around in disgust. "Here?"

"What's wrong with this place? I'll admit it's a bit rustic, but we're on the road. We're gonna get some of that out here."

She seemed to be sizing up the place.

"I know it's not what a high-fashion model like yourself is used to—"

"It's fine," Morgan said a little too quickly.

"You sure?"

"Yeah, I mean, you only live once, right? Might as well experience everything."

He felt the mischief playing on his face. "That's my motto," he said, thinking of all the ways he planned to make verbal love to her. As they approached the hostess's station, they paused, but only briefly. A sign that looked as old as Van read *Have a seat*. So they did. They chose a booth on the right side of a room that was much bigger than he first imagined.

The waitress took her time coming to their table, and if she wasn't a dead ringer for Flo from the television show *Alice*, Van didn't know who was. This Flo, however, had aged significantly and gained a few pounds. No, not a few pounds, a truckload of them. But she still knew how to wear her hair in a beehive hairdo and grind chew like a major-league pitcher.

"Y'all thirsty?" she asked, staring at her pad instead of at them.

"I'm not," Morgan said.

Van laughed. That woman had been making him feel silly and horny for the last fifteen minutes.

"I'll take a water," he said, winking at Morgan. She stuck out her tongue to offend him, but all he could think of was a more imaginative use for that slick pink muscle.

"Be right back," Flo said—although her name tag read *Marjorie*.

"Where did you say we were?" Morgan asked, taking another leery glance around.

"Spencer," Van responded and followed her eyes all around the restaurant.

The inside of the place was accented by dark, dull, wood-lined walls that looked like they had never been polished, a high steepled ceiling, several dead animal heads framed around the neck and protruding from the walls, and wallpaper so faded, the original color might have been white but was now a muddy beige color.

An older couple came in. It took them five minutes to shuffle to their seats. Regulars—Van could tell by the familiarity with which they entered the place and the way they were received by Flo—the only server in the entire restaurant.

Another couple sat near the kitchen. Midfifties, maybe. They chatted and squawked like chickens. The man attacked his burger and fries like a Viking at vanquished-enemy time. And the woman was just as energetic an eater as he was. The two were a sight.

"What I wouldn't give to eat like that," Van said. He thought he was talking to himself, but obviously Morgan had heard him.

"Like what?" she asked, then followed the direction of his stare. "Oh, man. I hear you. But guys eat like that all the time, or so I thought."

"Some guys," he said and waited a beat. "I used to be a porker when I was a kid."

Morgan's gaze traveled up and down his body so lavishly, it felt like hands. "Really?"

"Yeah. My metabolism is still turtle slow. Most guys I know eat like horses and then, if they want to keep from getting fat, they run or swim or something. Me . . . I have to pay attention to what I eat *and* run or swim or something."

"Well, you look darn good, Mr. Wrong. Darn good. I know a few agencies that would love to get ahold of your face *and* your body."

Flo came back with his water. It was in a brown plastic cup with a bubbled surface. Definitely tacky. Morgan smiled and gave him an "I told you so" stare. He ignored her and looked up at Flo.

"Y'all ready to order?"

Van could have sworn he saw a thin line of brown

juice hanging in the corner of the waitress's mouth. *Maybe this is too much of an adventure for me, too.*

They'd barely looked over the menus but felt relatively safe ordering a couple of cheeseburgers and fries.

"Comin' right up," Flo said, and waddled off.

"Did you see—"

"Yes," he said. "I'm trying to ignore it. Besides, where's your sense of adventure?"

"It left when the chew drool came."

Van laughed for a moment, then took a sip of his water. The last remaining sense of adventure he had leaped from his body as he tried to keep from spitting out the water.

"What's wrong?" Morgan asked.

"The water is bad," he said, swallowing and longing for peppermint, toothpaste, or a sandblaster—anything to get that lousy taste out of his mouth.

"Taste it," he said, offering her the glass.

"That's all right," she said. "I believe you."

The water tasted like an equal mixture of dirt and metal, as if it had been siphoned from a liquid steel mudslide. He ran his tongue across his teeth, not because he wanted to but because his brain insisted on knowing if there was gritty buildup on his bicuspids.

A slight smile curled across Morgan's lips. She was enjoying his misery. "Wow, that must have been pretty bad."

"I think you should see for yourself."

Van scanned the large dining area. He'd bet one hundred folks could eat comfortably in the place. It was slim pickings now. But a couple that had just come in and sat down not far from where they were seated had pulled what looked like a place mat from the side of the table. The couple unfolded it between them. It was a checkers mat, complete with two-inch round pieces rolled up in the middle.

"Want to get your butt kicked while we wait for the burgers?"

"What?" Morgan responded, with that look black women gave a brother when her mind was asking *Have you lost your damn mind?* and *Don't think I won't dust you off* at the same time.

When Van pulled the mat away from where it was tucked on the side of the table and opened it, she rolled her eyes and blew out a breath.

"Are you kidding?" she said, helping him set up the pieces. "When I was little, I was the checker champion. The only person in my family that will play checkers with me now is my brother, Zay. Everyone else is afraid."

"Yeah, well, I ain't everyone else."

Morgan fidgeted with the last round piece lodged between the table and the wall. "We shall see."

She gave the piece a hard tug and the piece snapped free, but not before the table sprang back, catching the end of her finger. Morgan howled, yanked her finger free, and shook it.

"Let me see," Van said.

Skeptically, she extended her hand. He pulled it closer and looked at the injured finger. The skin wasn't broken, but the tip of the finger was already red.

He couldn't help himself. He did what any red-blooded American man would have done when faced with the sexiest finger on the planet. He wrapped his lips around it.

Van got the response he wanted. Morgan released a gasp so soft and sensual, desire burned like wildfire in his veins. He wanted to do something, anything to hear it again.

Closing his mouth around her finger softly, slowly, he sucked and pulled with his lips until he felt the throbs of pain subside and the pulse of need build.

Their eyes locked the entire time. No blinking, no

turning away. Just a gentle reminder of what they'd shared between them and could share again.

Morgan moaned once more and Van shuddered with the memory of all that came with a sigh like that the last time he'd coaxed one from her lips. His blood rushed molten through his veins. If he didn't stop, he would have no choice but to grab her, push her against the closest wall, and thrust himself deep into her core until she grew wet with need and sang "Do Me Baby" at the top of her lungs.

He pulled back, giving her finger one last warm swirl of his tongue for good measure. Morgan's finger hung in the air for several seconds before she dropped it down in front of her and smiled.

"Thank you," she said, the sultry voice he'd grown accustomed to hearing, suddenly lowered an octave.

"Better?"

Her eyes flickered appreciatively. "Yes."

"There's more where that came from," he assured her.

Neither one of them noticed Flo hovering beside the table. They moved the game cloth and sat back while she lowered plates in front of them. Big juicy burgers, fat crinkle-cut fries, and a setup of lettuce, tomato, and pickle spears.

"Are you ketchup people?" Flo asked.

They both shook their heads, but it was more than her question they were responding to. The moment to recapture what they'd had last week had passed—all too quickly. Flo walked away, leaving them with randy silence and greasy cheeseburgers.

Somewhere a radio played. Instrumental country-western. Van didn't know that kind of music even existed, but song after song droned on with slide guitar, banjo, or both. It was the first time in his life he longed for twang vocals or just a straight-up yodel. The music alone was making him crazy. Or was it sitting across from Morgan and ignoring an attraction between them that was as large as a football field? The ball had been in play for a hot second. But now it was out of bounds.

They began to eat, and when Morgan finished, she said, "Well, it's not peanut butter, but it still hit the spot."

Van eyed the glass of stank water still sitting on the table, almost thirsty enough to take another drink. Morgan's plate was clean.

"You didn't even leave a fry."

"Oh, I can eat, now. Don't think I can't. It's just that I know what goes along with a meal like that. Lots of—"

"Physical activity," he finished, eager for the mood again. He didn't want it to get so far away from them that they couldn't see it or remember it once was there.

"Men!" she snapped. "Always thinking about sex!" For a moment Van was concerned, but the expression on her face was playful and a little sneaky.

"What I want to know is what's wrong with you women," he said, playing along. "Why aren't you thinking of sex more often?"

"We have better things to do with our minds and bodies."

"What's better than sex?" he asked, and honestly wanted to know. "What's better than being so close to someone with no barriers, showing them every emotion?"

"Most men just want to screw and that's it."

"Oh, so you're an expert?"

Morgan glanced around. Her scan paused at each animal head on the wall before she spoke again. "Men are so simple a species, you don't have to be an expert, just a keen observer."

Van didn't laugh. "You think you know something, but let me tell you—" For some reason his eyes looked down then. He couldn't look at her. And his hands found the salt and pepper shakers and slid them back and forth on the table. "It's not like that for all men. Some men just scab over after they open up so completely. It keeps the feelings under control."

Morgan raised his gaze with a question. "What about you?" she asked. "You're a player's player. Got a player's set of rules. Is that what *you* do?"

Her eyes were bright, liquid with curiosity. But he was afraid she already knew the answer to her question and he was much too angry with himself for having what seemed to be growing feelings for her to answer her.

"Gordon talks to my sister. My sister talks to me. So, with so many conquests, Van McNeil, do you really open yourself and allow yourself to be vulnerable or do you scab over like some others?"

Her eyes bore into him for the truth, a truth he was too ashamed to give her.

Van looked away, not wanting her to see that before he had slept with her, he had been one of those men. Sex was pleasure, not connection. It was feeling, not emotion.

"That's what I thought." Morgan's words came out in a rush of disappointment.

Flo came over. She hesitated a moment before speaking. Maybe she ran into the thick fog of tension suddenly rising between Van and Morgan.

"Y'all want dessert?"

"No," they said together.

"Thanks a mill," she said, leaving the check. "Come back and see us, now."

Van shook his head. Having never in his life regretted his carefree lifestyle, it felt strange to regret it now. But then again, if he had been serious and found a woman to settle down with, he wouldn't have had that great night with Morgan.

And that had been his plan all along, to hold the angel in his arms and kiss her. Who knew he would have trouble letting go?

Picking up the check, Van heard Flo's words echoing in his head. "Come back."

No, Flo, he thought. He hoped he and Morgan never had to come back to this place ever again.

"How was everything?" the cashier at the front asked. She could have been Flo's cousin, smacking and staring at the register.

"Everything was fine," Morgan said.

Van took his wallet out of his back pocket. "Except for the water."

"Well, *yeah*," Flo's cousin said, as if this fact was something they should have known. "Well water." She took Van's twenty-dollar bill. "Lots of wells around these parts. Makes the water the same color as the cup. I won't drink it, myself."

He remembered the brown, cloudy plastic cup the water was served in. He guessed people who were used to that kind of water didn't mind.

Van took the change and they left the rustic cool of the air-conditioned restaurant for the sultry heat of the day.

By the time he got inside the car, Van had already started to sweat both physically and emotionally.

The damned thing wouldn't move. Morgan and Van sat in his SUV on the onramp, waiting for a deer to cross the road.

After Van paid for their lunch and they headed back to the highway, they realized it wasn't as easy as turning around and going back the way they came.

"Leave it to you to pick an exit with no reentry ramp."

"I didn't pick it," she protested.

"Sure you did. The moment your bladder made you

scream 'Pull over!' that was the moment you chose the exit."

Van laughed. She didn't think it was funny. They traveled for twenty-five miles to the next town, which was even smaller than the one they'd just left, to find a ramp back to the highway. The roads were narrow and a few weren't even paved. When they finally made it to the onramp, Morgan breathed a sigh of relief. She had no desire to get lost in Small Town, USA. She glanced into the backseat. Ashley's gown lay in the garment bag, waiting to be worn. She was eager to get back on the road. And that's when she saw it. They both saw it. The deer smack dab in the middle of the most narrow on-ramp she'd ever seen. When the animal saw them, it looked up, blinked, and stared.

"Well, I'll be. . . ." Van said.

He inched the SUV forward. The deer didn't move. It only looked like it was searching for something.

"Can you go around?" Morgan asked.

"Not without flipping down the hill. The Explorer is bad, but it ain't that bad."

She scanned their surroundings. Wooded hillside on the right, ravine on the left. "I guess four-wheel drive won't keep you from sliding down a hill, huh?"

Van smirked and honked the horn. The deer's ears twitched. It blinked a few more times and stood its ground.

"I don't get it," Van said.

"Me neither. Should we back up?"

"No."

Now the little deer had the nerve to take a step forward.

"I don't believe it," Morgan said. "You got a camera?"

"In the back," Van motioned, his neat, manicured fingernails strumming against the steering wheel.

She grabbed the camera, but after seeing it, handed it over to Van.

"That camera looks more expensive than my car."

He smiled, obviously proud of his equipment, then put the car in park. "It didn't cost that much, but it's probably close. The only thing it doesn't do is give back rubs."

Van switched on the camera and snapped a picture of the little orphaned deer standing close enough to touch. It stared at them with big inquisitive eyes and pawed lightly at the ground.

"I wonder . . . " Van said, unlocking his door.

"What are you doing?" she asked, concern rising in her throat.

"I think it's tame. It's probably a pet." He got out and closed the door behind him.

Morgan pressed the button and rolled down the window. "But if it's not tame, there could be a mother lurking around!"

She watched with amusement as Van tried without success to get the deer to move.

"Here, deer," he said. "Shoo, shoo!" He flailed his arms.

He searched around for a moment, picked up a stick, and waved it like a magic wand in front of the animal.

"I don't think it's going to disappear, Houdini!"

"Shut up!" he shouted playfully. Then he threw the stick down the ravine. "Fetch!" Morgan snickered. Van had lost his mind.

He walked to the edge of the road, patted his leg, and whistled. "Come on, deer!"

The deer tilted his head to the side as if to say, "What the hell is the matter with you, man?"

"Morgan, throw me your peanut butter!"

Yep, she thought. *He's lost his ever-lovin' mind.* "You must be crazy!"

"Look, it's got to be tame. It probably just wants to be fed."

"What about your jerky?"

"Deer are herbivores!" he shot back. "Hey, little fella." Van approached the deer.

Morgan shook her head and out of the corner of her eye caught a flash of movement. Panic turned her blood to ice.

Antlers.

The bull charged up the embankment so quickly, she couldn't believe she had time to react. But she did. Jumped out of the car and rushed toward where Van was speaking baby talk to Bambi.

As the bull galloped over, Morgan thought she was Warren Sapp for a moment. She tackled Van as if it were the Super Bowl, and he was on the opposing team.

Van hit the ground and rolled. When she landed, she landed flatly on top of him. In another situation, she would have loved to stare into his eyes and have him stare into hers. Feeling her flesh catch fire from his hard muscles tightening beneath her, she realized this wasn't the time and quickly rolled away. Both of them stared up and over at the wild kingdom they were close enough to pet.

The buck ran past, missing them by inches. It stopped, pawed loose grass and dirt, snorted, then trotted away with the younger deer. Van on the other hand was clutching his knee, rocking from side to side, and howling.

"Van! What's wrong?"

"Before I rolled I landed on my knee. I don't think it's broken, but it hurts like hell."

"Let me see," Morgan said, though she didn't know why—she couldn't tell if it was broken, sprained, fractured, or anything else.

They both sat up. The only thing she could see was a blood-soaked rip in Van's jeans.

A wave of guilt made her a little sick to her stomach. "I'm sorry," she said.

"Don't worry about it. You kept that buck from goring me. Between an antler in the gut and a scrape on the knee, I choose the scrape."

"Can you walk?" Morgan asked, standing.

Van stood, too. "Yeah. Come on. There's a first-aid kit in the car."

"Let me help you," she said, grabbing him by the waist. He slung his left arm over her shoulder and together they ambled to the car.

Van opened the rear of the SUV and opened a black storage container the size of a small trunk. Favoring his right side, Van rummaged through jumper cables, flares, flashlights, and a tow rope to retrieve a small white box. She extended her hand.

"Thanks, but I know how to dress a wound."

Morgan wasn't havin' it. "Drop your pants, Mr. Wrong."

"Now, there are two phrases I never would have imagined hearing in the same sentence."

She took the kit and opened it. The antiseptic spray, bandages, and alcohol wipes lay on one side, tape Band-Aids and tweezers on another. While Van unbuttoned his jeans, she picked up a few alcohol pad packets. She watched closely and unashamedly as the jeans dropped from his hips to his ankles. Brown-olive muscled legs, glowing even browner in the sun, stood like massive temptations before her. The sight weakened and exhilarated her at the same time. One day soon, she had to get Van's skin back in her mouth. She just had to.

To fight off her growing urges, she folded her bottom lip in and bit down. The only thing preventing her from running her hands up and down Van's legs was the blood now trickling from a gash in Van's right knee.

"Elliptical machine, level five, forty-five minutes a day," Van said.

She snickered at her own behavior. "Have a seat," she said, gently giving him a shove backward. He sat down in the back area of his SUV.

Morgan squatted before him and ripped open the alcohol packet. For a second she imagined what a sight they must be to passersby, if there had been any. There weren't. The only hint of civilization around them was the whoosh of the occasional car driving past at the top of the ramp on the freeway.

Morgan cleaned the wound and Van's leg. After wiping away the blood, she took a good look at the cut. It was a fairly deep slash that extended left to right in an almost perfect line across the middle of his knee. She took a square gauze pad and pressed it firmly against the wound to stop the bleeding. Van only winced once.

"You know you can't drive with this," she said.

"I've got cruise control. I'll be fine."

"Even with cruise control you still have to brake and speed up. This thing isn't bleeding too badly, but it could. The last thing you need is to bend your knee over and over. The cut will never heal, or, worse, it could get infected."

"It's just a little cut."

"Van, I'm looking at this thing head-on and it's not little. I don't think you need stitches, but from the looks of this you need to be careful. Real careful."

"Nobody drives the Explorer but me."

Morgan pulled the gauze away. The bleeding had stopped, mostly. Dabbing the area once again with an alcohol pad, she doused it with the antibacterial spray and taped a fresh gauze pad over it.

"Okay, stand," she said.

Van did as he was told. Even though she would much rather have been pulling them off, she pulled up his jeans. The clean, manly scent of his skin intoxicated her. She wondered how she would recover from its effect on her.

Van tucked in his shirt and fastened his jeans.

"Thanks," he said. Honest appreciation shone in his eyes. She couldn't tell which was brighter, the appreciation in his eyes or the sun in the sky. Either way, she was warmed by both.

Morgan put the first-aid kit back in the box and closed it up.

"Think you can walk?" she asked.

"Yeah," Van said in typical male fashion. Never hurt, never sick, can handle everything.

He took one and a half steps and groaned so loudly, it sounded like a wild animal.

"Hand over the keys," she said.

Chapter Ten

"You all right?" Morgan asked.

She and Van had made it to the highway and were back on course to Atlanta. They'd entered a stretch of road where the pavement was being resurfaced. The ride was bumpy and several times Van moaned, groaned, or uttered a quick, hot expletive.

"I'm fine," he said. He'd had a frown on his handsome face ever since she'd taken the wheel of his precious SUV.

"Are you mad because I'm driving?" she asked.

"No," he said.

"Is it the road?"

"That and the fact that my knee is doing some crazy throbbing. It's like a cartoon throb. Like my knee has blown up to balloon size and is pulsing so hard I'm surprised you can't hear it."

"I've got some ibuprofen in my purse," Morgan offered.

"I can't take that stuff. It messes with my system in weird ways."

"How weird?"

"Like I've smoked a joint or something. It's strange. I usually don't take anything for pain. But if I absolutely have to take something, I take regular, old-fashioned aspirin."

Morgan nodded, wondering what Van would be like high. She couldn't imagine it. Even the night they were together, they'd ordered a bottle of wine, but neither of them seemed more than simply relaxed by it.

Out of the corner of her eye, she saw Van clenching his teeth. She could tell he didn't want to talk; the expression on his face was too intense and angry. *Sometimes a man just wants to be left alone,* she thought.

From the passenger's seat, she'd thought the view of the terrain was interesting. She'd found things to look at. But now, in the driver's seat, there wasn't much to see. Grass browning under the scorching heat, hills rolling with more brown grass, and the occasional car driving to who knew where.

They'd long since grown tired of country-western music. The only sound in the car was the air conditioning and Van's frustrated blasts of hot air forced out between his lips. In the background were his occasional grunts and groans.

Her right foot rose and fell with the demands of the road. She didn't like cruise control. It took all the fun out of driving and eliminated at least half of the concentration it took to stay alert. So she did what Van could not; she drove without cruise control through sun-parched Indiana back roads on the way to Georgia. *Midnight,* she told herself. *We'll be there by midnight.*

"Jesus!" Van said, his voice mirroring the frustration on his face.

Morgan's soul flooded with concern for him. "What's wrong?"

He took a deep breath. "Where's your purse?"

With one hand on the steering wheel, she reached behind his seat for her purse. She placed the small Fendi bag in his lap. "You'll have to get it out."

He unzipped the bag and smiled for the first time in almost an hour.

"I always wondered what women kept inside their purses. Let's see . . ."

"Don't worry about anything except the ibuprofen. It's in a gold pillbox."

"Hmm," he said. "Pillbox? Pillbox? I don't see a pillbox yet. But I do see a makeup case, a mirror . . ."

"Don't go through my things, Van. That's rude. Just get the pain reliever."

"They say you can tell a lot about a woman by what she carries in her purse. What does it say about you?"

"None of your business," she said, wondering why it bothered her so much.

"I'm a man after adventure, and I'd say that going through a woman's purse is the ultimate adventure, second only to sharing her body."

"You've had one; you don't get the other." She laughed.

"I just took my pants down, outside, and let you clean me up. One gesture of vulnerability deserves another, wouldn't you say?"

"Not really," she said, but felt herself giving in. "You find the pillbox?"

"Yeah," he responded, reaching for her water bottle. "You don't have cooties, do you?"

"If I do, you've already got them," she said. Their kisses had been more passion-driven than passion could define, and they'd exchanged enough bodily fluids to swap cooties a long time ago.

Van threw back four pills and washed them down with quick gulps of water.

"Four! I thought you said they make you loopy."

"They do, so get ready."

"Oh, God. If you get any worse than you are now, I warn you, I'll bust up your other knee."

"So you don't think you've done enough damage already?"

That shut her up. She already felt bad about Van's injury. Her head dropped a bit with regret.

"Hey," Van said. He placed a hand on her thigh. It was warm and forgiving. "I was joking. Don't feel bad. It really is just a cut. I'm just having a little fun rubbing your nose in it. That's all."

"I really am sorry, Van."

"Look, let's not talk about it again. All right?"

She nodded.

"Good. Now tell me something. Where did you learn to tackle like that? Reggie White? Grant Wistrom? Dick Butkus?"

First there was silence, then the car erupted with their laughter.

"I mean, really. The deer never had a chance. It's a good thing you weren't aiming for him!"

"Okay, okay!" she said, giggling.

"You call me Mr. Wrong. I should call you Don Knotts. Your whole body's a weapon!"

They were laughing so hard they could barely breathe.

Van grabbed his knee to keep it stable while he laughed. "The bad part is, the ibuprofen hasn't even kicked in yet!"

"Shut up, Van!" Morgan managed to say. She blinked back tears and spoke between chuckles. "I'm not going to be able to see!"

"I'll stop," he said. "Heaven forbid we survive a deer attack only to have an accident now."

She used one arm to cradle her mini six that was beginning to ache as if she'd done her eight-minute abs again. "Oh, God. Are you sure the pills aren't making you silly?"

Van fell silent. "Well, maybe I am feeling a little something."

Her laughter subsided. "I tell you what. Looks like

you've got some CDs in the back. If you've got something slow, let's pop it in. That way, you can relax, keep
your knee still, and let the medicine work. And I will
have some mellow music to cruise to. Deal?"

"Deal," he said. "And just so you know, as soon as the
medicine takes the pain away, I'm driving."

Yeah, right, she thought, but kept that to herself.

Van reached into the backseat and shifted around
the items on his side to fish out a square leather CD
case.

He flipped through the selections. "What's your poi-
son? I've got a few R&B cuts, some slow fusion, or . . .
some Marc Anthony."

"Now you're talkin'!" Morgan said.

"I made this myself. Seventeen of his slow cuts."

He inserted the CD into the player. She slid him a sly
glance. "Why, Van, I didn't picture you as the sentimen-
tal type."

"I'm not. This is, well . . ."

"Don't tell me—your booty-call tape."

He smiled and closed his eyes. "I call it 'The
Soundtrack.'"

"I'll bet you do."

While Marc Anthony sang "Sin Te Vas," Van yawned
repeatedly and loudly. "Golly," he said. "I might be sleepy."

"Ya think?" she responded. "Why don't you just go
ahead and take a nap?"

"Nah. There's so much to see."

Morgan glanced around. Grass. Lots and lots of
grass. Patchy grass. Sparse grass. Grass that was mostly
dirt. Oh, wait a minute—an RV was coming up behind
them. Now there was excitement. "So much to see" was
an interesting statement coming from a man who'd had
his eyes closed for the last six minutes.

Morgan noticed Van was still holding her purse.
"Before you drift off," she said, "can you dig out my cell
phone and check it for messages?"

Van's groan was unmistakable. He opened his eyes.

"What's the matter?"

"You and your sisters. Do you *ever* do anything without them?"

"Of course."

"Really? Name something . . . anything."

Morgan racked her brain. She must have been flustered and Van must have caught her off guard, because at that very moment, she couldn't think of a thing.

"That's what I thought."

"My sisters and I are close."

"Too close," Van mumbled.

"What's that?" she asked, frustration thinning her voice.

"I'll bet I know as much about what's going on in your family as you do. Why? Because my best friend's conversation these days is 'family business.' Why does he tell me these things? Because Ashley is always telling *him*. And why is she always telling him? Because she is always up in 'the sisters' business' the same way 'the sisters' are all up in hers." Van wiped his hand down his face. "I feel sorry for my man."

"Why would you feel sorry for a man who is marrying into a family that loves him?" she asked, trying very hard to concentrate on the road and not strangling Van's throat.

He blew out a loud, relenting breath and opened her phone. "You have six missed calls." He scrolled down the list.

"Ashley. Ashley. Roxy. Marti. Ashley *again* and Clyde."

"Thank you," she said, still feeling insulted.

A strange expression came over Van, one she hadn't seen before. She guessed he really didn't understand about family. Especially one as close as hers. Oh, well, he'd learn, she thought, then corrected herself. Van probably wouldn't be around long enough to learn a lesson as important as that. He would only be around until midnight tonight when they pulled up at her place. After that, the only time she would see him would be on the channel WAGA Fox5 news.

"You want to return any calls?"

"Yes," she answered, reaching for the phone.

It rang before he handed it to her. Ashley.

She pressed TALK.

"Hey," Morgan said, trying to sound like all was well with the world. If she didn't, Ash would recognize the unease in her voice and call her on it.

"Are you all right?"

"Yes, Ashley."

"Are you sure? I feel something."

Her sister was famous for her cosmic experiences. They made most of her family members a little crazy. But she meant well.

"I'm fine."

"No, you're not," Van said. "You're on the road with a man who would like nothing more than to rip your clothes off and ride you so slow and easy you scream in Spanish."

"Is that Van?" Ashley asked.

Morgan sucked her teeth. "That's him. He fell on his knee and took some ibuprofen. Girl, the stuff is making him spacey."

"I didn't fall! You knocked me down!" He leaned over as if he'd had five too many drinks. "She tried to hump me, outside, in broad daylight! Tacky. Just tacky."

He shook a finger in her face, then leaned back to his side of the car.

"Ash, I can't talk now. Van is trippin'."

"Okay, I'll let you go. As long as you're all right."

She glanced at Van. Four ibuprofen had him feeling no pain. Peace, serenity, and straight up dizzy warred for control of his face.

"Yeah, we're all right."

"Call me when you get in."

"I will," Morgan said and hung up. "Can you put this back in my purse for me?"

Van's head lolled back and forth against the headrest. "Sh-bure!" he said, sounding like a drunk Mushmouth.

She handed him the phone, but should have known better. It slipped right through his fingers quicker than water. "Uh-oh," he said.

The phone fell between them and dropped between her seat and the armrest. With her left hand on the steering wheel, she reached down. She felt the phone with her fingertips, got a grip around the top part of the phone, and pulled. It wouldn't move. She pulled again. It still wouldn't move. Instead, it started ringing.

"Phone ringing, Lil," Van slurred.

"I hear it," she said. She noted the familiar rise of frustration and realized that frustration had been her best friend since starting this trip with Van.

Morgan reached around the phone with her fingers, trying to figure out what it was caught on. Part of the phone was wedged against the seat back extender. She pushed, shoved, turned, slanted, and tilted the phone. Nothing worked. It was caught really badly and still ringing.

"Lillian, get the phone," Van said.

"I will!" she responded, wondering how many times Van had seen Eddie Murphy's routine about his mother, Lillian.

The frustration finally turned to anger and with a burst of strength, she yanked the phone free.

"Lillian, hang up the phone," Van said, obviously responding to the loud dial tone filling the air.

Morgan pressed END and checked to see who had called. Roxy. She hit REDIAL and the loud dial tone returned.

"What?" she said, then realized that the speakerphone function must have come on when she yanked the phone loose.

"Hey, girl," Roxanne's voice said.

"Hey, Roxy. Hold on," she said. She pushed the speakerphone button, but nothing happened. It was still activated on her screen.

"Say something," Morgan said, then yanked the phone away when Roxanne responded, "Something"—but it came across as if broadcast at Level Ten over Bose speakers.

"Why do I sound funny?" Roxy asked. "Did you put me on speakerphone?"

"No. Yes. My phone is broken," she said, pressing SPEAKERPHONE repeatedly with no success.

Good thing this stretch of highway is fairly straight and uneventful, she thought, passing a Cadillac.

"What's going on?" Van asked, raising his head.

Just what I need—Van to come out of his stupor.

"What's this I hear about you humping Van outside? Ashley said you attacked him!"

"Not attacked, tackled. And it wasn't for—"

"What are you talking about? And who are you talking to?" Van said.

"Is that Van? Hey, weatherman! How's it going? I guess you and my sister are getting along pretty good, huh?"

Van swung his head around with much effort. "Who *is* that?"

"Roxy," Morgan said, dread lining her voice.

"Dang, heifer! You don't have to sound so excited."

"A sister," Van responded, running a hand down his face.

"Yeah, I'm a sister!" Roxanne shouted.

Morgan wanted to cover her ears, but she had to keep both hands on the wheel.

"You got something against black women?"

"No, Roxy," Morgan said, "he meant sister as in *my* sister. But I don't even want to get into that now. Look, I'm fine. Tell everybody I'm fine. If anything changes, I'll call. Okay?"

"Are you telling us not to call you?"

Van's eyebrow went up. He stared at Morgan, waiting.

She wanted to prove to him that she could do some things without her sisters.

"Yeah," she said. "That's what I'm saying."

"Wow. You must really like him."

What Morgan wouldn't give to close her eyes and forget the whole conversation.

"You call me when you get home, you hear? As soon as you get home!"

"I will. I promise."

"Okay. I'll tell everyone not to bother you."

"Thanks, Roxy!"

Whew! she thought, grateful for that ordeal to be over. Van had fallen silent again. She looked over. His head was down and rolling in time with the motion of the car. He was out and not a moment too soon.

Morgan couldn't help herself. Now that they were back on the road, and Van was out cold, she glanced periodically in the rearview mirror. It was funny how Brax had been behind them at the beginning of the trip. It was comforting to know that a friend was on the road with them. But he was probably miles away by now, maybe only stopping to refuel. He probably had a refrigerator in his rig and didn't bother much with truck stops. *I'll be in the area for a few days*, she heard him say.

Oh, what do I care, she asked herself. He was just another man she would probably never see again. Ships passing. She turned up Marc Anthony just a tad. She didn't want the volume to wake up Mr. Wrong, but she wanted to hear Marc when he held his notes for so long she wanted to gasp for him.

The hottest part of the day was approaching. The dashboard clock read two P.M. She'd just gotten behind the wheel two hours ago, but it felt like she'd been driving all day. They were still in Indiana. At this rate, it would take longer than twelve hours to get back.

Morgan remembered the map and tried to recall a shorter, faster route. She might be able to take Highway forty-six to the interstate. Ah, she thought. The familiarity of four lanes and the luxury of seventy-five miles per hour instead of sixty-five and, on some stretches, fifty-five.

She glanced at Van, who was sleeping like a wino in the seat next to her. He looked passed out, completely oblivious to everything. And his knee—she took her eyes off the road long enough to check out his knee. He had his jeans on, but she could tell the knee was swelling. If it got too tight against the fabric, they might have to cut the jeans to get them off.

That interstate sounded better and better. She kept an eye out for the exchange that would lead her to it and hoped Van would stay asleep long enough for her to get them far enough along on the interstate that it wouldn't make sense to go back to the slow, two-lane gig.

Latin rhythms urged her on. A guitar, a marimba, and Spanish syllables sung so beautifully, the inside of her mouth tasted spicy and flavorful—as if she'd just eaten authentic Mexican.

The interchange was coming up quickly. She grabbed the map to get a closer look. She was right. She would have to take Highway forty-six for one hundred or so miles to get to Interstate Sixty-Five. Once on sixty-five, she could drive straight through to Kentucky. She couldn't wait; they would be home in no time. Ashley could stop worrying about her wedding dress and Van could get his knee taken care of.

In the back of her mind, she knew there was another reason she wanted to get home quickly. She wanted to be free of Van, or at least his influence. Being this close to him was eating away at her resolve. If she wasn't careful, she really would be humping him on the side of the road, bad knee or not.

"Whew," she exhaled and turned up the air conditioner. The visual on that thought gave her a hot flash.

Highway forty-six was straight ahead and the merge was on the right. She took a deep breath and turned the car, hoping Van would understand once he woke up. After all, the king of adventure couldn't object to the change in plans now with his knee injury. Even so, she was still glad he was asleep.

Flat lands and cornfields stretched out on either side of the highway. She hadn't seen so much farmland since she was a kid on a family vacation. Even with the latest equipment, farming still looked like a lot of work to her. She'd take a month of eighteen-hour shoots before she'd take a day of farming. Unless it was a peanut farm. Maybe she would make an exception for that.

Speak of the devil, she thought. Lo and behold, a big red tractor prattled amiably along on an access road at the top of the upcoming hill. Well, driving that thing wouldn't be too bad. She kept her attention on the road and her eye on the tractor as she approached. With enormous wheels on the back and smaller wheels on the front, it resembled a metal monster with its snout stretched out before it. But instead of pulling some other piece of equipment, it was just rolling along as if the driver had suddenly decided to take it out for a spin.

Morgan kept watching the equipment as it traversed the dirt road; she was getting close enough to see the driver. Would it be the stereotypical farmer with wrinkled, sun-leathered skin in Oshkosh overalls and cap? Maybe it was a woman or a young adult. Just as she was about to find out for sure, the tractor turned and took the road headed toward the highway intersection.

What is this guy doing? she wondered. She didn't have to wait long for an answer. The slow-moving machine pulled out in the middle of the highway and took off down the road . . . right in front of her.

She braked quickly. "No, no!" Morgan pounded her fist against the steering wheel. Van shifted in his seat, groaned, and fell silent. A lot of help he'd be if they were in trouble. "Ooh!" she said in an exasperated breath. The tractor toddled along at twenty miles per hour, taking up almost both lanes. A SLOW-MOVING VEHICLE sign was nailed to the back. Morgan had no choice but to keep her distance and grit her teeth until the next passing lane came up.

She was nothing like Van, she realized. Van would have been fascinated by the machine and curious about how it worked and where the guy was taking it. He would have played some lively music to pass the time, or checked the weather. Better yet, he would have stared into the clouds, as she'd caught him doing from time to time, and taken a moment to appreciate the current conditions.

All Morgan wanted to do was honk and make the old coot move over.

To Morgan, the world and everything in it had suddenly slowed down. Especially anything that had to do with her. She shook her head sadly. Her career had slowed down. Her relationships with men—definitely slowed down. Her time with her sisters, now that they all had men to tend to, had slowed down. Her enthusiasm for life . . . slowed down.

She had to admit it to herself: she was in a rut. Even with her audition for commentator and hanging out with Clyde in all the swanky "in" places from New York to L.A., the only excitement she'd experienced recently involved making her sister's dress and sleeping with Van. She blew out a sad breath. Her eyes looked straight ahead, but her mind was a million miles away.

They passed three intersections before mercifully coming to a passing lane. She took it gladly and bid the old farmer adieu. She retracted all the times she wanted to throw something at the back of his wrinkled head and shout, "Get a move on!" and resumed her drive down the highway. The route change would be coming up soon.

Van stirred in his sleep. Morgan chanced a glance in his direction. He looked so comfortable and charming, except for the disgusting line of slobber sliding down the side of his chin. If it hadn't been for that, she might have stolen a kiss from his silly butt.

Stay asleep, Van McNeil. Stay asleep. Just a little while longer. We'll be on the interstate and there will be no turning back.

The merge was just ahead. She flipped on the turn signal and veered to the right. The road was a long, slow curve winding upward to the highway. She could tell by the gradual increase of cars and buildings that this area was more populated than the one they'd just left.

"Civilization," she muttered under her breath. At least, she thought it was under her breath.

"What about civilization?" Van asked. His voice sounded like it had been caught in a fog and was struggling to come out. He sat up, went into the glove compartment, opened a toilette packet he found inside, and wiped his face. "Where are we?"

"On our way home," she said, wondering why, just this once, things couldn't go her way.

Marc Anthony was still singing. The CD had started over, but somehow his soulful voice was not as soothing.

The sign was an average highway sign, but when they passed it, it looked as big as a billboard.

"Interstate sixty-five? How'd we get here? Are you lost?"

Take a deep breath, bite the bullet, she told herself. "I'm getting us back to Atlanta faster."

"You're what?" Van said, grabbing the map from between their seats. "Morgan. . ."

The exasperation she heard in his voice made her regret her action—almost.

"Van, how's your knee?"

"It feels like a sixteen-pound bowling ball with millions of sharp needles sticking out of it. Other than that, it's fine."

"We should probably find a hospital, or a local doctor somewhere, and have your knee looked at. We can't do that if we're traveling in backwoods America."

Van checked his watch and scanned the sky. It was bright with sunlight. Not a cloud in sight.

"I know you were expecting a storm sometime today, but as you can see, clear skies ahead."

"You should have asked me, Morgan. There are two of us and this is my car. Don't forget, I'm giving *you* a ride back to the city. Not the other way around."

Morgan chuckled. Such bravado from a man with a gimpy knee. "You really *are* Mr. Wrong. Look," she began, and took off her sunglasses so he could see that she was serious. "We don't need to waste time here. We need to get home. I see all your fancy equipment here, but there's no storm to track. And besides"—she said, putting her glasses back on—"if you haven't noticed, I'm driving now. An hour ago you didn't know your own name. You were in no shape for me to ask anything."

"That's not true," he huffed.

"Not true? Do you even remember anything from an hour ago?"

"Of course." He fell silent for a long moment. "I remember complaining about my knee, you making me take those stupid pills, getting sleepy, and falling asleep."

"You don't remember anything else?"

"What else is there to remember?"

"Nothing," she said with a smile. "Nothing at all."

He stared at her for a long moment. "Used to getting your way, aren't you?"

He just couldn't leave it alone.

"No, I'm not. As a matter of fact, I'm used to fighting, sometimes clawing and scratching, for everything I get."

"What do you take me for? The only clawing and scratching you're used to doing is against the back of whatever man candy is in your life at the time."

"Van, don't make me pull this car over and bust up your other knee."

"Just be honest. You are drop-dead, eyes-buggin'-out, knock-'em-over-with-a-feather gorgeous. Everything in your life has been easy. Or at least a heck of a lot easier than it is for most folks. This is a man's world, baby, but men take one look at you and hand the world right over. So the fact that I wanted to do something you didn't, like take my time getting back to Georgia, got under your skin like a splinter. Even something as simple as that worked your nerves until you had to figure out how to get your way."

She opened her mouth to speak. Van cut her off.

"Don't even try to lie to me, Morgan. I know you too well."

"You don't know me," she retorted. Anger boiled just below the surface of her resolve. "Cumulatively, we've been in each other's company for all of what . . . ten hours, including our faux date and our tête-à-tête last week. What do you know about me besides what my sister may have told you? Nothing! That's what. Now prop up your knee and shut up, please. I'm trying to concentrate on the road."

Van's jaw snapped closed and he stared straight ahead. But Morgan knew he was right. God help him, or God help her—he had hit the nail on the head. And there was something else: he did seem to know her. It felt as though they were a couple in this car, they'd been dating for years, and were just having a disagreement they would resolve later by having soul-shattering make-up sex.

It was spooky.

"We need to stop," Van said.

"Right now? Why?"

"At the next rest area or something. I've got to take a leak."

Crass. "No problem," she said, still simmering warmly from their exchange. Maybe he'd just woken up on the wrong side, so to speak. She wanted to ask him if he wouldn't mind taking another pill or two; she liked him better when he thought he was Eddie Murphy.

The sign said *Bear Diggers Next Right*. She didn't know what "Bear Diggers" was, but, judging from the expression on Van's face and his fidgeting, they would find out and pray that it had a restroom.

Morgan took the right and traveled up the hill to the mouth of the exit. At first glance, she was disappointed and nervous. Then she saw it, a large building made of old brown wood planks. It was like something out of a movie. The place looked deserted, except for an old sky-blue pickup that had definitely seen better days. She parked beside it and they stepped out.

"I hope someone's home," she said, trying to lighten the mood. The brick wall that had fallen between them had gotten old already.

"If not, I'll just take a walk around back," Van said.

Morgan shook her head. Men.

Van tried the door. It was locked. He knocked hard and they waited.

"I'll be back," he said. "Get in the car."

"Do you need some help?"

"I'll manage."

"Okay," she said, watching Van hobble around back. She wanted to be agreeable, but she had no intention of getting back in the car. It was hot, yes, but standing up felt so good. She stretched, shook out her legs, and wondered what was going on in the world. Was O'Hare still on high alert? She'd be sure to turn on the radio and find a news station when they got back in the car.

Even in the intense sun, the place was so brown and dark, she wondered if it could even be seen at night. The side wood slats were assembled haphazardly, nailed askew, like an ochre house of cards about to fall. The wood had deep groves and contours as if Mother Nature had raked it in circles and curves with her fingernails. It couldn't possibly be safe. No one in their right mind would go inside for longer than two minutes for fear the whole structure would collapse around them. It was a good thing Van had decided to go around back.

Van had only been gone for a few minutes when a man came around the opposite side of the building with a portable billboard.

"Can I help you?" the man asked.

"No, thanks. I'm just waiting for my friend. We knocked but there was no answer, so he—"

Just then Van and a middle-aged woman came out of the building.

"Mort, I caught this guy snooping around out back."

"You did?" he said, anchoring the billboard in place. It was yellow with large black letters that read COUNTRY FRIED WING BASKET $7.99, LINE DANCING FREE, KARAOKE $500 PRIZE.

"Yep," she said. "Right around the horseweed."

"Is that a fact?" He flipped a switch and the yellow sign lit up. He turned it off and wiped his hands as if he'd been working in a garden.

"Well, you know what we do with snoopers."

This conversation was making Morgan uneasy. The last thing they needed was to get mixed up with a couple of crazies in the middle of nowhere. She'd seen *Pulp Fiction* way too many times.

Before she could protest or apologize, the couple spoke in unison.

"We invite them inside for a drink!"

Morgan blew out a grateful breath. Van laughed. He'd known what was up the entire time.

"Thanks," Morgan said. "But we really don't have time to stop."

"Sure we do," Van said. "We have plenty of time now."

Morgan knew he was referring to taking the interstate.

"Besides, I'm hungry," he said.

"Well, if it's food you want, you'll have to take the Fifty-Six down two miles to Franklin's General. Our stuff's put away until we open again this evening at four-thirty."

"Okay, thanks," Van said, walking toward Morgan. "We'll check out Franklin's."

"You can't miss it," the man said. "Take the first exit to the access road."

Morgan walked toward the car. Van followed.

"Y'all come back sometime when we're open. We have a good time!" the man called after them.

"I don't think we'll be back this way, Pop," Van said.

Even in his disabled condition, Van opened the door for Morgan. They both smiled at the kindly couple. "Bye."

When Van was inside, she started the car and they were off to find Franklin's General. Morgan slid Van a smile. "So you got caught, huh?"

"No. When I walked around to the back, she was there hauling boxes in from a storage shed. I helped her with the boxes and she let me use their restroom. Even trade, I'd say."

Van sat back, adjusting his sunglasses.

"What's it like inside?"

"Huge. Remember the bar from the movie *The Blues Brothers?*"

"Yeah."

"Multiply that by ten and you've got it. As sparse as this area looks, I can't imagine it ever filling up with people. I wonder how they keep it open."

"Did you see the parking lot? There must be enough spaces for three hundred cars."

"Maybe it was a factory once."

"Good explanation."

Van was fidgeting again, clenching and unclenching his jaw.

"Look, Morgan," he turned toward her and even with sunglasses on, she could see the earnestness in his eyes, "I was abrasive back there. I didn't mean to be. I woke up stupid."

"Well, the thing is . . . you were right. All I've wanted since I got in the car with you was to get home as soon as possible. That dress in the backseat is more than just a dress. I wish I could explain what it means, how important it is."

All the emotion, prayers, thoughts, feelings, blessings, and love Morgan had poured into making that dress came bursting to the surface. Her voice quivered as she continued.

"I'm going to be anxious until the dress I made is in my sister's hands, ready for her to wear on her wedding day."

"I hear what you're saying, Morgan, but something tells me it's not all about the dress. When you can be honest about that, you can stop being so anxious."

This twelve-hour drive was starting feel like a really, really bad idea. Her sisters were right—she really didn't know who Van was. He could be some volatile sicko just waiting to get an unsuspecting model-type away from civilization and do who knew what. She was about to reach for her broken phone and call Marti, Roxy, or somebody for reassurance, when she saw the exit they were looking for. She took it and headed straight for the rustic general store just off the main road.

Chapter Eleven

Van felt hungover. Like he'd thrown back twenty-some bottles of beer or maybe just one really bad one. His head felt like one solid mass, heavy and thick. *No more ibuprofen for me—ever.*

Some food would do him all kinds of good. It would take his mind off the pain and the fact that no matter what she did or said, he still felt that Morgan Allgood was the sexiest, most fascinating woman he had ever met. She was complex, a puzzle to be solved. He could spend forever figuring her out.

Damn. Forever.

The general store was just as deserted as Bear Diggers. One lone car outside. He decided to test his injury, so he put his full weight on his right leg first. He paid for that silly idea with a bolt of pain that shot from his knee to his head and exploded into white light.

"I said I would help you," Morgan admonished him coming to his side. She slid an arm around his and helped him stand.

"I don't get it," he said. "It's just a scrape."

"I think you've just proven it's *not* just a scrape. Let's grab enough food for the rest of the trip and push the speed limit home. You got a fuzz buster back there?"

"Yeah," he said.

"Why don't you wait here while I go in?"

"Bad idea. My knee may be stiff because I wasn't on it long enough back there. Walking on it might help."

She gave him a look, a look he'd seen Ashley give his best friend on more than one occasion. It was the battle face. The face that said he was in for a fight.

She studied him for a moment and then a miracle happened. The battle face went away. What was left was a smirk of indignation.

"You're not going to wait in the car no matter what I say, are you?"

"Nope."

"Come on," she said.

Being out on the road was such a huge contrast from the city. So much room and so much silence. He stretched, let the sun warm his skin that had been chilled stiff by the air conditioner. A steady wind blew in from the north. It was hard not to think of things in terms of barometric pressure and air currents. Where most people saw cloud movement, he saw jet streams and warm fronts.

Someone asked him once if knowing the physics of climate took away the magic and mystery of it. But it didn't. On the contrary, because he understood how the magic worked, he was even more in awe.

"At this rate we won't get to Atlanta until three in the morning."

"But we'll get there, Allgood. We'll get there," he said. Then, without a clear thought in his head, he slung his arm around her shoulders. Not for support. Just to touch her, pull her close, remember how a heat hotter than fire radiated between them. Instead of the icy rejection he expected, Morgan responded by wrapping her arm around his waist.

It was as natural as the sun shining in the sky.

Why hadn't they done this sooner? This little piece

of intimacy changed the tension between them. Dissipated it completely.

She held him tighter and together they tottered into the general store.

Time machines do exist, Van thought, walking inside. It wasn't quite the 1800s, but it was close. Touches of modern technology—overhead lights, refrigerators, and an ATM machine—amidst wood floors, an apothecary, wheat barrels, an antique coffee grinder and scale, potbelly stove, and a sewing thread bin with more colors of thread than Van knew existed.

His sensitive black man's nose took in tobacco, chocolate, and Murphy's Oil Soap.

The only missing elements were two buddies at the porch entrance in rocking chairs, playing checkers.

"Afternoon," a man behind the checkout counter said.

"Afternoon," Van and Morgan said together.

"Something I can help you find?" the man asked.

His face was a pleasant blend of happy eyes and a big smile. "Big" was the operative word. The man wasn't very tall, but he was very, very round. Round eyes, round nose. His two chins were round. Round tire of a midsection. Pudgy, round fingers. Round man. Van couldn't see them, but he'd bet the man had small round feet that barely looked long enough to balance his weight.

"Do you have Peanut Butter Bing?" Morgan asked.

"As a matter of fact, I've got some in the candy aisle. Down toward the bottom on your left."

Van limped alongside Morgan. "What's Peanut Butter Bing?"

"Have you heard of Cherry Bing?"

"Yeah."

"Same thing, only instead of cherries, the main ingredient is peanut butter. Before Peanut Butter Twix and Peanut Butter M&M's, there was Peanut Butter Bing."

"I should have known."

Country music piped in from hidden speakers. Despite his sore knee, Van almost whistled. Something in his soul turned, like a plant to sunlight. It was turning toward Morgan. And what he wanted was more than one night could provide.

Then the thought of her sisters popped into his head. He gritted his teeth. He had walked out on that idea eight months ago.

Van watched Morgan's face light up as she found the small bag of candy she was searching for and thought that maybe, just maybe, being with Morgan and all that came with her might not be so bad.

"I thought we were buying *real* food," he said.

Morgan kissed the package and spun around. "Right, Mr. Wrong! Peanut butter *is* real food!"

He laughed. "You know, I'm going to come up with a name for you."

Morgan picked up a hand basket at the end of an aisle and threw her candy in. "Go right ahead. I'm sure I've already been called worse than anything you can come up with."

"By who?" he asked, picking up a bag of pork rinds. If Morgan was going to go for a crazy back-in-the-day snack, so was he.

"Tabloids, mostly. Between the *National Enquirer* and the *Star*, I've been a hooker, a drug addict, and a man in drag. Of course, I'm not well known enough to merit my own story. It's always attached to the man I'm dating."

"Like Murder One."

"I think I mentioned that Clyde and I are just friends. We like to hang. It's comfortable. And it's useful, too. It keeps most people away from both of us."

They maneuvered around barrels of dried goods and bags of flour piled in rows. The hard soles of Morgan's pumps clacked against the wood floor. They threaded through the rows crowded with foodstuffs like a couple shopping for dinner for the hundredth time. When Morgan discovered a box of Peanut Butter Crunch cereal, she was beside herself. Van had to convince her not to buy two boxes.

She laughed. Her happiness touched him, all the way to his womanizing soul. Even his busted and swollen knee felt a little better.

The bell above the general store door rang just as it had when he and Morgan had come in. They picked up a few more items, cashews for Morgan, beer nuts for Van, ham and cheese sandwiches for both of them, and headed for the cash register and the roly-poly man behind the counter—the man whose pleasantries seemed as big as his size.

"Hold on there, Will and Jada," a voice said. The voice belonged to a young man with long blond hair, a beard like a cactus plant stuck to his chin, a body as thin as the man behind the counter's was large, and sad gray eyes. *Shaggy,* Van thought immediately. *He looks like Shaggy from Scooby-Doo.* He wondered what his problem was until he saw the gun coming out of his pocket. Instinctively, Van stepped in front of Morgan.

"Don't you have something to do?" the man asked, training his gun on Van and Morgan but speaking to the cashier.

The large man narrowed his eyes and slowly lifted twenties, tens, fives, and ones from his register and put them in a plastic container that looked like Tupperware.

"Hurry up!" the skinny man said. Then he turned to Van and Morgan.

"Wallet, billfold. In the box."

"Van," Morgan said, eyes bright with concern.

"Let's do as he says," Van said. His heart pounded like a Japanese drum in his chest. It wouldn't take much to tackle him. A good block, like the one Morgan threw on him earlier, would do it. But with a gun, and Van's bad leg, it was much too risky. Van couldn't take the chance that in the struggle, the gun would go off and injure someone or worse.

With the basket in his left hand, Van reached in his pocket with his right. Morgan dug in her purse.

"Stay here," Van said, taking her billfold. He put it and his wallet in the plastic container with the money.

Van glanced at the cashier, who didn't look so good. He was as red as a tomato and seemed as though he were trying to kill Shaggy with his stare.

"Good. Very good," the young man said. Then he smiled, revealing decayed yellow teeth, rotted most likely by methamphetamine—which he might even have been on at this moment. "Nothing personal," he added, staring at Morgan for far too long.

The cashier shouted, lunging his portly body across the counter. Of course, he was too large and too slow to take advantage of Shaggy's momentary distraction. The young man simply sidestepped the thick hands reaching for his throat and swung the butt of the gun up against the cashier's forehead.

The thud of gun against skull sounded like a fist squishing into a deep-dish pie. The force of the blow knocked the man backward, where he hit his head against the wall and slumped to the floor.

"Oh, my God!" Morgan shrieked. She grabbed Van's arm. He could feel the tension coursing from her into him.

"Hollywood!" the young man yelled at Van. "Make sure he's not dead."

Van gave Morgan a reassuring touch on her arm. Her eyes grew wide with anxiousness. "Stay here," he whispered.

He limped over to where the man lay in a heap on the ground. He checked for a pulse and other things as well—like a panic button to signal the police, an alarm of any kind, or a shotgun like the one that's always behind the counter in the movies.

Nothing.

But the man was breathing.

"He's alive," Van said. His forehead was already red from the blow. He would wake up with a nasty headache.

"Thank Jesus," Morgan said.

Even Shaggy seemed relieved. Van guessed he had planned a clean getaway without loss of life.

"What's takin' so long, Billy?" A scraggly woman in worse shape than the robber stood holding the door open.

"Don't use my name, you idiot!" he shouted at her. "Now turn over that sign and get back in the car!"

The woman's gaze roamed over Van's body like dirty fingers. He shuddered. He usually liked it when a woman found him attractive. Not this time. Definitely not this time. She left without a word and turned over the sign in the window to read CLOSED to anyone who would happen by.

"All right, Hollywood. I need to make sure me and my girl get a nice long chance to get away. Now, I don't want to hurt you, but I will," he declared, his body tense and jittery.

Billy glanced over at the man still unconscious on the floor, then his eyes traveled back to Morgan with an unholy stare. The smile that took over his face looked pulled straight from hell. It sent Van's flesh crawling in all directions.

"Strip," Billy said.

Van stepped toward him. "Now, wait a minute—"

"You, too," he said.

"What!" Van and Morgan said at the same time.

He cocked the gun. "I said *strip*, both of you!"

Morgan looked at Van, cold dread filling her eyes. Van looked at her.

"Look, man. We're not going to call anyone, okay."

"Yes, you will. As soon as I step out that door. I'm just going to make sure you don't get the chance for a long time. Now, strip!"

The guy was getting shakier by the minute. Van nodded to Morgan to do as they were told. But no matter what, he was determined that even if it meant his life, this crazy drug addict would not lay a finger on her.

"Move!" Billy said, motioning them aside to an area away from the front door.

Van soon found himself unbuttoning his shirt. He glanced at Morgan, realizing that it wouldn't take much clothing removal before she would be naked. If this crazy fool had any notions about trying anything with her, one of them was going to die today.

The gun shook because the robber's whole body was a shaking and quaking mass of twitches. And it seemed as though he was the only one in the room who hadn't noticed.

"You two are taking much too long!"

"Jesus!" Morgan exclaimed, pulling her top over her head.

"Just do as he says," Van admonished her. He didn't want shakin' Shaggy's forefinger to jump or twitch a bullet out of that gun.

Morgan's expression was brutal. "Shut up, Van!"

He blinked with surprise. "Morgan, calm down."

"That's hard to do with a gun pointed at my chest."

"Look—"

"No, *you* look. If you hadn't been so determined to take your sweet time about getting back home, we never would have stopped here."

She was yanking off her clothes now, fury rising from her skin like steam.

"Are you crazy?" Van asked. He unbuttoned his pants, let them fall, stepped awkwardly out of them. The pain medication was starting to wear off. "Don't forget, I'm giving *you* a ride. If it weren't for me, your"—he took an eyeful of the derriere she was exposing by unwrapping her skirt—"big butt would still be in Chicago. Now, if you think you can do better," he said and removed his boxer briefs—"go for it!"

Despite the cold steel pointed in their direction, Van's mind registered Morgan's reaction to him standing naked beside her. Hmm. They'd talk about that later, assuming there was a later.

"Shut up and take it off! Sunglasses, too!" the young man said, referring to Morgan's thong. "Better yet, let me help you." Before Van could move to grab him, the man slid the barrel of the gun under the elastic of the thong and pulled.

Morgan's body shuddered and her eyes bore into Van's as the last article of clothing was removed from her body, including her shades.

"Now what?" she asked, crossing her arms over her breasts and cocking her hips as if she were fully clothed instead of standing buck naked at gunpoint.

Mr. Jumpy kicked their clothes away and looked around. Outside, a car horn blared like a siren.

"Stupid wench," he said. "Go on! Over there!"

They followed his directions past the chips, candy, and beer into the back of the store. At first, Van thought they were headed to the bathroom. When they walked past the bathroom, dread pounded in Van's chest.

"Get in," he ordered, motioning toward the freezer.

"Oh, my God," Morgan said. Goosebumps were already popping out on her skin.

"Don't worry," Van said as they stepped inside.

"And now if you'll excuse me, I'll be gone. I'm gonna give the big guy another conk on the head, then me and my lady are takin' off. We'll be halfway to Timbuktu before you all get outta here."

He was delusional. Van could see it in his eyes.

Probably imagining he was the star of some crime-spree movie. Van wondered if even detox and extensive therapy would help.

"Be cool," Billy said and closed the door. They heard scratching metal and fumbling on the other side of the door and then what sounded like running.

Van guessed the juiced-up youngster didn't realize that modern freezers had a mechanism inside so that stockers couldn't get locked in. He just hoped that the freezer's old-fashioned look was only a façade.

It wasn't.

"Help me look for the release lever," Van said.

Marching around to relieve their feet from contact with the cold floor, Van and Morgan searched for a release lever. The only switch they found was to the overhead light.

Unless the unlock button was camouflaged really well, they were in trouble.

Van shoved his weight at the door. Nothing. Just the icy smooth surface of steel that felt bolted in place. "Keep looking for a release," he said. "Keep your body away from any place on the metal that's frosted."

Among rows of frozen pints of ice cream, ice cream treats, pizzas, pizza rolls, frozen vegetables, and dinners, they searched behind the shelves for a lever, a button, a spring, anything that would unlock the door. Morgan took one side, Van took another. By the time they'd searched to the middle of the freezer, he knew it was futile. There couldn't possibly be a release this far away from the door.

"I can't believe you just let that guy lock us in here," Morgan grumbled.

"Did you say *let* him?"

She was silent. Van kept looking for a lever in order to keep his mind in a safe place. He shoved a bag of frozen French fries aside. "Did you see the gun? 'Cause I sure as hell did!"

"You're so much bigger than he is. You've got to be twice his size. You could have taken him."

His head snapped around to stare at her. "What do I look like, Vin Diesel?"

Her gaze slid down his body, serpentlike. "No. You look nothing like Vin."

He swung completely around. "So the tabloids were right. You dated him."

"We didn't date. It was all sex. Burned itself out real quick."

"So what am I, just a vowel change?"

Morgan's eyes flashed anger, but her laughter belied her fury. Van struggled against it. Eventually, Morgan won and he laughed along with her.

"Okay, look. With this bum knee, I couldn't take a chance that Mr. Jittery wouldn't kill someone. Namely you. Now can we forget about all that for now and concentrate on getting the hell out of here and calling an ambulance for the man out there?"

"Okay, should we push together?"

"Let's try it."

They pressed their weight against the cold door and shoved. The enclosed space filled with their grunts and machinations of strain as they pushed so hard their bodies shook.

That didn't work either.

"Stand back," Van said, prepared to try and kick the door down.

"Wait!" Morgan said. "There's already something wrong with your right leg. If you mess up your left leg, we'll be in a world of trouble."

Van glanced at the bandage on his knee with a fresh stain of blood on it. "I guess you're right."

Morgan clutched herself. Rubbed her hands up and down her arms.

"Are you cold?" he asked.

"Two words: *naked* and *freezer*."

"Smart aleck. Come here." He opened his arms and she walked right into them. He didn't know if his shiver was from the fact that he was holding her again or the chill on her skin.

"You really are cold."

The thermostat on the wall read minus two-degrees, but the temperature in his body had just jumped up significantly. At that moment, he wanted to do anything but moan. But what did he do? Moaned like a lovesick schoolboy.

"Don't even think about it, Van."

"Why not? You can't tell me you haven't thought about it. You can't tell me you aren't thinking about it right now. Can you?"

"Van—"

"Can you?"

"No. But we've been locked up at gunpoint. In a freezer, of all places. And there is a man outside lying on the ground who probably needs a doctor."

"I understand that. I'm simply saying there is a chemistry between us that I'm not asking you to act on, only acknowledge."

She pulled tighter against him, her body beginning to shudder. Van tried to create heat by running his hands over her arms, her sides, her back. He nuzzled in closer.

"Are you fishing for a compliment, Mr. Wrong?"

"Damn, Morgan," he said, staring at her piercing eyes. "I'd just gotten comfortable. Why do you keep backing away from me?"

"I'm not backing away from you. I'm backing away from the lifestyle you represent."

She spoke in clipped tones, but her embrace never faltered.

"How is my lifestyle different from the way you've been living since the day you became a model?"

"I'm freezing," she said. "Can we move around?"

"Sure, and you can answer my question while we're moving."

He wouldn't have thought that ice and cold had a smell. It did. He tried to discern it. A crisp, dry frost. White light and air. Or cold paper. It all meant the same. They had to get out of there before their extremities were frostbitten.

The hum of the freezer motor droned loudly in the silence between them. Morgan held on but turned her head against his chest. "I need a change, Van. I'm not a kid anymore. I can't keep living fast and furious. After a while, it gets old. You and I are in two different places in our lives. You're still in 'The Life.' I'm trying to get out of it."

"Why?" he asked, genuinely wanting to know.

She pulled back and looked him in the eye. "How many models do you know who are my age, Van? It's time I get serious about life and start trying to plan for a stable future."

"Morgan Allgood, are you thinking about turning in your player card?"

"Yeah," she said, resting her head against his chest again. "So if I want to make a clean break, find a man I can settle down with, and, who knows, maybe even have some kids, I can't afford to get tangled up with you—Mack Daddy of the Century."

Van let out the breath he'd been holding since Morgan started talking. A fine time she picked to decide to become a one-man woman who wants a one-woman man.

"Why now?" But he knew the answer to that before he even asked the question, because in a week, all her sisters would be married except her. And now she was starting to feel bad about it, especially since she had always been dubbed the beauty of the family.

She sighed heavily. He didn't think she realized how

much tighter she held on to him. He only knew that an inferno was raging inside his body now and it was demanding to be quenched by the lips he hadn't been able to stop thinking of in more than a week. She took her time and finally said, "It's just time, Van. It's time."

She let go then and they searched again for the elusive lever, button, knob that would unlock the door and get them out of their frozen purgatory. He pushed aside broccoli, carrots, and brussel sprouts and pounded his fist against the steel walls.

For ten minutes they shouted separately and together for help. Nothing worked. Van was so cold he expected his words to come out frozen solid when he spoke.

Morgan shuddered against him. "Is it necessary to keep food this cold? This isn't frozen, it's frigid!"

They blew into their hands, waved their arms—but in the end, they came back to each other, to the only warmth that mattered. Van tried hard not to add his own shivering to Morgan's. Time and the steady whir of the motor defeated him. Soon they shook violently against each other as if attempting to shake apart instead of hug together.

"Say something," she said.

What could he say? The only thing in his head besides the cold was the fact that Morgan had made up her mind about him. The worst thing anyone could do was tell a man like him "no." Now all he could do was focus on how to turn that "no" into a "yes."

"I'm sorry we're here," he said.

"Me, too," she responded, clinging tighter. "How's your knee?"

"I can't feel it."

"My toes are starting to go numb. Fingers, too." She waited a beat and then, "Wake up, store-clerk man!" she shouted. "Get us out of here!"

Even if he was awake, Van realized it would be hard to hear anything coming from inside the freezer with the motors going.

"We've got to keep shouting," she said, as if she'd just plugged into his thoughts.

"Maybe there's a way for us to shout and keep warm at the same time."

"There you go again, turning something serious into something sexy. You men *must* think about it all the time!"

"For the record, sex *is* serious. And yes, we do. Like it or hate it, I don't see men changing anytime soon, so the best thing for you to do is deal with it."

"If I wasn't damn near frozen solid right now, I would . . ."

"What?" he asked and kissed her neck. "Tell me how much women think about it, too?"

Van didn't give her time to answer. Instead, he blew his breath on the crook of her neck and her shoulder, and the place at the base of her chin that made her moan like crazy. His efforts were not without their reward. She was quiet, sucked in a breath, and let it out slow.

"How do you feel?" he asked, moving his lips against her shoulder blade.

"Warmer," she said. "Sexy."

His hands trailed down her back, stopped at her butt, cradled it, kneaded it, pulled it toward him.

"I've been thinking about a name for you," he said, with his head against the side of her face. His hands continued to knead as he spoke. "You know, to go with Mr. Wrong." She drew in a breath. He kept on. "I'm going to call you Mahogany. But not for the wood, for the movie. You're beautiful, ambitious. You're involved with one of the most handsome men on the planet—"

"Ple—"

"No. You've done enough talking for a while. Just listen."

He kissed all the cold places on her neck and sucked them until they were warm. Her body loosened and some of the shivering subsided.

"Just like Tracy, I don't think you really know where you're going or what's really important in life. But I have no doubt that you'll figure it out."

They took small steps together and swayed as if there were music playing and they were working on a slow waltz.

He kissed her cheeks. "I'm going to tell you where we are right now. We're at your place in Atlanta. We're there because I know how you like to be in control. And I'm there to let you control me. To do whatever you want."

"Van."

"Let me know I'm right. Don't speak it. Just moan. All right. We're lying on your bed. Tito Puente is playing. Candles are burning and the moon is claiming the sky. If I touch you here," he said, massaging her round behind, gripping it firmly. "If my hands make promises to you of the pleasure to come, would you want me then, Morgan?" he asked, kneading the flesh of her buttocks. "Do you want me?"

"Yes," she whispered.

"Say it right," he uttered gently.

"Ummm," she moaned.

"That's right, baby. Just like that. You say you don't want me in your life, but I think you do. Don't you want to be with a man whose touch is like a key that opens the door to your soul?"

His lips brushed lightly against her ear. He whispered softly just behind it. *Please, God, let this warm her body.*

Her body temperature rose, as did his. He felt the heat generating between them. Almost enough to forget where they were, why they were there, and the tingling in their extremities. He needed to create a different kind of tingle. A more intense kind of heat. Something Morgan would never forget.

Chapter Twelve

Van's body had swallowed Morgan's. It covered her like a blanket and his words devoured her. Took her inside a cave and burned like a fire. She couldn't move away from the warmth.

His words generated a heat that started at her ear, tracked downward through her body, and spread. She listened and longed as each syllable brought her closer and closer to the brink of explosion.

"If you let me, I will make love to you like a perfect prayer. Until your body grows weightless with pleasure. Until you abandon your soul to desire. Until the walls of the room sweat from the inferno of passion in the bed. You have had sexual partners before, Morgan, but you have never had a lover. A man that coaxed your body to sweet bliss with the touch of his hand. A man whose lips strike like paradise against your flesh and who you abandon your soul to with a yearning so glorious that ecstasy bursts inside you and fills your every sense with his essence. I am that man, Morgan. I am that man."

Morgan pressed her face against the corded muscles of his chest. His grip tightened as he poured his words into her more urgently.

"I'm a good lover, Morgan. I can fill you with rapture so intense, each moment of climax will pass like an eternity with your body writhing within the throes of its release. Let me take a journey to the center of your soul, my beautiful one."

Her breathing escaped her lips in uneven gasps as his lean body molded into the contours of her curves and his words continued to torment her.

"My mouth burns with fire for you, Morgan. Let me brand you with its heat on your breasts. Suck the tight buds of your nipples while passion inches through your veins. Every time I look at you, I starve for the taste of your body. Let me dine and feast where your arousal flows wet and sweet for me when I touch you. Let me drive desire deep within you until your body vibrates with warm shivers against my hand."

Morgan moaned and locked herself in his embrace. His touch was firm and persuasive. She clamped her teeth as his hot breath against her ear sent channels of fire straight to her soul. His thigh brushed against her hip and she felt the hard length of him. Her entire body ached from the contact.

"See, baby, your mind can experience pleasure your body could never imagine. And afterward, after I take you again and again and you whimper helplessly, consumed by golden waves of passion, love made so well all you can do is tremble and cry, I will pull you close, rock you like a baby in my arms, and hold you until you fall into the sweet bliss of sleep."

At his last four words, soft explosions erupted like pulsing hands inside her and all her moans culminated into a note that sounded like it came straight from a love-ravaged opera scene. She held it for a long, long time.

When the sound of the note faded and her breathing returned to normal, she realized that her legs were shaking, but not from the cold. For a few moments, the freezer felt hot enough to melt ice cubes and cook the vegetables that surrounded them.

Van kissed her forehead, her nose, her mouth. Then he said, "Pretty good, huh?"

"Whatever!" she said, trying to dismiss the fact that a man could whisper and make her come. But she knew Van wasn't just any man.

"Hmph," he said, fondling her behind. "If you doubt me, I can do it again."

The burning heat returned, stronger this time. It rushed eagerly to her nipples and tightened them into hard pebbles. The flame of her lust for him licked tongues of desire between her thighs, turned her need into a volcano . . . waiting. "Again?" she asked weakly, her pulse quickening to the thought of the pleasure she knew he could bring her.

Van lowered his head, whispering into her left ear this time. "This time is on my turf. A beach in St. Lucia—no, Tahiti. The sun sends its red-orange glow that bathes us both in its light. We are alone. You are lying on a blanket. I am prone before you. Finally, after staring into your eyes, and using them to tell you everything I feel in my heart, I bend down, slowly, slowly, slowly and take my time to kiss your—"

The ruckus from outside the freezer startled them. Their heads snapped in the direction of the sound.

The freezer door swung open, sucking out cold air with it. Instinctively, Morgan clung tighter to Van. Certain parts of her body throbbed with regret. The large cashier and a sheriff stood in the shadow of fluorescent light that didn't quite reach past the door. They looked like ghosts, unwelcome specters. Van's body relaxed, but hers could not.

"Thanks for the rescue, guys. Leave us alone for a moment," she said, then stared at Van.

Van glanced at her curiously, then nodded his head.

"The sensation building between us are radiant, spectacular . . ." Van went on.

As she closed her eyes, Van continued to whisper and she prepared for the delicious shudder that was only moments away.

It was the best hot chocolate Morgan had ever tasted. She hugged the mug against her chest as if it were salvation itself. Of course, it wasn't. Salvation came in the form of Harley-James Hines and his wife, Verleen. Harley-James, who preferred to be called Harley, was cashier, stocker, maintenance man, and owner of Franklin's General Store.

"You all comfortable over there?" Verleen asked.

"Yes, ma'am," she said. Morgan was sitting on Verleen's couch, wearing something called a petticoat that was ten sizes too big and three sizes too short. But the blanket covering her hid it so well that she didn't have to think about it.

Their home was a small prefab house with two bedrooms and more country-style decorations than any home deserved. Ducks, geese, chickens, you name the wild bird, and it was on the wall, sitting on a table, or staring up from the carpet.

In all the fabric stores and designer warehouses Morgan had been in, she'd never seen so many ruffles and so much lace in her entire life.

If it weren't for the fact that the Hineses were generous with blankets and hot chocolate, she would have run from the house screaming.

Van and Harley had gone with the sheriff to make a report about the robbery. Morgan was with Verleen, warming up and resting from the ordeal.

"Are you sure you're all right, dear? I could bring you another blanket or put more chocolate sauce in your hot chocolate."

If she had some chunky peanut butter, they would have been in business. As it was, it really was the best hot chocolate she'd ever had because it was real hot chocolate. Not powder from a packet, but from fresh milk and real chocolate. If it weren't for the frilly stuff, Morgan would almost consider moving in, she was so content.

"I hope they find your car. It sounds like such a nice car. You know, my Harley is good at finding things. You leave it to him, you'll be back driving your—now, what is it, a VUS—in no time."

Morgan hoped so. Otherwise, they'd be hitching home. Bonnie and Clyde had taken not only their money, but their clothes, cell phones, sunglasses, car, and whatever hope they had of getting back to Atlanta within twelve hours. After spending nearly an hour in the freezer, and another at the Hines' house trying to warm up, Morgan's mind fixated on her sister's dress and tried to stave off the panic she felt building at the loss of it. What she really wanted, besides all the stuff they lost, was to call her sisters and tell them to wire some money so she could get the heck out of Dodge. Better yet, she should just call Marti and have her send the Williams family helicopter after them. If Van didn't return with Harley soon, she was going to do just that.

"Here you are, dear," Verleen said, handing her a fresh cup of steaming hot chocolate. It was a sky-blue cup with smiling white ducks on it. Yuck! But what was inside was the bomb.

Verleen scuttled off. She was only a blink smaller than her husband. Together, they resembled Mr. and Mrs. Santa Claus. If a gaggle of elves had suddenly appeared in the living room with tools and toys, it wouldn't have surprised Morgan at all.

"I hope you're hungry, dear."

"I am!" she called back, realizing it was true. She was ravenous. The only bad thing about peanut butter was if she ate it by itself, it didn't stay with her long. She always ended up craving a heavier meal an hour or two after eating it.

"Since we have guests, I'm cooking just about everything we have in the house. Now, I know you look like one of those model types—for all I know, you might very well be one—but I hope to goodness you don't eat like one. No, sir. I won't have it. Not in this house. Besides, I'm the best cook in three counties. One taste and you'll unbuckle your belt."

Verleen Hines talked on and on while she cooked in the kitchen. Morgan couldn't see her, but she could hear her loud and clear. Must have been from years of calling out to her husband.

The aroma coming from the kitchen was wonderful. If Verleen wasn't the best cook in three counties, it certainly smelled like it. Morgan hugged her knees closer to her chest and tried to pay attention to what was on television. It looked like *Little House on the Prairie*, but the show was interrupted by an update on the High Alert at the O'Hare airport. The alert had been canceled for Chicago but had been extended to Minneapolis and St. Louis. What was going on in the world? she wondered.

Morgan pulled the quilt closer around her. Pink, lavender, and a soft subdued yellow surrounded her in a patchwork kaleidoscope pattern she tried hard not to stare at for fear of getting dizzy. Tiny geese had been embroidered into the corners. A fine sewing job. She snuggled in, placed her fresh cup of cocoa on the table next to the couch, and closed her eyes.

There was no hotel in Smithfield, Kentucky—population one hundred. Only families scattered throughout a fifty-mile radius. The nearest real town was about an hour away, Verleen had said. She and her husband had gracefully offered to take Morgan and Van in while the sheriff investigated the robbery and she and Van made arrangements to catch a bus, try to rent another car from somewhere, or did something to get themselves back home. Everything was up in the air right now until Van and Harley returned.

Her lids felt as though there were bricks attached to the lashes. She could barely keep them open. The next thing she knew, she was dreaming about being back in the SUV with Van.

They were speeding down the interstate, windows down, wind whipping her hair around her head. They laughed. Morgan didn't know who said what, but it didn't matter—their laughter filled the car and competed with the wind for force and velocity.

The world was right.

"We'll be there in plenty of time, Morgan."

"I know," she said. She saw Georgia coming up fast. The outline of it lay flat against the horizon as if God had painted its borders on the land in inky brown lines as wide as a river. "I see it!" she proclaimed.

"Morgan," Van said, his voice lowered with a hint of huskiness, "I know about you. I know your secret and you know what? I love you anyway. I know that the only thing you've ever wanted in your entire life was to be married and stay at home with a house full of kids. I know that your sisters are strong-willed and independent and that you aren't. At least, not in the way that they expect you to be. I know that if the right man came along, you'd throw away your modeling career in a heartbeat and the truth of that terrifies you. I know. You hear me? And I love you anyway. So, it's okay. We can do this and it will be all right."

Her chest rumbled with a dizzying combination of fear and relief. *Did I tell Van everything? I must have. And now that he knows, he still loves me.*

She couldn't breathe, yet it was the first time she'd been able to breathe, really breathe, in a very long time.

She stared across from her at the man who was able to bring her the first true sense of peace she'd ever had. And suddenly she felt sexier than she ever knew she could feel. Sexy, desired, complete. She couldn't wait to share that feeling and express her gratitude. One more glance at Georgia, the brown lines looked closer, they were almost there.

She smiled, determined to make their homecoming special. In her dream, she began to unbutton her blouse.

"Morgan, what are you doing?" He asked the question, but his tone told her he knew exactly what she was doing.

She unwrapped her skirt and let it fall open in the seat. Morgan thought for sure she had put on a thong, but when she looked down, she only saw skin and that area of her body growing hot and needy.

"Morgan?" Van said, impatience lacing the edge of his voice.

She answered him by moving, turning toward him and tracing her fingers, her hand, against his right arm. So powerful. The muscles were tight and his veins bulged against his skin, leading to a hand that gripped the steering wheel in the same way she wanted to be gripped.

"Umm," he moaned. She moaned, too. Making him feel good made her feel good.

He reached over, touched her where her blouse fell open. She gasped. Van's touch electrified her and calmed her at the same time. He coaxed her nipples to harden at his feather light caress. Her boldness grew.

"Van," she tried to say, but instead it came out breathy and full of lustful yearning.

"Yes, baby," he said, emitting his own gasp as she maneuvered over the middle console and slid onto his lap.

His goal never faltered. They continued racing toward Atlanta, approaching the edge of one state and into another.

Morgan ground her hips against his lap and sank her teeth gently into the side of his neck. "I can whisper, too," she said.

"Morgan," he said. "Are you hungry?"

"Yes, baby. Mommy's hungry. Let me show you what mommy's hungry for."

"Morgan?"

"Feed me, Daddy!" she shouted, grinding her hips with fury. "Feed me!"

"Oh, deary me!" an older woman's voice said.

At that, her eyes snapped open. Van, Verleen, and Harley stood over her. Their shocked expressions told her everything she needed to know. She'd been dreaming. And talking in her sleep.

"Let me get you a cold compress, dear. I think you've warmed up now."

Van's shock gave way to the widest smile she'd ever seen.

Harley jabbed Van in the arm, said, "Lucky dog," and followed his wife into the kitchen.

"You dozed off for a second, dear!" Verleen called out.

"A second?" she said. The dream felt more like an hour-long episode of *Sex and the SUV*. Her nipples were still hard.

Van sat beside her on the edge of the couch with a smile one hundred yards wide. "I see you've been dreaming about me." His expression was smug.

Morgan looked at Van and wanted to crack up. Along with his smug expression, he looked like a black Mr. Green Jeans from Captain Kangaroo, complete with plaid flannel shirt and overalls, both several sizes too big for him. The only thing missing was a straw hat and a bandana. Give him a pitchfork and he would look right at home in a barn bailing hay. Both of them wore flip-flops from the store, but Van's flip-flops were too small. Morgan wished she had Van's camera.

"Why on earth would you assume that I was dreaming about *you*?" she asked, fighting with the smile threatening to reveal her delight in seeing him.

"Because only Daddy Cool can bring out that kind of response in a woman. You were darn near pornographic up in here."

"Whatever," she said, throwing off the quilt with her right hand and sighing in embarrassment when she discovered where her left hand was buried.

"Tell me it wasn't me," Van said.

"What happened at the sheriff's office?" she asked, changing the subject.

"First, look me in my face and tell me you weren't dreaming about me."

His voice had suddenly taken on a serious, cavernous quality she hadn't heard before. Despite the fact that she thought he was actually ordering her to do something, it was sexy as hell. Damn, there was something about a confident, self-assured man who knows exactly where he stands with me. Morgan took a deep breath. "I was . . . sitting in your lap . . . you were driving."

He kissed her on the neck. She melted instantly, but kept up a good facade. "Damn, woman. I like the way you think!" He stood up. "Let's get some food and me and Har will tell you everything that happened."

He extended his hand. Morgan took it and allowed him to help her up. For a moment, a very long, intense, desire-filled moment, they stood in front of each other, staring. She wanted to kiss him so badly. She wanted to see if she could re-create the feeling in her dream, if he could really make her feel uninhibited and careless . . . again.

"Well, what are you waiting for?" Harley said. "Kiss her! After that dream she had, you better come up with somethin' to cool the lava, son. Otherwise, no telling who it might spill over on, and as much as I'd like to, I'm old and married."

Well, Van didn't need any more cajoling. He kissed her. And anyone would have thought it was the "I now pronounce you man and wife" kiss. Morgan did everything except lift her leg. Van did everything except dip her.

She would never be cold again.

"You two come on in here and eat now, before you set fire to my Mallard Pond carpet," Verleen said.

Reluctantly, they did as they were told and the four of them sat at a small rectangular table in the Hines' kitchen, saying grace over a feast fit for three families.

"My Verlie loves to cook, so dig in! You won't be sorry."

Everything was covered in gravy or some kind of sauce. All Morgan could think about was how to be polite and eat just enough so that she wasn't rude.

Please, oh, please, God. Let this food be good and flavorful. Any food other than Southern soul food was suspect to her. She had already made up her mind that the food was bland and tasteless.

One forkful of something Verleen said was pork schnitzel and she knew once again that God answers prayers. It was so good, she blinked in surprise.

"Wow!" Morgan said, already cutting herself another piece.

"You're not kidding," Van said.

"It's the bomb, right?" Harley asked.

"Harley!" Verleen said, slapping her husband at the elbow.

"Well, that's the hip way to talk, isn't it?"

"Hip-hop!" Morgan said, giggling. She really couldn't believe how delicious the food was.

"If illegal drugs are anything like this, now I understand how people can get addicted," Van said.

Harley patted his rotund stomach. "I know that's right!"

Van and Morgan stared amusingly at Harley.

"City Slang," Verleen said. "He studied it in a Pinkerton's correspondence course. This is the first time he's been able to try it out."

"It's the language of the future!" he said and lifted a glass in salute.

While Van and Morgan got their grub on, they listened as Harley gave Verleen "the four-one-one on what went down with the sheriff."

"So, I was, like, Mr. Sheriff, dude, man, how can a brother be down? Of course, Rusty isn't part of the slang correspondence course like I am, so he had no idea that I was asking him when he would have more information about the case. He didn't understand a word I was saying." Harley shook his head as if that was a crying shame. Morgan shoved a chunk of biscuit in her mouth to keep from laughing.

"*I* don't understand a word you're saying," Verleen responded. "Can you please translate so that us rural folk have an idea?"

Harley placed his fork on his plate, slightly irritated. "If you'd just read the pamphlets like I ask you—"

"Harley!"

"All right. Basically, Van and I gave the sheriff detailed descriptions of the two who came in and what they took. Van provided information about his big car and that the woman called the guy Billy. As far as we know, there's an APB—that means all—"

"I know what it means, Harley," Verleen snapped.

Harley gave them a knowing glance. "She's trippin', ain't she? Anyway, the authorities are on the lookout for them. In the meantime, Van and Morgan here need to get back home. Rusty will contact them if anything turns up, but he's pretty sure the first thing the robbers did was spend the Ben Franklins from the register. Right, Van?" Harley winked.

"Right," Van said with a mouth full of food.

"Can I get you some more schnitzel?" Verleen asked, getting up from the table.

"No," Van and Morgan said in unison.

Van closed his eyes, licked his fingers, and burped. "I've had too much already. I never eat this much, ever."

"Me, too," Morgan said, sighing with pleasure.

Onion pizza, goulash soup, cabbage salad, pork schnitzel, spätzle noodles, and brotchen bread. Verleen could have fed a small town with all the food she had prepared.

"It's time for dessert," Verleen said, coming back into the room. She carried a large silver tray heavy with three different desserts.

"The dessert is the best part," Harley said, rubbing his beachball stomach.

"We've got German chocolate cake, apple streusel, and peanut butter fudge."

"Ms. Verleen," Morgan began, "I couldn't possibly . . . did you say *peanut butter* fudge?"

"I sure did. It's my specialty!"

Harley elbowed Van. "Any dessert she makes is her specialty. But the peanut butter fudge is, uh, off the fence."

Well, that was it. Morgan and Van devoured dessert as if it were their last meal. When they finished, Morgan's stomach hurt so badly, all she could do was sit back and moan in bittersweet pain.

"Verlie and I always take our after dinner coffee on the lanai. Would you like to join us?"

Morgan rubbed her distended belly and groaned with discomfort. "I can't move."

"I can't move, breathe, or think straight." Van put his head on the table where, moments ago, heaps of food on plates had been in front of him.

"Come on out if you change your mind," Harley said as he and Verleen headed outside.

Van groaned. "I never want to eat again."

Morgan closed her eyes. "I think I'm going to be sick."

"Really?" Van asked, lifting his head awkwardly as if it weighed eighty pounds. "I can't help you." He let his head fall back to the table with a soft thud.

Bloated was not the word for what she felt. She had to do something to take her mind off the agony.

"Why did we do that?"

Van's voice muffled his response from his head down position. "Because we never do it."

"What?" Morgan asked. Even her mind couldn't function properly.

"It was a binge. Probably brought on by the fact that we always watch what we eat and the trauma we just experienced."

"I wish you would have told me that before my third helping of schnitzel. What the hell is schnitzel anyway?"

He turned his head and clamped his eyes shut. "I have no idea."

"But it sure was good!"

"You got that right." Van laughed. "This must be what it feels like to be on *Fear Factor*."

"Not even." She moaned. "I've been on *Fear Factor*. The stuff they make you eat tastes horrible for all of thirty seconds and you never eat enough of it to get full."

"I forgot about that. You were on there with that chick who ate the live maggots."

"Yeah," Morgan said, trying to stand. Maybe she could walk it off. "I copped out and ate them blended."

"Barfing Beauties. That's what my homeboys called that episode."

"I still walked away with ten thousand for my charity. It was worth it for a few swallows of puréed larvae."

"Stop! Don't say any more! My stomach can't take it."

She made it to the middle of the living room and

tried to make it to the couch. There were too many ducks on it. They made her stomach rock and lurch. Instead of collapsing on the couch, Morgan sank down right were she was and stretched out on the floor. "I hope this woman keeps a clean house," she said.

"Oh, my!" Verleen came rushing to Morgan's side and knelt down as best she could. She had no idea how long she'd been lying on the floor. Fifteen, twenty minutes maybe.

"Are you all right?"

"No," she and Van groaned in unison.

"Too . . . much . . . food," Morgan said, actually starting to feel better.

"We got some Pepto tabs," Harley told us. "How many do you need?"

Van sat up as if he were coming out of an alcohol-induced stupor. "Eighteen thousand," he said.

"Hold on there, partner—uh, homies. I'll be right back."

"Let me help you up, dear."

Morgan stood with Verleen's assistance, slow-footed it to the couch, and sat down carefully. She thought the worst of it had passed, but to be on the safe side, the off-brand Pepto was a good idea.

"Mr. Van, can you manage?" Verleen asked.

"Yes," he said, finally sitting straight up.

"Why, land sakes. I've never seen anyone enjoy my food quite like you two. I'm flattered, really. But if I've made you ill, I'll just never forgive myself."

Van's smile was weak at best. "Don't sweat it, Mrs. Hines. No one forced that food down our throats. We pigged out because we lost our minds for half an hour. I'm sure we'll recover."

Verleen headed back into the kitchen. Her husband arrived with a pink bottle in his hand.

"Did you hear that, Verlie? He said, 'Don't sweat it.' There really is another language out there like I've been telling you all these years!" He turned to the two. "My wife . . . she can cook, but some of the lights on the tree are dim, if you know what I mean." Harley winked at them playfully, then ran across the room, grabbed Verleen, and hugged her. The room vibrated with his footfalls.

"But she's mine and I love her!"

"Harley! Put me down! You gonna give yourself a hernia! Now, let's give them their medicine and let them have some peace and quiet while their stomachs settle."

Verleen gave them water. Harley gave them two pink capsules each. They swallowed them and prayed for quick relief.

Chapter Thirteen

Men will be men, but there are exceptions to every rule. While Morgan and Verleen talked in the living room, Van and Harley put away the food and cleaned up the kitchen. Now and then, Verleen would leave to attend to the load of clothes and bedding that was washing in the laundry room. Other than that, Morgan got the story of Verleen's life with Harley—how they met when Verleen and a few of her girlfriends stopped at the general store on their way to a shindig in town. It was love at first sight, and after buying gum, peppermints, and dental floss, Verleen decided to stay at the store and let her friends continue to town without her.

When her friends stopped to pick her up on the way back, she and Harley were already promised to each other. On the day after they graduated from high school, they were married in a Shelbyville church. Harley took over the store when his father passed away. He'd been running it ever since. Today was the first time they had ever been robbed.

Morgan smiled; inside she was a little sad. All around her, couples seemed to be having happy endings. She wondered when her turn would come.

Verleen filled her full of the story of her life. Morgan imagined Van getting the same earful from Harley. They would have a lot to tell when they finally got back home.

Over the next several hours, Morgan and Van watched *The Jim Nabors Hour, Lawrence Welk,* and *Hee Haw* while their stomachs did what they could to digest all the food they'd consumed. For a while, all Morgan could do was rub her belly, burp, and struggle to keep her eyes open. It had been a long day.

Van, on the other hand, actually seemed to be enjoying what the Hineses chose to watch. They all perked up when an official news bulletin interrupted the programming to provide updates on the alert status of the country. All airports involved had gone from Red Alert to Yellow and, so far, there had been no incidents. Thank God.

According to Harley, they were probably seven hours from Atlanta. That matched what she had guesstimated in her mind. They still needed to decide what they were going to do if there was no news on the car. All other transportation was still about an hour away. The only thing was, she didn't think she could wrap her mind around anything that serious until her stomach settled. Until then, nothing mattered except the end to the bloat.

"How's your knee?" Morgan asked, letting her head loll to the side in the direction of where Van was sitting beside her on the couch.

"Still sore. But I'll live."

The credits rolled on "Mayberry R.F.D." and Verleen waddled up to the television and turned it off. "Well, time for bed," she said.

Van checked his watch. "It's eight P.M."

"Is it *that* late?" Harley said, hoisting himself up.

"Sheriff Taylor said he would take us to the motel in Frankfort. We'd better give him a call," Morgan said.

Verleen held her hands up in a stopping motion. "Oh, no. It's much too late for that. You can stay here the night. We'll call Rusty first thing in the morning to find out if there's any word on your vehicle."

"And if not, he'll take you to Frankfort then. All right?" Harley asked.

Morgan and Van looked at each other for consideration. Exhaustion etched Van's face. She had no doubt that hers looked the same way. She decided to follow his lead; she was too tired to do anything else. She nodded for him to decide.

Van swallowed slowly. "Thanks for the offer. We'll take you up on it."

"Wonderful!" Verleen clapped her hands together. "I would have been so worried otherwise. Now, Morgan, you come with me. Van, you go with Harley to the spare bedroom."

Morgan frowned. "What?"

Van's face paled. "If it's all the same to you, I can sleep on the couch."

Morgan laughed. Along with the gaggle of geese and the flock of ducks decorating the home, crosses also dotted the walls and appeared on throw blankets and pillows. It was obvious these lovable country bumpkins weren't racist, thank goodness, but fornication was obviously against the rules under this roof.

She could live with that. "Oh, buck up, Mr. Wrong. Like you said about your knee . . . you'll live."

Van's eyes narrowed to slits. He was angry and sexy at the same time. Now Morgan knew she was feeling better—she'd stopped thinking about how much food she'd consumed and started focusing on the fact that Van McNeil was the sexiest man alive, and with soft, silky words, he'd caused a small eruption inside her she would never forget.

That realization also shot a bolt of fear through her

good sense. It was scary for her to be near a man who had that much control over her body, or her soul for that matter.

Van McNeil was not just Mr. Wrong. He was Mr. Dangerous.

After an hour and a half, they had all taken showers and were ready for bed. Morgan put on what could only be referred to as a muumuu. The tent-sized caftan fit for a queen came to an inch below her knee. The flowers on it were so big and loud, she didn't know how she was going to get any sleep. She bet when she turned off the light, she would still be able to see them.

One person's fashion disaster is another person's couture, she thought. Connie would take one look at what she had on, slap a wide sequin belt around it, and call it a hit.

Her muumuu was blue. Verleen's was lavender. Together they looked like a billboard for *1-800-FLOWERS.*

"Lights out?" Verleen said.

"Yes," she replied and settled into the California king-size bed. A good choice for the couple. That way they would have enough room to maneuver, toss and turn, or whatever else they did in the bed. The sheets were fresh-from-the-drier clean. They smelled good. Morgan inhaled deeply to take her mind off the aroma of schnitzel that still lingered throughout the house.

"Good night, dear."

"Good night, Verleen."

When Verleen stretched out fully on the bed, the mattress tipped like a seesaw, and Morgan clung to the side to keep from sliding into her.

It's going to be a long night, she thought and closed her eyes. Then next thing she knew, she was waking up.

* * *

Verleen had decorated the spare room in a way that would make any home-interiors consultant weep with glee—plenty of wall sconces and lots of illustrated relatives of Donald and Daffy displayed prominently on the walls and fabric patterns. The room was a perfect square with a full-sized bed in the middle of the room, one wood end table, and a small lamp with an embroidered shade. It was well kept, neat, and tidy, like it was waiting eagerly for visitors, relatives, and friends. For someone like Van who'd had a long day, the sight of the bed, even with all the birds on the linen, was welcome. Looked like it wasn't disturbed often, but was always waiting for someone to come and make it useful.

Van couldn't wait for dreamland and fell back on the rollaway bed like a boulder.

"Morgan, Morgan, dear." Verleen stood over her and patted her forearm gently.

She opened her eyes. A light peered in from the hallway. It was still nighttime.

"Yes," Morgan said groggily. "What's wrong?" Then she sat up. "Is it news about the car?"

"No. I'm afraid you'll have to take the guest room after all."

"Why?" she asked. Her mind was still groggy with sleep.

"Well, dearie, it's flatulence."

"What!"

"I'm sorry. It's just that, well, you've been asleep for half an hour and your colon has been busy. Frankly," she said and blinked as sweetly and innocently as a young girl, "it's keeping me awake."

Self-consciousness burned Morgan's cheeks. "Are you telling me I have gas?"

"Yes, deary. Maybe Van is used to it. Or maybe it's all

the food you ate, but in either case, you'll have to sleep in the guest room. With him."

She was so embarrassed. "I'm sorry, Verleen."

"That's all right, dear. I've already spoken to Harley. We're going to switch as soon as you get yourself together."

Morgan got up and gathered the big gown around her. "I am so, so sorry!"

"I understand. But what I am curious about is why you didn't wake yourself up."

She kept her mouth shut and headed toward the door.

"Just follow the light, dear."

Morgan padded down the hallway. Harley waited in the doorway to the guest room, concern blanketing his round face. "Did that Pepto tab work for ya?" he asked under his breath.

"Yes, it did. I feel much better."

He moved aside and she stepped into the room. Van was on his side, sheet pulled up to his chin, eyes closed. *Won't he be surprised to wake up and find me beside him.*

"Good night, Miss Morgan."

"Good night, Harley."

She stood for a moment listening to Harley make his way toward the end of the hall. After a few seconds, the hallway light winked out. A thin shaft of moonlight from a window at the end of the hallway guided her. She walked quietly over to the smaller bed, grateful that Van wasn't awake. If he knew the reason she got kicked out of the master bedroom, she'd never hear the end of it.

Sliding in beside him, Morgan pulled the cover around her, and closed her eyes. When she heard the snort come from the other side of the bed, her eyes snapped open.

Van's shoulders shook as though shock waves moved them.

"Go on. Let it out," she said.

His raucous laugher filled the room. He sat up, smiled at her, and laughed some more.

"According to Verleen, the government should take your ass to Afghanistan. The fumes would flesh ol' Osama right out."

"What*ever*! She did *not* say that!"

"She might as well have." Van gripped his washboard stomach. "And it was just starting to feel better. Now it hurts again."

"Good for you!" she said, yanking the covers around her and turning away from him.

"Don't you dare point that thing at me!"

Morgan didn't move. "You know, if I was crass, I would force one out right about now."

"Keep your mushroom clouds to yourself," Van said, settling back down into the bed. "Otherwise, I'm headed for the couch."

"Oh, no, you're not!" she protested.

"Really? Why not?" His voice grew softer. Less playful.

Darn it. There go my silly feelings. Coming right out of my mouth. She was so happy to be lying next to Van, flatulence or not, she didn't want him to go.

"You can't leave me alone in a strange house."

"I can, and I will. If it's as bad as Verleen says."

"I'm sure she's exaggerating." Truth be told, Morgan was holding gas in right then. In a few moments, she would be off to the restroom to relieve the pressure, but she couldn't do that all night. Rather than prolong the inevitable, she got up.

"Where are you going? And by the way, what are you wearing?"

"Never mind, and a muumuu!" she said.

Van laughed so hard, he coughed several times.

Serves you right, she thought.

She didn't make it to the restroom, and she had no doubt that Van heard everything. When she came back to the room, he was under the covers, quiet, but his shaking shoulders were a dead giveaway.

"Good night, Van," Morgan said, sliding back under the sheet, facing him. She vowed she would never overeat again.

He turned to face her. "Good night? Now that you're in here, you don't think I'm going to let you go to sleep, do you?"

"We need to rest up for tomorrow," she said, but felt tingly nonetheless.

"What for? Tomorrow we'll probably take a Greyhound or an Amtrak home. Someone else will do the driving. We can rest then. Right now, I would much rather help you work off some of that food."

"Me? You're the one who had two slices of German chocolate cake."

"Three, but I'm trying not to count them."

"Three? When did you have the third piece?"

"About half an hour ago. Harley and I got hungry."

"Hungry?"

"Okay, so we're pigs. The point is, there are calories to be burned, and I think we should get busy burnin' them."

Morgan couldn't help herself. She snuggled closer to him. "You seem to be taking this whole getting-robbed thing very well."

He slid a finger down the side of her face. The memory of his exquisite touch sprang back into her mind, her body. She was instantly wet.

"Don't get it twisted, I'm upset."

" 'Don't get it twisted.' Harley would *love* that," she commented.

"He sure would."

"What's *up* with that?"

Van's fingers brushed lightly through her hair. "It's a correspondence course."

There was silence in the room, but only for a second.

They both laughed so loudly, Verleen and Harley must have heard them.

"Oh, damn!" Van said. He waved his hand in front of his nose. "Is that you?"

"Sorry," she said. "I laughed too hard."

"Oh, hell no! On second thought, you can't sleep here tonight. Get out of this bed."

"No," she protested.

"I mean it." He nudged her with his arms. "Get out!"

"No!" she insisted, hanging on to the bed.

He tickled her side. She giggled and slid closer to the edge of the bed. "Stop!"

"Shh," he said. "You'll wake up the Hineses . . . again."

She slapped his hands away, but they kept coming for her. Touching, traveling, tickling. The sensation no longer made her laugh—just long for more.

Van slid back the sheet. "Take that thing off, *please*."

She loved a man who knew what he wanted. "You take it off for me."

"You ain't said nothin' but a word."

Van gathered the yards of fabric.

" 'Nothin' but a word.' We ought to write these down for Harley."

"Will you get serious? I'm trying to seduce you."

"Mmm." She lifted her hands above her head. "Seduce me, baby."

Van took the sheet from around them. He was wearing nothing but the most powerful, rippling birthday suit she'd even seen. Even in the dark of the room, heat blazed through her veins at the sight of him.

"Were you sleeping like that?" she asked breathlessly.

"Nah. I tossed the big bloomers when you stepped out to fart."

"Will you get serious?" She traced her finger along his six-pack, now a seven-pack as a result of dinner. "I'm trying to be seduced."

The large dress came off easily enough. Nothing but naked flesh underneath. Van climbed in front her and stared at her as if he hadn't eaten in days.

"Damn, M," he said, his voice heavy with passion. "Tyra ain't got nothin' on you. And I know. I had a thing with her once."

"You're kidding," she said, fresh jealousy tinting her words.

"There's one thing I don't kid about and that's women. Now shut up and kiss the hell out of me."

If only that were possible, she thought. If a kiss could change a bad boy into a prince, she would have pressed her lips to Van McNeil the second she laid eyes on him. No, it would take more than a kiss to tame this scoundrel, but she leaned up anyway and challenged the devil.

Van tasted so sweet. Better than her dream. Better than *any* dream. Morgan tasted more and more, sucking his tongue, licking his lips, clinging close. She couldn't catch her breath, didn't want to catch her breath if it meant pulling away from Van for even one second. At the same time, she knew their lust affair could only exist in the mini reality of this road trip. When they got back home, things would go back to business as usual.

"What's wrong?" he asked. "What are you thinking about?"

She lowered her eyes. "Nothing." And why was she suddenly so coy with this man? Usually she was the assertive, straightforward, no-holds-barred kind of woman. But with Van . . .

His large hands massaged her shoulders, scorching her skin, and traveled toward her chest where the sensation blazed within her like a midnight bonfire. Lingered there. "I was only kidding about you leaving the bed. But you're gone anyway." His fingers teased her nipples, brushing them rhythmically back and forth, drawing them into tight, aching pebbles. "Tell me," he said.

She could barely speak, let alone tell him what was in her heart. "Let's just have sex, okay?"

"Sex?" he said. Van leaned way over, reached down toward the floor, and picked up a condom. "We can do better than that."

"Where'd you get that?"

"Harley and I stopped by the store before we came back from the sheriff's office."

"So you knew this was coming."

"Let's just say I had high hopes."

"What about your knee?"

"Forget my knee!"

He tore the packet with his teeth. She watched as he sheathed his burgeoning manhood with such practice, it seemed as though he'd done it a million times. More systematic than sensual. She sighed sadly.

"Now about that sex thing," he said, lowering her down to the bed.

"What about it?"

"I'm more into making love right about now. Aren't you?" His fingers fondled her moist feminine opening. When he found her love spot, his fingers slid in slow, sensual circles, getting her wetter than she could ever remember being.

She moaned. "What do you know about love, Mr. Wrong?"

"You know what they say, Mahogany. Actions speak louder."

With that, he slid himself inside her. The first joining, her mind whispered. His hard body on top of her; inside her, it felt like she'd never been with anyone before Van. Something about this exchange felt different. She couldn't wait to find out what.

She circled her arms around his neck. Stared up into

his eyes. Took on the weight of his body. Sighed out in pleasure.

He braced himself with the headboard of the bed, closed his eyes, and ground his hips. He pushed into her slowly, steadily, and pulled himself out with intensity and control. Whatever control Morgan thought she had over her body or her soul before she met Van McNeil caught fire and went up in flames.

Van's deft attentions tossed around her sensibility and willpower like a rag doll. It was a hurricane, a cyclone, a landslide. Van touched her inside and out as if he'd invented skin and created intimacy. Each kiss was a lightning strike in her soul. Every caress, every stroke of his hand against her flesh released an avalanche of energy so strong, she was nearly paralyzed by it.

He moved inside her and she held on tightly. Van's lovemaking was a force of nature. And he was thunder itself. She didn't know whether to run for cover or open herself and be drenched.

"Tell me something," he said.

"W-what?" she asked, struggling to speak.

He moved his hips in a gyrating motion. Sent her to the moon. "Anything," he moaned.

Morgan gazed into his eyes. They stared back as dark as storm clouds. "I missed you," she admitted. "For eight months. After our date."

He slid his hands beneath her. Lifted her thighs. She wrapped her legs around him. He moaned appreciatively. "When you left me, I missed you," she said, and buried her head into his shoulder.

He smelled like wild earth and manly intensity. She breathed deeply, wanting all of Van inside her. Even his scent.

"I'm sorry," he said, kissing her shoulder, pushing slowly into her. "I won't ever do that again."

She sighed, clung tighter, kissed his arm. Stroked his

back. If he could make her feel like this, like heaven floating, she didn't want him to leave her ever.

Van kissed her eyelids. Moved in and out. He kissed her cheeks. Moved in and out. He kissed her forehead, her nose, her chin. Moved in and out.

Morgan's head thrashed from side to side. Her hips ground up into his. Fulfillment felt like a slow-moving train. Dominant. Deliberate. Somewhere off in the distance, the power was coming. The roar and thunder, quaking and steam was on the way. She rolled her hips to coax it faster. She dug her nails into Van's back to summon him closer.

"Mahogany," he whispered. "Sweet, beautiful, mysterious Mahogany. Uhhh. Do you feel that?"

"Yes," she whispered back.

"No, you don't," he said, driving harder. Riding strong, steady. "Do you feel it, baby? Do you feel me? Loving you? Do you?"

"Yes . . . Van . . . oh, God!"

"What's your name?"

"Mahogany!" she screamed.

Van plunged deeper. The train pulled in. "What else, baby?"

"*Van's* Mahogany!"

"You got that right! You like this?"

"Yes!"

"You love it?"

"Yes. . . ."

"Tell me you love it!"

She should have been embarrassed by the answer that came out. She wasn't, though. She just closed her eyes and let everything come.

Van loved making love to Morgan. She was all woman, but a seductress in her own right. And he was about to erase all her sexual boundaries.

"Tell me!" he said again. And he heard it. Faintly at

first, but her voice came in loud and clear while he took her in long, languid strokes.

She was singing.

She'd done it in the hotel room. She'd done it again in the freezer. Some women spoke in tongues. Some kicked and scratched. Morgan sang, and Van wanted her—needed her—in full voice tonight. He had to know if she was feeling what he was feeling. And this, by God, would tell him.

He smiled inside.

Her voice was low, barely perceptible. He kissed and caressed. She hummed "You Bring Me Joy" and crooned "Ain't Nobody." After the chorus of "Love TKO," he had his answer.

"Think I better let it go," she whispered.

"Let it go, baby," he responded.

She grabbed him. Quick. Hard. "Van!" she screamed.

"I feel it, baby. I feel it," he moaned in her ear.

The strong muscles inside her throbbed and thrummed against him, pulling out the last remaining strength he had before the explosion claimed him and he collapsed on top of her.

"I love you, Morgan," he admitted against his better judgment. "I always have."

Her orgasm felt like waves crashing against him. Van was instantly addicted. He craved the sensation of bringing Morgan to ultimate pleasure.

He adored it.

They fell apart, exhausted, but he couldn't stand being separate from her. He kissed the sweat from her neck, chest, and stomach. He tasted the oasis of flesh that was her thighs as they trembled and quaked in aftershocks. With a deep moan, his tongue flirted with her core—darting and dashing in quick circles, suckling Morgan's sweet essence.

When he'd brought Morgan to the brink of ecstasy,

he slowed down, tasting more deliberately, more skill-fully, more artfully. This time there were no songs, only soft sobs and his name on her delicious lips over and over and over.

He never knew his name could sound so good.

He was going to make sure Morgan would never for-get the name on her lips.

"Oh! Van!" she screamed. If she gripped the back of his head any tighter, he would be screaming, too.

He had a feeling the whole house would shake with this orgasm. But he was wrong. Morgan released the most delicate sigh, a sigh more fragile than a butterfly's wings, but it lingered in the air like perfume. In every way possible, Van was intoxicated.

He lay beside her while she panted and fanned her-self. In the slated glow of moonlight pouring through the window blinds, she looked more beautiful—with the thin veil of sweat glistening against her honey-brown skin—than he had ever seen her. He stared up at the ceiling. Even in his boldest of fantasies, he hadn't imag-ined this.

Morgan rolled over, laid her head on his chest, and stroked his abdomen.

"What did you do?" she asked. The words came out breathy and sultry. "Spell my name?"

"No." Van said. "I spelled mine."

She craned her neck up and kissed him. He smiled, sensing the bliss threatening to wash over him, and ac-cepted it like a man.

If this was perfection, he'd wanted it for a long, long time, but then . . .

"Morgan! Was that you?"

"Sorry," she said, burying her face in his chest. "I couldn't hold it."

Van tousled her hair, wrapped her in his arms, and kissed her forehead.

"I'm never gonna let you live this down. You know that, don't you?"

"Just don't put me out of the bed."

"Never," he said out loud and in his heart.

Chapter Fourteen

Morgan slept beautifully in Van's arms. A more wondrous picture could not have been painted by the finest artist in the world.

There was a soft rap at the door, breaking the paradise Van had enjoyed for hours.

"Yes," he said. Morgan stirred a bit. He stroked her hair.

Harley's round face smiled at them through a crack in the door. "I hope you don't mind, but I called a doctor friend of mine to come have a look at your knee. He'll be here in about an hour."

"Thank you," Van said. After last night's activities, his knee felt like the head of an Olympic torch.

"Breakfast will be ready soon," Harley said, backing out and closing the door behind him.

Van breathed deeply. Last night had been a marvelous fantasy. Now it was back to the real world.

"Morgan," he said, shaking her slightly and kissing her forehead. "Wake up, baby."

"Ooh, no," she moaned, eyes closed. "I can't come anymore, Van. I have to get some sleep."

He chuckled. They *did* have a late night. "No, baby, it's morning."

"Umm," she moaned, then a smile brightened her face. "You were in rare form, last night, Van McNeil."

"It was the Pepto. It made me crazy."

"Please! You can tell that lie if you want to. I know it was my body that made you crazy." Her eyes were fully open now and were casting a warm gaze in his direction.

Van sat up on his elbow and leaned over her. "That's where you're wrong. *Everything* about you makes me crazy. Don't you know that by now? The way you think. The way you react to things, especially me. Your attitude toward life." He slid his lips against her cheek. "I'm practically certifiable."

"Well," she said, thrusting her chest out in a way that ignited his libido. "I *am* perfect." The timbre in her laughter played like cool jazz in his ears.

"Yes, you are. Except for that one strand of red hair growing on the side of your face, the diamond-shaped mole on your left shoulder, the tan discoloration behind your right knee, and the fact that your left breast is slightly bigger than your right one. Other than that, you are the definition of perfection."

Morgan slung a long silky leg across his thighs. "You're not too bad yourself. Even though you're wrong about the weather an average of thirty percent of the time—not forty-five—that blue Prada suit you love to wear clashes with the weather map something terrible, you can't say 'meteorologist' without tripping over the syllables, and every time you say it's going to be partly cloudy, it always ends up being mostly sunny."

"Is that right?"

"Yeah. Work that out, will you?"

"I'd rather work you out."

"Come on, Casanova. Let's get up."

Van glanced down at himself. "I *am* up, Lady Mahogany."

* * *

They showered, dressed in clean, bulky clothes, and joined the Hineses in the kitchen—Van with the shadow of a beard and no aftershave, Morgan without her designer clothes and makeup. "Bumpkin" didn't begin to describe how country they looked.

He leaned toward her for a much-needed kiss. Morgan pulled away and frowned as if she'd just sucked the juice from a pickle. "I'm not kissing you!"

His heart caved in. "Why not?"

"Because you didn't brush your teeth this morning!"

"I gargled," he said, leaning closer.

She pushed him away playfully. "I don't care."

Van couldn't take his eyes off her. "Hmph. If we were married, you wouldn't be so standoffish." Reflexively, his hand clamped over his mouth. *I must be nuts.*

Morgan eyed him suspiciously.

"Sorry. I don't know what came over me."

Verleen smiled and interrupted them. "Are you hungry?"

"No," Van and Morgan asserted at the same time.

"I'll take some coffee," Morgan said.

"Let's make it two," he added.

Harley and Van made fresh coffee. Then Van and Morgan added cream and sugar to their steaming cups while Harley and Verleen filled their plates with potato pancakes and apple streusel. It sure smelled good, but right now the aroma of breakfast wafting to Van's nose just made him want to swear off food, at least for a while. He could tell by the scoff on Morgan's face that she felt the same way.

"Harl? It's Cecil."

The man they were introduced to as Cecil Hines came through the front door. Two spitfire boys ran in behind him. He looked like a door-to-door insurance salesman, with his wrinkled gray suit, straw hat, and loafers. The small medical bag he carried with him had seen much better days. The boys acted as though they were part of a gymnastics act. Rough and tumble all the way.

"Didn't mean to interrupt your breakfast," Cecil said, removing his hat.

"You know there's plenty," Verleen said.

"I don't mind if I fix me and the boys a plate, then," he replied and helped himself in the kitchen as though he'd been doing it for years.

Morgan and Van had reached a new level of understanding. They communicated without even using words. He slid a quick glance her way. But his glance said, "*This* is the doctor?"

She gave him one back that said, "Why are you surprised?"

"Van, Morgan, this is my brother Cecil and his boys Jeb and Tauny," Harley said.

As if on cue, the boys, running from opposite sides of the room, slammed smack into each other and fell to the floor. There came a series of *ows* and head shaking, then they were back at it again. Neither Cecil, Verleen, nor Harley paid them any attention.

Van had to fold his lips in to keep from laughing. Morgan wasn't so successful at staving off her laughter. She excused herself and headed toward the bathroom.

Although Dr. Cecil was about Van's height and build, he could put away some food just like Harley and Verleen. It made Van's stomach hurt all over again just to watch. The boys were more fickle, preferring to throw their food rather than eat it.

When Morgan came back, she and Van excused themselves from the madcap scene to call the sheriff to see if there were any leads since yesterday.

The deputy Van spoke with said Sheriff Taylor was out investigating a call about the case. She didn't know when he would check in, but as soon as he did, she would give him the message to call.

"There's a lead," Van said, hanging up. "Don't know

what it is yet, but the sheriff is investigating it." He turned to Morgan. "So, what do you think? Should we wait to see what happens or should we head back now?"

Concern turned her face into a mask of wrinkles.

He put his arm around her reassuringly. "I know you're worried about the dress. I'm surprised you haven't been on the phone to your sisters, telling them all about what's going on here."

"Me, too. I thought about it, but . . . I don't want them to worry." She swallowed hard. "But the wedding is four days away. If we don't get the dress back with everything else, I need to let Ashley know so she can go buy . . ." Her voice trailed off.

That dress must really mean a lot to her. Van slid even closer to her on the couch. His knee was really hurting him, but he could see Morgan's pain was greater.

"Come here," he said, and wrapped her in his arms. She felt good. "They'll find the car, Morgan. The dress and everything else will be there. We'll drive back to Atlanta, your sister will get married, and she and Gordon will live happily ever after."

She looked up at him. Her eyes looked younger than he had ever seen them look. "Sounds like a fairy tale. Nothing's that perfect."

He kissed her cheek. "Some things are. You'll see." Although he had a good feeling about the car and his best friend's wedding, he wasn't so sure about him and Morgan. After everything, he still felt a barrier between the two of them.

Van had never been one for relationships. It was even hard for him to say the word. But what Morgan and he had was much more than proximity, an easy lay, a booty call, or just plain old convenient sex. But it wasn't a commitment either and something about that worried the heck out of him—the fact that he wanted it to be.

"So, are you the one with the knee problem?" Cecil asked, coming into the living room after checking Harley's injury.

"I suppose so," Van said.

"Sit back," he said. "Light!"

The Hineses quickly turned on darn near all the lights in the house. The scene resembled a beat from the three stooges. Van sat back and winked at Morgan and she nodded in agreement.

Cecil took a dry sniff and opened his case. Van's eyes grew wide when he saw the name printed on the front of the bag and stenciled on all the instruments he pulled out of it.

Pinkerton's.

"Pinkerton's?" Morgan said, reading Van's mind again.

"Yes. Cecil graduated from the correspondence school, too. He has a certificate in medical administration assistantship."

Van didn't know whether to stay put and humor them or to refuse treatment.

"He's really good," Verleen said.

Her sincerity made Van trust him. If nothing else, he'd clean the wound and apply an antibiotic.

"Van—"

"Don't worry, Morgan. It won't hurt a bit. Right, doc?"

Cecil strapped a combination stethoscope and magnifying-glass light to his head. "Never say never, I always say."

Van rolled up the right leg of the overalls and removed the bandage he'd applied earlier that morning. His knee looked like Jeb or Tauny had gotten into the finger paints and done a number on his knee cap.

"Oh, my Lord!" Morgan said.

Verleen's eyes grew large. "Morgan, dear, let's take Jeb and Tauny outside to play."

Morgan nodded. She and Verleen rounded up the boys and herded them onto the porch.

Van was starting to get concerned about the cut. It was obviously infected. He didn't want it to get any worse. Nor did he want to take any chances with a knockoff doctor.

"You know what, Cecil? I'm going to put some peroxide on this and go see my physician as soon as I get back to Atlanta."

"Is that what you've been doing?" he asked. "Putting peroxide on your cut? And I must say, it's an ugly cut, Mr. Van. Yes, indeedy. Ug*ly*!"

"Thanks," Van said.

Cecil rummaged through his bag again and pulled out the thinnest pair of tweezers Van had ever seen. "What we've got to do is clean *inside* the wound."

Unease made a vein in Van's neck throb. "That's okay, Cecil."

"Have you looked at your knee? It is surely not okay." The man with the certificate in medical treatment opened an alcohol pad and placed it between the tweezer prongs. "Now, you might want to hold on to somethin','cause this is going to hurt a *lot*."

Van took a deep breath and prayed the man knew what he was doing. One second later, Cecil squeezed the skin on his knee, opening the slit that had been dealing Van a fit for nearly twenty-four hours, and swabbed it out with the pad.

The pain was grandiose. A red-hot star-burst of agony shot from Van's leg to every part of his body. If Cecil's boys hadn't been within earshot, he would have hollered an expletive or three. As it was, he wanted to break Cecil's jaw.

"Well, what do we have here?" Cecil asked.

Quickly, he removed the puss-stained alcohol pad and moved the tweezers back toward Van's knee. Van was about to protest when Cecil said, "Mr. Van, I am about to make your day."

He inserted the tweezers. Van gritted his teeth. A moment later, he pulled out a piece of metal about a fourth of an inch wide and about half an inch long. It hurt for a second and then the most wonderful feeling set in. A feeling of no pain. Van's knee was extremely sore, but the acute pain was gone.

"Must have slid into a nerve," Cecil said.

Van didn't realize how tense he'd been until then. Van took a breath and thanked him, while Cecil applied an antiseptic cream and a fresh bandage.

"Give your knee as much rest as you can for the next twenty-four hours. Irrigate it every morning and apply an antibiotic twice a day."

"Thanks," Van said again, noting that the man sounded like a real doctor.

At that, the whole gang came in. They must have been listening at the door.

"See, I told you he was good," Verleen said.

Morgan trotted in after the boys. They must have bonded in the short time they were on the porch. All three of them ran around the living room, playing cops and robbers.

Van had heard the metaphor about a heart melting many times. He never knew it was possible for a man. But he would have sworn on a stack of Bibles that a sudden internal heat had just reduced his heart to Silly Putty. If anyone asked, he would have said the experience only lasted for a split second, but in that second it was *his* sons Morgan was indulging in that living room. Or, rather, *their* sons. Morgan's and his. They were tall and muscular like their father. Smart and good-looking like their mother.

He was elated and apprehensive at the same time— elated to discover that all that love stuff really was all it was cracked up to be, now that he was in it; apprehensive to realize that he couldn't see himself with another woman. Ever. Not after Morgan.

His player's card had self-destructed with her smile.

Jeb, Tauny, and Morgan settled down. Verleen, Harley, and Cecil talked in the background. Van was some place else entirely.

"What's wrong?" Morgan asked.

"What?" he said, snapping out of it.

"You were staring at me."

"I like to look at you. I guess I just got carried away."

The knock at the door startled them all. It was heavy and urgent. Harley marched over, pulled the door open.

"Rusty!" he said. "Any news?"

"I wish you would call me Sheriff Taylor like everybody else, Harley."

"Sorry, guy."

"Sheriff!" Van said, interrupting the moment and trying to forget the Kodak moment of his own he'd just had.

"I need you and Miss Allgood to come to the office and identify the couple one of my deputies pulled over this morning. I'm pretty sure they're the ones we're looking for."

Van rolled down his pant leg. "Let's go."

They couldn't leave without thanking Harley and Verleen, who had opened their home and made them feel like family, and allowed them to act like ravenous pigs in their dining room.

Van shook hands with Harley and hugged Verleen. Morgan hugged them both.

"There are no words, Harley," Van said. Harley slapped his palm and left a twenty-dollar bill in it.

"And, Verleen, I'm still full from your wonderful cooking."

"Glad to do it," she said with a wide grin.

"F'sho," Harley said.

Cecil and Sheriff Taylor stared at Harley. Morgan and Van just smiled and nodded. They were ret-ta-go.

They walked solemnly toward the porch, each in their own thoughts, when Verleen said, "Oh, Morgan?"

"Yes?" Morgan responded, and turned toward the door.

"You have a lovely voice, dear. You really must take up singing."

Van laughed so hard, he thought he might lose his balance. Morgan's eyes grew wide in surprise. "Thanks, Verleen. I'll think about that."

"You two look a sight better than you did yesterday, but not much."

African-American Gothic, Van thought, but remained quiet.

"The Hineses are good people. It's a good thing you ended up there. I know they took good care of you."

"They did," Morgan said from the front seat.

Van stared out the window and focused on the fact that he'd been right: they were going to identify the lowlifes that robbed them and get back on the road in no time.

The sheriff's office was forty-five minutes away. It was the longest forty-five minutes of Van's life. Only the sight of his Ford Explorer in relatively good condition in the back lot of the sheriff's office cooled his nerves nicely.

On the way, the sheriff had filled them in on the details. "The suspect's names are Billy McLean and Susan Gulfoyle. Billy has a rap sheet as long as the Great Wall. Petty theft, numerous counts of drug violations, even prostitution. Susan's record isn't so extensive, but she's got similar infractions. They've been doing a dance and dash with the law since they were both eighteen. It's the first time either of them pulled anything with a gun, though."

The sheriff escorted Van and Morgan inside. Van was eager to get this over with. Things were looking up and if everything went smoothly, they would have plenty of time to get to Atlanta before dark.

He stepped out of the car and the heat hit him like a prize fighter. It was just approaching noon, there were three hours to go before the hottest part of the day, but it had to be ninety degrees already.

The inside of the building reminded him of a combination lodge and visitors' center. Lots of wood, an information board, and a deputy who was not at her desk.

"Over here," the sheriff said, heading down a hallway on the left.

He led them to a holding-cell area. It was like nothing Van could have prepared his mind for. It was neat, very low-tech, and austere.

"We're pretty sure they took the money and got loaded last night. First thing this morning, they drove to the nearest pawn shop and tried to hock all the electronics in your SUV. One of my deputies found them at Saul's Jewelry and Loan in Louisville."

There were three holding cells in the back. The guy who robbed them was in one. He was dirty. His eyes bloodshot. He stared at the wall as if they weren't even there. Van's clothes, the ones he'd taken off yesterday, were on him and ruined.

The sight in the other cell made him gasp and drop his jaw. The woman, Billy's accomplice, stood gripping the steel bars and screaming obscenities. Worst of all, she was wearing Ashley's wedding gown.

The woman looked to be in a lot better shape than her male friend, except for the fact that Morgan wanted to choke her and slap the profanity out of her mouth for even touching her sister's dress, let alone putting it on.

Morgan looked away from her.

"Tell me this heifer is *not* wearing my sister's dress!"

Astonishment and rage warred for control of Morgan's emotions. The thought of her most personal creation on the body of a stranger almost choked her.

"Van," she said, the fury boiling inside her making her voice menacingly low. "Get my dress."

"I take it that's a positive ID?" Sheriff Taylor asked.

"It sure is," Van said.

"I don't want your stupid dress! That idiot got cranked out of his mind and made me put it on. I just want out of here!"

The woman pulled and thrashed against the bars like a wild animal.

"Give up the dress and we'll see what we can do," the sheriff said.

They walked back down the hall. The man hadn't moved.

"Is he catatonic?" Van asked as they followed Sheriff Taylor back to his office.

"No. Just crashing from a drug binge."

The word "binge" made Morgan cringe. She and Van sat down on the other side of the sheriff's desk and waited. The office was as sparse as the jail cells. No plants. No photos of family. No pictures on the wall. No decorations of any kind. Just a desk, a lamp, a file cabinet, and a computer.

After a few moments, the sheriff pulled a file from a locked drawer. There were several forms inside. A couple handwritten, the rest computer printouts.

"I understand you two are traveling to Atlanta."

"Yes," Morgan spoke up, trying to convey the urgency in her voice.

"Well, you got two options. You can press charges, in which case we'll have to impound your SUV and everything in it for evidence. We'll go to trial. You'll testify that they were the ones who robbed you. If they're found guilty, and I don't see why they wouldn't be, you get your things back."

"How long will that take?" Van asked.

"Best case? A few days. Worst? A month or so."

A cold knot of dread formed in Morgan's stomach.

"What's our other choice?" Van asked.

"You cut your losses and leave with your car and whatever they didn't sell."

Morgan blew out a breath of exasperation. "And they go scot-free."

"Not at all. Harl will press charges for the store robbery. Bonnie and Clyde in there will see time. About five to ten years' worth."

Morgan nodded. Van touched her forearm reassuringly. "Let's get the dress and go."

As if they'd ordered it, the deputy came in, wedding dress in hand. "Sheriff?" she said.

Morgan released the breath she'd been holding since she sat down in the office. "We're going to go, Sheriff. Thank you . . . for everything."

Sheriff Rusty studied them for a moment, then nodded. "I just need you to sign these forms and you're free to go."

Free to go. The most beautiful three words in the universe right then. But free to go how, she wondered? Unless Van had a wad of money stashed somewhere, they had no cash, no credit cards, checks, nothing. Even if Van's gas tank was full, which she highly doubted, it wouldn't get them all the way to Atlanta.

Morgan had a sinking feeling that although they were free to go, they weren't going very far.

The sheriff led them back to the lot where Van's SUV was parked and left them alone to deal with the mess. A big, nasty mess. It was all over the backseats of the car. Everything they'd left in the car had been ransacked and thrown around with no regard for anything.

"Oh, my God!"

Van just shook his head.

The sheriff came back a few minutes later. "I forgot to give you this," he said, handing Van a box.

Van's scanner, laptop, and digital and video cameras were inside.

"Thanks," Van said with a grateful breath.

Morgan stroked the dress on her arm like a beloved pet, like a thing alive. She hugged it close. She never would have considered dry-cleaning it, but it would have to be cleaned if her sister was going to wear it. And that was a big *if.*

Morgan had to call Ashley as soon as possible. The thought of searching through all the strewn items in Van's backseat area was almost depressing, but she had to know if her cell phone was among the wreckage.

They sifted through clothes, some clean, most not. Shoes, makeup, shaving supplies, deodorant, sewing kit, seminar handouts, maps, batteries, flashlight, and . . . cell phones! Both of them. Her favorite treat was gone, though.

"My Peter Pan . . ." she said, feeling miserable.

Van shot her a sideways glance. "I'll buy you some more."

Morgan put her modeling brochures in a pile. She always carried them with her whenever she traveled. They functioned like business cards and there was no telling when she would need one.

"Hey . . . what's this?" she asked, pulling out an eight by ten glossy. It was her when she did print ads for Pink Moisturizer. "I don't remember bringing this." She picked it up only to find another photograph of herself beneath it. "Did I pack my portfolio by mistake?"

She wasn't asking Van. It was a rhetorical question, but he answered her anyway.

"Maybe you did. You know how it is with last minute packing. Sometimes you throw everything into a suitcase."

"Do I seem like a last-minute packer to you?"

He scratched his head. "No. Not really."

She continued to pull pictures out of the pile. Then newspaper clippings where she appeared on the arm of whatever famous man she happened to be dating, and finally a cutout of her on a box of hair relaxer. That small sample of her work looked like something from her agent's file.

"Where did you get all this?"

Van ran a hand down his face and let out a hard sigh. "It's mine."

"Well, that's kinda obvious. What I asked you is *where* did you get these? Van, some of these photos were taken years ago."

She held all the representations of herself in her hand then let them all fall in disgust.

"I've been fascinated by you for a long time," he admitted.

She put her hands on her hips. If Van was some sick stalker, she wanted to know now so she could get the heck away from him. Thank goodness they were at the sheriff's office. She bit her lip, praying he had a good explanation.

His face closed as if guarding a secret. "When I said I remember the day we met, I meant it. I remember it like it happened three seconds ago. I've never been able to get it out of my head. You were so beautiful. I'd never seen a girl so beautiful. Morgan—"

Morgan's stomach tightened like a fist. Van reached out to her. She moved out of the way. She didn't want to be touched by him right now. Right now, Van McNeil was suspect.

"I was a fat, extra, shy nobody. And then I saw an angel. You changed my life. I told myself that if we ever met again, I would be worthy of your attention. So I lost weight. Took care of myself. Made sure I looked good at all times.

"When I started modeling for Williams Brothers, I thought I'd hit the lottery. We were together again, kinda. I knew it was only a matter of time before you and I hooked up in some kind of way. I just had a feeling."

He appeared sincere, but Morgan kept her distance.

"In the meantime, I would run across your picture from time to time in the paper, in a magazine. So I saved a picture or two. It was my way of keeping up with you. Keeping in touch."

She relaxed a little. His tale sounded reasonable. Except for one thing.

"What about our date? You apologized, but you never did explain why you left. Did you really have a weather emergency?"

Van looked away, gritted his teeth, and then faced her. "No. I didn't."

His truth relieved and saddened her at the same time.

"Going out on that date made you real. Not the fantasy woman I had admired for years. Of course, in my mind you were more or less like most of the women I'd been dating. Demure, easily influenced, sexually open.

"Not only were you none of those things, you came with a family I was one hundred percent sure I wanted nothing to do with."

"My sisters," she said.

"Your sisters. From what I've observed with Gordon, any man who becomes involved with an Allgood woman has to deal with her sisters. I wasn't ready for anything that heavy." Van's face grew pensive. "But more than that, I realized that you really were an angel and a person like you deserved much better than a person like me."

His words came out strained and tight. Suddenly Morgan felt sad and tired. She nodded, more hurt now than she was when she discovered the photos. The thought of anyone rejecting her partly because of her sisters, or just flat-out rejecting her sisters—

"But things have changed," Van said.

"Now there's a player's line if I ever heard one," Morgan said, unconvinced.

Van just stared at her, saying nothing. His eyes, however, appeared wounded.

"Okay, look, let's just get back on the road. I guess I understand the pictures, and I don't think you're a pervert. Can we shove all this to the side and deal with it when we get back in town?" she asked, wondering if she really could put Van's revelation to the side.

Instead of waiting for him to answer, she handed Van his cell phone and checked hers.

"Dead," Van said, wiping a bead of sweat from his brow.

Morgan flipped her phone open. A sliver of power flickered on the screen. "I've got enough juice for two, maybe three short calls."

"Okay. Let's save yours. Mine we can recharge with the cigarette lighter."

"If we go back inside the station to change, I can plug up my phone. Ten minutes is ten minutes," she said, fishing her AC cord from beneath her open suitcase.

The inside of the car smelled like someone had slept in it. They opened all the windows, hoping the wind would help air out the car.

Van blew out a frustrated breath. "Now I know what women mean when they say they've been violated. Part of me wants to trade in this car for a new one and the other part wants to rip Billy a new one."

"Well, it's all we've got right now. What do you say we straighten this stuff up, throw away the cigarette butts and beer bottles, then go inside and get changed?"

Van wiped his hands on the overalls that hung off him like loose skin. "Sounds like a plan to me."

Chapter Fifteen

Half an hour later, they were on the road with less than a fourth of a tank of gas. The sheriff had told them there was a gas station less then a mile down the road. Even with money the Hineses had given them, she prayed they had enough to get them back to Atlanta.

"That twenty dollars isn't going to get us very far," Van said, speaking her thoughts.

"We'll make it," Morgan said.

"Morgan, this is an SUV. Twenty dollars will buy what, eight gallons? Nine at the most. If we're lucky, we'll get as far as the Georgia border."

A cold fist of dread closed over Morgan's heart. She had no choice. She would have to call her sisters. Ask one of them to wire enough money so she and Van could drive the rest of the way home.

Her body slumped in emotional anguish. For someone who claimed to be trying to change her life, she was slipping right back into her old habits. Maybe Van was right. Maybe she and her sisters had grown way too dependent on each other. She had to prove to herself—and to Van, too, if she was honest—that she could stand on her own.

"I'll call Gordon. Get him to wire us some money."

"No!" she cried in a voice too full of emotion.

"Why not?"

The last thing she needed was for her sisters to hear about their predicament from someone other than her. There had to be another way.

"Look," he said, "I don't want to be stranded again."

"And you think I do?"

"What else can we do?"

"You could hock your equipment."

"And you could pose for pictures. Next idea."

Morgan scoffed. "Pull over. Let's not waste gas."

Van pulled the car over to the shoulder and cut the engine. "Okay, Morgan. What do you have in mind?"

She thought for a moment, hoping to be struck by brilliance. Instead, Verleen's last words to her echoed in her head like a ghostly whisper.

She turned to Van, feeling excited about the potential of their future for the first time that day. "Let's go back the way we came."

Van gawked at her in disbelief. "Are you crazy? What for?"

She could only smile when she thought about it.

Van looked puzzled for a moment, then the dawn of realization relaxed the wrinkles in his brow, their telepathy intact. "No. If it doesn't work, we've wasted gas going in the wrong direction."

"In which case, I'll pose for pictures—fully clothed, that is."

Van didn't look convinced.

"Around here I think the chances of this working are really good."

"Morgan—"

"Trust me."

He threw up his hands. "All right," he said, turning on the ignition. "But if this doesn't work, I am *not* hocking my equipment. Got that?"

"Got it," she said, smiling.

And she had a right to smile. She and Van were about to be five hundred dollars richer.

They arrived at two P.M.—way too early. Bear Diggers' owners were just starting to get ready for the evening's festivities.

"Back so soon?" the man asked. He was sweeping up trash in the parking lot. The heat of the day was just beginning to peak, evidenced by the beads of sweat dotting his weathered face and arms.

Morgan stepped out of the car, eyeing the yellow sign. It still said KARAOKE $500 PRIZE, but the evening's special was ALL-YOU-CAN-EAT RIBS. After going all day without eating—a feat she was not accustomed to—her stomach was finally beginning to growl.

"You have contests every day?"

"Nope. Just Tuesday, Wednesday, and Thursday. On Friday and Saturday most folks like to ride into the city."

"Mind if we hang out until you open?"

"I sure do," he said.

"You do?" she asked.

The man stopped sweeping and stood up straight. He adjusted his hat and stared at them. "You want to hang here, you help out. That's the deal. You go on inside where it's cool. Sarah will find plenty for you to do. Otherwise, you wait for the doors to open like everyone else." Then he winked.

Morgan and Van exchanged glances. He went back to his work and continued sweeping. "In exchange for your help, you can eat and drink all you want for free. How's that for a deal?"

They smiled. A little food was sounding better and better.

"I like it."

"I do, too!" Morgan said.

Little did they know it would be two hours later before they would have a break to actually eat something. Until then, Morgan endured several "I hope you know what you're doing" comments from Van while they arranged chairs, cleaned off tables, and stacked dishes. All their activity made her wonder how the owners—the Robinsons—would have gotten ready without them. She started thinking maybe getting help from locals was a usual thing with them. And they seemed real easy and nonchalant about offering them food and drink in exchange for in-kind service.

Eventually they ate, but they didn't let themselves go like the previous night. They had healthy helpings of the ribs the Robinsons were preparing to serve that night. When they asked about side dishes, they were told there weren't any.

"You mean all you're serving is ribs?" Van said.

"Yep. All you can eat. It's simpler that way."

"Of course, folks can order whatever they want to drink. We have the best-stocked bar for fifty miles in each direction."

"What about bread, coleslaw, baked beans?" Morgan asked.

"Wet-Naps," Mr. Robinson replied.

Van gave Morgan a look that said, "Shut up asking questions and eat." She did as his expression suggested.

At four-thirty there were people standing at the door, waiting to get in. They looked like the folks she and Van had been watching on television the previous night at Harley and Verleen's house: farm, country, rural folk. They filed in by the dozens. Within thirty minutes, Bear Diggers was half full of dancing, laughing, and hungry patrons. The transformation from barnyard warehouse to bar and grill amazed Morgan. She and Van both had stout beers and sat at the bar staring in amazement.

"Where are they all coming from?" she asked.

Tommy Tucker, the man they'd come to know as the

lovable bartender, leaned toward them and said, "They come from miles around."

They laughed at that, then he clarified. "Seriously, Bear Diggers is the only game in town. *Any* town for miles. It's *the* community activity. Some folks come darn near every night. Everybody else comes at least once per week. It's a tradition."

Van scoffed. "Whatever happened to cookouts and family reunions?"

"I'm tellin' ya, by five-thirty this place will be standing-room only."

Van and Morgan clinked their bottles in response and drank up.

Tommy was the hippest person they'd come across since they left Chicago. In fact, he looked as though he belonged in Chicago or any major city. He was hip-hop cool with his oversize shirt, sagging baggy jeans, bounce in his walk, and hat to the back. Bright-eyed and wide-grinned, he looked barely legal enough to be pouring drinks in an establishment like the one they were in.

As sure as he spoke, by five-thirty there were more people in the warehouse than the law probably allowed. They were loud, boisterous, animated, and made Morgan's and Van's shovel-fest the previous evening look like they'd eaten birdseed with chopsticks.

"It's a madhouse," Van declared.

"You ain't seen nothin' yet. Wait till the contest starts. Now that's wild."

"How so?" Morgan asked, not sure if she liked the insinuation in Tommy's voice.

"Like I said, we got a tradition around here. The same people sing the same songs night after night. Sometimes they'll sing a different song, or someone new—such as yourself, Ms. Morgan—will get up and sing a song."

She licked her lips apprehensively. "So?"

"So, if they don't like you, you get heckled and booed something awful. I mean, these folks can be rude. If they really don't like you, they might throw food or, worse, throw you out on your keister."

"Keister?" Van said.

Morgan was as shocked as Van was. She didn't know people still used that word.

"You ready for that?" Van asked.

She turned to him, sat her beer on the bar. He looked good sitting on the stool, like he belonged in a place like this. Carefree and reckless. She let herself take inventory of the man. Van was supa-dupa fine. She kept trying to put that fact out of her mind. It was impossible. Every time he opened his mouth, she just wanted to put her tongue in it.

He'd changed into a ribbed silk sweater and black trousers that hugged his legs at the thigh. He looked . . . mmm-mmm good. Despite everything, being with him was doing her body good.

"Thank you," she said.

"For what?" he asked and took a sip of beer.

"For not treating me like all the other men I've been with."

"How do other men treat you?"

"Like I'm their own personal supermodel. I'm so used to men wearing me like jewelry that being appreciated for just being me—your stash of photos notwithstanding—is a refreshing and pleasant way to spend time with a man. Do you know you're the first guy I've been with who hasn't pulled out a camera right away and wanted to take pictures of me or asked me to model clothes or wanted me to strut in front of him wearing nothing but red high-heeled pumps—or worse, put on a string bikini and pose beside their sports cars while they 'roll camera?'"

"Mmm," he said and nodded.

"You wouldn't believe all the things men have asked me to do."

"Yes, I would," he said. "And don't think I haven't thought of them, too. But I respect you beyond my own perverted thoughts, so I would never ask you to do anything like that." Van wiped away a trickle of condensation running down the side of his bottle. "Now, if you want to *volunteer* to do any of those things for me, you go right ahead."

They shared a laugh. For a man like Van, she might not mind at all.

"I should thank you, too," he said.

"For what?" she asked, her eyes sparkling like champagne.

"For not treating me like a weatherman—aside from the name-calling thing."

"What name-calling thing?"

"Mr. Wrong."

"Oh, that."

"Definitely that. Anyway, when I tell women I'm a meteorologist, they start treating me as though I'm a weather instrument instead of someone who uses them."

"What do you mean?"

"You know, asking me the temperature as soon as we step outside, asking me what time it's going to rain while we're having dinner, wanting me to predict the weather weeks, sometimes months in advance."

"You're kidding."

"I wish I was. Matter of fact, one woman I dated—the woman you rescued me from in Chicago—said she was planning a trip to Madrid next year and wanted to know if I could tell her if it was going to rain during the third week of June when she was scheduled to be there."

Morgan started to laugh and then her eyes narrowed speculatively and she said, "That's what happens when people see you as what you do instead of who you are."

"Amen," Van said and looked past the beautiful model standing next to him—wearing a white dress that looked more like painted-on latex—to the woman he was pretty sure he wanted to be the mother of his children. The thought made him uneasy and content at the same time.

Morgan caught Tommy's eye as he passed to fill up a patron's empty beer glass.

"You know what, Tommy? I have every intention of going up on that stage tonight. I'm going to try my best to win that contest," she said and winked.

Tommy's eyes widened; he dropped the beer glass he'd been carrying.

"Sorry," he said, then bent down to clean up the mess.

Morgan laughed inside.

Van shook his head. "How do you *do* that?" he asked.

"I'll never tell," she said, and slid off the bar stool to check out the karaoke setup. "I'll be right back."

She expected all kinds of "what in tarnation are you colored folk doing here?" looks in a place like this. She and Van may have gotten a few, but most of the glances had been looks of appreciation. She had to admit, she and Van looked good together . . . damn good. Stunning even.

The truth was the truth and, for better or for worse, she and Van were members of the Beautiful People Club. Their genetic aesthetic edge gave them advantages, and it was times like this that removed Morgan's hesitation about using her looks to her benefit. They needed money, and if dressing up and spicing up her demeanor with sensuality would get them that five hundred dollars, then she was going to work the room.

Morgan made sure the route she took to the stage cut directly through the middle of the warehouse. That way, men on both sides of the room got a good look at her. She used her runway stride to draw attention to her hips but not to overexaggerate her walk. Lastly was her eyes. Her eyes had been dilated so many times for print ads to make them more appealing to men that she could simulate "I want you" eyes on command. Morgan added that look to her arsenal and approached the stage, where a man who looked to be about her age was giving the karaoke equipment a final check before the six P.M. contest.

"Excuse me," she said, using a voice like her favorite on-screen seductress, Lisa Carson.

The man turned from where he was swapping one microphone for another and let everything in his hands fall as though his hands had suddenly lost their gripping ability. He stared at her, mouth gaping, eyes stricken with surprise.

"Y—yes?" he stammered.

"I was just wondering . . . how does this karaoke thing work?"

"Work?" he asked. The man hadn't moved a muscle—not to reposition his hands after dropping the mikes and chords, not even to pick up the equipment from the floor.

"Yes, I mean, I was thinking about entering the contest and I"—she stepped closer, hoping her presence would fill the space between them—"thought I should check out the equipment first." She thrust her breasts forward.

One crash. Two crashes. Three. Four. For about ten seconds, the warehouse filled with the sound of things dropping, breaking, and women slapping their men upside the head.

Morgan wanted to laugh so badly, but she didn't. She just stood there while the guy, who finally found his words, introduced himself as Hank and explained the karaoke basics. She listened but didn't pay much attention. She'd done it before. It had been a while, but she was sure it would all come back to her. What she wanted was to ensure that if Hank had anything to do with the voting, his influence would go her way.

She had a wedding to get to.

After Hank's explanation, she picked up one of the song books, exposing just a little bit of cleavage. "May I take this?" she asked as sultrily as possible.

"Yep, y—yes, I mean, go ahead."

Morgan smiled sweetly, touched his elbow, winked, and said, "Thank you, Hank." Then she turned and walked back to the bar in the same manner she had come. Van's expression was unmistakable: lustful, like so many others in Bear Diggers. In a past life, she would have thrived on all the attention in the room. But right then, and probably for longer than she wanted to admit, the only man's attention she wanted was Van McNeil's. Mr. Wrong was starting to feel mighty, mighty, mighty right.

Six P.M. came faster than she had anticipated. Hank slipped right into his emcee role and pumped up the audience by singing an opening song to get them ready for the contest. There was a sign-up sheet to the left of the stage and folks were lined up to add their names.

"You better get on the list," Van insisted.

"In a minute," she said. She didn't want to be in the first bunch of people to sing. She wanted to assess the competition to see what she was up against. This could be a crowd of fun-loving amateurs who didn't mind making a fool out of themselves in the name of having a good time, or it could be a bunch of hard-core show-business wanna-bes with some talent who took their performances very seriously. She wanted to know which group she was facing before she got up onstage.

When it was time for the first singer, Hank said, "He was born Barney Lipscomb, but we all know him as Bo! Singing your favorite and mine, 'Born to Be Wild'!"

One would have thought by the applause that Hank had just introduced Bruce Springsteen. Bo took the mike, the music started, and the words appeared on two televisions on either side of the stage. When he started to sing, a little voice in Morgan's head said, *Uh-oh*. Bo was terrific. Maybe better than the original. The man was record-deal material, for sure. She hoped this wasn't a trend.

"He's good, huh?" Tommy said, drying off a glass with a brilliantly white towel.

"He's good," Van said.

Morgan nodded in agreement. Tommy walked to the other end of the bar to serve a customer. Morgan sighed nervously.

Van leaned toward her. "I've heard you humming in the car during this whole trip. And when the spirit, or a certain handsome man, moves you, you belt out a song like nobody's business."

"I thought we agreed not to talk about that," she said, the heat of embarrassment stinging her cheeks.

"I don't remember an agreement like that, but anyway I just need to know you can blow. 'Cause if you can't, we need to get the hell out of here and pray we make it to Frankfort and get a wire transfer from Gordon."

"Don't worry, I got this," she said. But if everyone who took the stage was like Bo, she and Van just might be in trouble.

She started thumbing through the songbook, looking for songs she thought suited her voice. Anything by Anita Baker or Toni Braxton would do. Heck, she might even tackle a Whitney or Chaka song. But after flipping through a few pages, the bottom dropped out of her stomach. There would be no soul diva songs in Bear Diggers tonight; the songbook didn't have any. Not even an obligatory Aretha song. Apparently the book had been customized for the audience—an audience that lived in rural Kentucky, drove tractors, herded cattle, and ran feedlots.

The *Uh-oh* in her head turned into a *Holy crap*.

She changed her strategy and scanned the artist list

for Celine Dion, Madonna, Bonnie Raitt. She found a few songs, but nothing she thought would do her voice justice or vice versa.

Van slid her a cautious glance. "You're awful quiet over there."

"I know," she said. "Still trying to pick out a song."

"What are the choices?" he asked, leaning over to get a better look.

"Well . . . I'm thinking about . . ." she scanned the Madonna songs, looking for something recent, ". . . 'Ray of Light.'" She wasn't really thinking about it. It was just the first thing that came out of her mouth.

"'Ray of Light,'" Van said, sounding like the words were sour balls in his mouth.

"Or not," she said.

He reached for the songbook. "Let me see."

Morgan handed over the book and bit her bottom lip, waiting for his reaction. He didn't have one. Instead, his eyes scanned the pages with interest. When they stopped and he smiled, she perked up.

"What did you find?"

He pointed to the song title and grinned mischievously. Her eyes grew wide with hope and relief. She kissed him full on the mouth, feeling a win coming on. *Atlanta, Georgia . . . here we come!*

She forgot all about her seductress persona and rushed up to the table where the sheet was and signed her name with a flourish. Number thirteen out of fifteen. She swallowed hard and hoped that for her sake and Van's, thirteen would be a lucky number.

After six more singers and renditions of "Elvira," "Crocodile Rock," "I've Got the World on a String," "Young at Heart," and "Devil Went Down to Georgia," she figured out that the Bear Diggers crowd was a hybrid—some who went onstage just for fun and some who were serious and had real talent. But with the song Van chose, her confidence stayed intact.

But not for long.

When Hank introduced performer number ten, the response from the audience jolted her. They did everything except stomp their feet and light matches. The guy's name was Charlie Hartman. He could have been David Copperfield's twin brother. Morgan could tell before he even started singing that he and the famous magician shared something else as well . . . stage presence. He hadn't sung a note and already he had outperformed everyone who had come ahead of him.

The moment he started singing, "Start spreadin' the news," all cockiness and assurance Morgan had, drained away. He was good, real good.

Van's expression darkened with unreadable emotion. "Sounds like a pro."

"Sounds and acts," Morgan said.

"You can take him."

She remained silent, not as sure as Van.

He brushed his forearm against hers playfully. Reassuringly. "You can."

Morgan just hugged herself and sat at the bar, riveted by the guy who belted out "New York, New York" as if he were performing on Broadway.

The entire audience cheered and clapped. Someone near them shouted, "Bring it on home, Charlie!"

Morgan couldn't help it, and she guessed Van couldn't either. By the time Charlie sang the last phrases of the song, they both clapped and cheered along with everybody else.

There was no denying talent. And Morgan believed in showing appreciation for raw, honest talent.

One of the patrons came up beside her and signaled Tommy for a drink, smiling a *I just ate a mess of ribs and now I'm fat and happy* smile. "That boy's good, ain't he?" the man said.

"He sure is," Morgan said, returning his smile.

"You oughta try and sing a little something."

She drained the last sip of beer from her glass, thinking that maybe a drink before the contest wasn't a bad idea. "You know, I just might," she said.

The man paid for his Bud Light. "Looking forward to it," he said, picked up his drink, and headed back to his seat.

While the alcohol warmed her stomach and relaxed her nerves, two other singers took the stage. Both of them were good, but neither of them challenged Charlie for the top contender.

"Ready?" Van asked.

"No," she said, feeling sick. Suddenly the whole idea of entering the contest seemed ludicrous. She and Van could have driven to Frankfort by now, hopefully gotten the wire transfer, and been well on their way back to Atlanta. What was she thinking? Was she so desperate to prolong being in Van's company that she'd cooked up this silly idea?

They needed to get on the road. Right now. Forget the whole contest thing, they—

"Morgan!" Van said,

"What?" she asked, coming slowly back to reality.

"You're on."

The crowd had followed Hank's lead and was staring at her. The loud and lively voices and conversations that had filled the room for the past hour had dissolved to murmurs and whispers.

Morgan donned her fashion-face smile, realizing she had made her bed and would have to lie in it. And just when a bum's rush of doubts was about to capsize her nerve, Van grabbed her and kissed her silly.

Among the *oohs* and *aahs* of the crowd came Van's smoldering words of encouragement.

"Go sing about that," he said.

At that moment she wanted to say—no, shout—"I love you." But she didn't. Instead, she channeled Van's encouragement into her stride as she approached the mike and stood as a visitor in front of the hometown crowd. All eyes held on her as she removed the mike from the stand and prepared to tell the audience, à la Shania Twain, that she felt like a woman.

Chapter Sixteen

Damn, that woman could sway a hip. And every man with it. *Whew,* Van thought, running a hand down his face. If her singing was anything like her strut, she had the contest on lock.

Before the music came up, he scanned the room to see the crowd's reaction to a newbie taking the stage. Just as he thought, there were a few curious glances and even a few frowns. Most people, however, looked on with mild enthusiasm as they waited for the first few notes that would tell them if she was a contender or just another mediocre singer out for a night of fun.

She began to sing.

Hmm, Van thought. *Not bad. The girl's got some chops on her.* By the time she got to the second verse, he realized she had stage presence, too.

Morgan worked the mike as if it were a man, caressing, fondling, and dipping. All good-natured and playful motions—lighthearted, not overtly sensual, but sexy nonetheless.

Van nodded his head. He couldn't help it. He grinned. And he would pay a million dollars to be that microphone.

"Woo-hoo!" someone shouted from the audience.

"Sing it, sister!" came another friendly, appreciative catcall.

Van scanned the room again, and a curious thought struck him. There must have been a hundred females in the room, but as far as he was concerned, there was only one *woman*. Folks were leaning in, patting their feet, smiling, swaying. Clapping.

She had them.

The last part of the song was coming up. Tommy sidled over from the end of bar. "You are one lucky dog."

"You got that right," he said, thinking about how many times over the past few days he'd heard that and did some clapping of his own.

Morgan hit a note that not even Shania herself could reach, taking the song to another level. Then, suddenly, someone hurled something toward her. Something metal. It hit the stage floor and slid toward the mike stand.

Van jumped to his feet, prepared to beat the crap out of somebody, when Morgan reached down and picked up the object.

A key.

Someone had thrown their house key on the stage. Morgan worked it into her performance as if it had been planned.

Van had heard of underwear being thrown onstage, but never keys. No sooner had the thought left his head than a pair of silk boxer shorts went hurtling toward the stage. They fell just shy of the edge, but Morgan played it up anyway, mouthing the words "Thank you" to the guy sitting toward the middle of the floor.

"Who the hell would throw a pair of boxers?" Van asked Tommy.

Tommy smiled spastically. "My dad."

He gave Tommy a crazy sideways glance.

"Yep," he said. "He brings boxers every week, hopin' some young thing will sing a song the way it was meant to be sung. He's only thrown 'em twice."

"Really?" Van said, half listening but mostly keeping his attention on the last note of Morgan's song.

"Both times the women won."

Now Van was listening. And cheering. He stood and clapped a steady rhythm until Morgan brought her beautiful self down from the stage and back over to him.

Tommy patted Van's shoulder. "Congratulations, man." Then he went back to fixing drinks.

Van noticed that not many people had talked, drank, or did much of anything while Morgan sang—except watch and listen.

He grabbed her and hugged her hard and fast like she was his long-lost love.

"Mahogany!" he said. "You are . . ." He didn't have the words to tell her how full of talent she was or that he was proud of her. "Even if you don't win, it was worth it. Hearing you sing was worth it."

Whoa, he thought. *This love thing is a monster.* If he couldn't have this woman—the woman with a million talents—in his life for now and forever, he was sure he'd go nuts. Absolutely, completely, *get him a drool bucket and a diaper* nuts.

"This is crazy!" Van said, speaking his thoughts out loud.

"What?" she asked, her hands shaking a little.

"Nothing. Nothing."

Several people crowded around Morgan to congratulate her on a great performance.

"Thanks," she said. "I haven't done anything like that in a long time."

"Well, you need to keep doing it," someone said.

"Thanks," she said again. "Tommy! Can I get a towel?"

"Be right there!" Tommy called.

She was sweating and nervous and jittery. Van liked this side of her. He was so used to the confident, always in control, had-an-answer-for-everything Morgan that this new Morgan was refreshing and endearing.

Tommy came over with a cold, wet cloth.

"Let me," Van said.

He dabbed her forehead, her cheeks, her neck.

She moaned softly.

When he dabbed her shoulders, she tilted her head from side to side, allowing him access to all the places where sweat had formed like tiny glistening diamonds. The sight was so moving, he didn't want to ruin it.

Their eyes never left each other's.

"Thank you," she said. But he heard, "I want you, Van. I want you right now. Forget the contest. Let's find a secluded spot and go for what we know."

"Van?" she said.

"Y—yes," he answered, blinking. Was Morgan saying something?

"What do you think?" she asked, motioning toward the stage.

Wow. He hadn't even noticed the woman singing. Had they gone on to another contestant? And from the sounds of it, she was more than halfway through her song.

"Night the Lights Went Out in Georgia."

Van hadn't heard that song since he was a kid. The woman sang it well, although she didn't deliver a performance like Morgan. If it hadn't been for the fact that her left eye was almost twice as big as her right, she would have been kinda cute.

He smiled down at the top of Morgan's wavy hair, giving her a quick squeeze. "No worries, mate."

She nodded, but didn't look assured.

Hank introduced singer number fifteen. The last one on the list. Van held his breath, waiting to see if the crowd would erupt as one of the local favorites took the stage. He didn't have to wait long.

The applause was thunderous as three people, a man and two women, took the stage. They were dressed as though they had just stepped out of a *Blondie* comic. When the music started, he realized why.

They were singing "Love Shack" by the B-52's. And they were off the hook!

The aroma of fresh beer and a thin cigarette haze hung in the air. Morgan and Van exchanged desperate looks as the trio sang every note, phrase, and refrain in perfect harmony. The lead singer was just as zany as the original singer and just as entertaining.

Morgan looked sick.

Van hugged her closer. Stroked her arm. "I said no worries. After all, you got the Fruit of the Looms!"

Morgan chuckled a little, relaxed a little more.

"Don't sweat it, baby. You got this."

But in the back of his mind, the people onstage were hard to dismiss. He believed in his heart that Morgan had won it. He just hoped the judges voted the way of his heart.

"They've even got choreography," Morgan said.

"You had choreography, too. Just a different kind."

"Let's hear it for Mary, Joanetta, and Jeb!" Hank said.

"Dang," Morgan said, "is everybody around here named Jeb?"

At first he thought the sound he heard was even greater applause than when Morgan had taken the stage. It only took moments to realize that rain was hitting the tin roof. It sounded like hands clapping in the heavens.

"While the judges tally their scores, I'd like to do a little number for you called "'Wichita Lineman'!" said Hank.

Morgan signaled Tommy for a glass of water. "I had no idea karaoke could be so nerve-racking."

"It's not the karaoke, it's the fact that it's a contest," Van said.

"It's not the karaoke? I didn't see you up there singing. When you get up there and work the stage, then you can tell me what the most nerve-racking thing is about it. Until then . . ."

He conceded. "Point taken. Have you ever heard this song?"

"No. You?"

"No." He liked it, though. It had a haunting quality about it. The story of a man missing the love of his life because his work was so demanding.

There were some things in life that everything else was worth giving up for. Van glanced at Morgan, wondering if she knew that.

"Thank you! Thank you, everybody. It's been a pleasure being your host tonight at Bear Diggers! Be sure and stop by tomorrow when the dinner feature will be chili-cheese fries and—"

"Oh, for Christ's sake, tell us who won already, Hank!" someone yelled from the audience.

Van agreed with the heckler. Van wanted to hear his baby's name being announced.

Hmm. His baby.

Van's nerves jumped like intense calisthenics in his body. His mouth tasted dry and metallic as though he'd been licking the inside of a pop can.

Will you announce the winner, please?

"And the winner of the Bear Diggers evening contest is . . . a new name around these parts . . . Morgan All-good!"

"Wooo!" Morgan shouted, thrusting her hands straight up in celebration.

"I knew it," Van said, wrapping her in his arms and lifting her off the ground.

They exchanged a celebratory kiss that nearly seared

his lips. An inferno of emotion passed between them. Happiness, relief, and undeniable attraction. They pulled apart as if they'd been shocked.

Morgan strutted happily back up to the stage, moving to the rhythm of applause. Tonight a stranger had come among the hometown crowd and stolen the show. Van wondered if there would be hard feelings. Scanning the crowed, the faces he saw were smiling and happy.

Morgan accepted the five hundred-dollar bills Hank placed in her palm. They shook hands and she all but skipped back over to Van. They kissed again, quick and sweet.

"Okay, folks," Hank said. "Show's over. You all finish your drinks and eats so the Robinsons and I can get ready for the late show."

Hearing that announcement made it clear to Van and Morgan why serving one entrée per night made sense.

"You sure sounded good, Ms. Morgan," Tommy said. "This one's on me."

He placed a small flute of champagne in front of her. She eyed it appreciatively.

"Thanks, Tommy."

He smiled, nodded, and went back to his bartending duties.

Van's eyes drank in the radiant woman standing next to him. The joy dancing from her eyes cast a glow around her body as if the sun had decided to shine on Morgan and Morgan alone. "You are . . . magnificent." He hadn't realized how tense he was; relief suddenly flooded his body like cold water on a hot day.

Morgan took a sip of champagne, swallowed, then took another. "Thanks, Van. Now, you know what I think?"

"What?" he asked as her eyes ranged freely up and down his body.

She turned up the flute, drained it dry, and smiled provocatively. "I think we should get the heck out of here."

Hmm. *There's nothing sexier than a woman who's not afraid to be herself.* And when you combined that with a woman who knew exactly what she wanted, now, *that* was an aphrodisiac!

He took the twenty-dollar bill the Hineses had given them out of his pocket and dropped it on the bar for Tommy.

"Let's go," he said.

He took her hand and led her out of the building. On the way, they stopped to say their thank-yous and good-byes to the Robinsons. Then they stepped outside into the night rain.

It was coming down in a steady shower. Thankfully the temperature had dropped or it would have been a hot, sticky, uncomfortable rain.

Morgan hesitated at the entrance. "My poor hair," she said, attempting to cover it with her free hand.

"This is rain," Van said, "one of the most beautiful, peaceful, wondrous, natural phenomenons in the universe—besides you, of course."

He led her around the corner of the building back toward where they had parked. They stayed close to the building so the overhang would prevent a cool drenching.

"Allgood women don't get their hair wet," she insisted.

"Is that right?"

"Yeah. I wish I had a newspaper or something."

"I got something that will take your mind off the rain,"

"Really?" she asked.

"Yes," he said and pulled her out into it.

Large droplets fell on Morgan, illuminating the elegant angles on her face in the moonlight. She blinked and still seemed unsure until he wrapped her in his arms and kissed her with his entire soul.

She'd won his heart. He wanted her to know that. And all the things he'd been in the past, including a player, chronically single bachelor, he'd tossed out the window like bad trash.

The rain blanketed them with wetness, reminded him of all the things in life that were unstoppable. This thing with Morgan was one of them.

She pulled away, panting. Her hair, heavy with rain, looked sexier than ever. The raindrops glistened on her face like bright sparkles of energy. Her eyes bore into his. Her chest rose and fell.

"How's your knee?" she said huskily between the raindrops.

"Let me show you," he said, taking her hand and heading for the car.

The clouds had darkened the sky. Van wanted a bit more privacy. He switched on the four-wheel drive and steered the SUV toward an area behind Bear Diggers between a large storage shed and a grove of trees. Raindrops danced on leaves and fell onto the roof of the car. In the distance the hum of people talking, getting in their cars, and driving away sounded like ghosts in the darkness. And Van was horny as hell.

He couldn't turn the engine off fast enough. Morgan was all over him like they'd done this a thousand times.

In an instant she had climbed across the divider and hiked up her dress before he could say, "Damn, baby."

Although he was more than willing, there wasn't much room on his side for what she had in mind. "Morgan, I don't think . . ."

"Okay, keep up with me, baby," she said, and placed her hands on the sides of his head. Her lips hovered inches away from his. She planted a kiss on him to rival the one he'd given her. But it didn't render him so out of his head that he couldn't give in to her demands by unbuckling his belt and unzipping his pants.

He heard his blood pounding in his ears. Her eyes bore hotly into his. "Slide over. Now move your thigh, yes, that's right. Now slide down just a little, yeah. Okay, now lift your left leg and I'll put my right one . . . ah, yes . . . ooh, that's it. . . ."

Her words came out hot and breathy. Morgan's hands caressed Van's face, stirring him with their heat and deliberateness. He wanted to touch her back, but his mind was consumed with one prayer: *Lord, please let my player's emergency condoms still be in the side pocket of this seat. Please don't let those thieves have taken them. Please.*

Relief took over his body as his fingers found his stash. Three *just in case, you never know* condoms. He pulled one out.

"You always meet my expectations," she said, pausing from her onslaught of kisses and taking the square package from his fingers.

He adjusted the steering wheel so that it was as far away from Morgan as possible. Then he pushed the front seat back as far as it would go.

And there were no words. The time for speaking and verbal communication had passed. Their bodies needed to talk now. After everything they had gone through and all they meant to each other now, there was only one thing left to say. Talking wouldn't do.

Morgan slid down Van's pants and boxer briefs and sheathed his body where it was hard and desperate for her. Every touch from her hand was an invitation. He pulled up her dress even more, moved aside her thong, and pushed himself up into her as she slid down.

The moan they shared was aching, animalistic.

Neither of them moved at first, only stared into each other's eyes as if waiting for a signal to begin a journey they'd been waiting for their whole lives. His vision traveled downward to her mouth, her trembling lips. Her arms circled his neck and her hips circled over him, bathing him with white-hot urgency. His eyes squeezed shut. The pleasure was too great.

He didn't keep them closed for long. Morgan's dress was soaked with rain and he loved the fact that she never wore a bra. The hardened pebbles of her nipples strained against the fabric of her dress, begging for his mouth. He did what any hot-blooded, intelligent man would do. He descended upon them like a wild man.

Morgan's body jerked as if a thousand volts of electricity had passed through it. He loved that reaction. Determined to coax it from her again and again, he swirled his tongue deftly, giving attention to each tight orb and reveling in the sweetness of her skin. Morgan's tongue massaged his neck, uncoiled the tension that had settled there. The sensation drove him to move his hips gently against hers, creating synergy and a powerful sensual bond that weakened and strengthened him at the same time.

Her body sprang back and ground down against his thighs, the power of her movement pulling him apart.

He grabbed her waist, helped her move. Van gritted his teeth, trapped the growl threatening to break free. The hunger of passion drove them onward. Van felt possessed. He'd never experienced a woman this way. Every inch of Morgan's essence seeped into him. He shuddered with the overwhelming power of it.

The air around them thickened with their heat, fogging the windows, making them drunk. They were out of control. Morgan was definitely out of control, riding out her pleasure frantically, her breath coming in ragged gasps. Van moaned and held on, out of his mind with the need for completion. If the cops came knocking, they would be powerless to stop.

He assaulted her mouth, felt the blood beating feverishly in her lips. Watched her breasts rise and fall with his thrusts. Kneaded them with his hands. Pushed hard into her core as ruthless passion consumed him in strong, hot waves.

Morgan didn't know what had come over her. She only knew that she needed to tell Van how much she loved him. She needed him to know that she never wanted to be with another man, ever. Her body was his and his alone. Despite her strength, her resolve, her good sense, and her home training, she had fallen in love with a cad, a rapscallion, a player extraordinaire who had played her heart right from the start. All the love she felt surged through her in a sweet rush of ecstasy as her body, soul, mind, spirit, and heart gave over to him, surrendered all, frightened her beyond measure, and set her free.

Is this what it's like? Van wondered. *Never wanting this raging pleasure to end? This feeling of love and wanting and need and desire. A feeling I have denied myself for so long?*

He wanted to talk to her of clouds and storms and hot, drenching rain until the breath left his body. He wanted to empty his heart and soul and all that she would take of him into her body. But she was telling him, teaching him about hurricanes of feelings and floods of emotions with a direction to his heart so precise, no radar instrumentation could compare.

"Uhhh," he breathed, the noise of their wild exchange driving him closer to the brink. The slick, wet sound of him moving in and out of her, the sound of their lips smacking, the sound of the rain beating outside like a million tiny heartbeats . . . the music of passion. "Uuh," he moaned again.

Morgan's hips danced now, a steady, pulsing rhythm that heated his blood like liquid fire. Her eyes grew dark and predatory. She bounced and undulated, her breathing uneven with need.

Van pulled her closer as her movements saturated his mind and every inch of his body with pleasure. She had wanting eyes, intense eyes.

In his eyes he knew that every night for the rest of his days, he would see her face.

For the first time there was no verbal dialogue between them, only this silent, sweet talk of bodies and sweat, possession, and unquenchable obsession.

"I love you," their bodies said, moaned, shouted.

They thrust together body to body, mouth to mouth, and as the lightning streaked the sky and the thunder rumbled in the heavens, Van's emotional heart exploded.

Morgan's head dropped to his shoulders. Shuddering though her own release, she kissed him hard and long.

Through her ragged panting, she sighed and said, "Let's go home now."

Chapter Seventeen

They put their clothes back on in no time and agreed to stop at the next rest area to "freshen up."

It felt good to be back behind the wheel. Van's knee was almost one hundred percent and all he wanted to do was drive safely and see the familiar streets of his home city.

"Baby, get the scanner from the back and turn it on, will you? I want to know what we're driving into."

Morgan gave him a quizzical look at first and then did as he asked.

"What's wrong?"

She turned on the scanner. "Nothing."

"Don't play with me. You're tripping 'cause I called you baby. It means something now, doesn't it?"

"I am not tripping."

She could pretend she wasn't, but Van knew her too well. "Yes, you are. You're afraid you might get used to it."

She blew out a breath and ran her fingers through her wet hair. "Can we just get to the rest area?"

"Yeah," he said.

He watched for exit signs and listened closely to the weather broadcast. Severe thunderstorms raged all around them. From the National Weather Service, it sounded as though the storms he had been expecting the day before would escort them home. As soon as they found a rest stop, he would turn on his laptop and see if he could hook up to satellite radar. He didn't want to drive directly into a storm and not know it.

They drove in silence for a while. Morgan twitched and fidgeted in her seat as though she was nervous about something. The expression on her face was pained. *That was quick*, he thought. *She already regrets what we just shared.* He'd better get her back to the city quickly before she jumped out of the SUV and hitchhiked back just to get away from her feelings.

When the low-fuel light came on, his jaw tightened. They had about a mile, maybe two, before they ran out of gas.

"Uh-oh," Morgan said, noticing the dash.

"I know," he said, and kept driving. "Any juice left on your phone? We may need to call for help."

As soon as the words left his mouth, signs for a truck stop appeared on the right. Food. Gas. Lodging.

"Thank you, Jesus," Morgan said.

"Amen, sister," he said.

Van and Morgan headed for the showers, which, thankfully, the gas station had for five dollars a shower. After changing into fresh clothes, they stepped back out into the rainy night together.

Van's eyes lingered on all the places on her body that weren't covered by fabric—which was most of her body.

"Good Lord, woman! Do you ever wear any clothes?"

"No," she said, challenging his question. His eyes darkened.

"Good. Now get in the car before I'm compelled to take you again."

Van turned on his laptop and filled up the gas tank while Morgan sat in the passenger seat, snacking on a

Reese's Peanut Butter Cup and staring blankly out the window.

"What's it look like?" he shouted through the window as he replaced the pump nozzle.

Morgan glanced behind her. "I don't know too much about that radar stuff, but the red zones don't look too good."

Van hurried into the car, avoiding the rain. He checked the radar. Morgan was right. If he were on the air, he'd be telling folks in outlying areas to take shelter.

Wind whipped around the SUV. The rain intensified and pelted the car with its fury.

"Let's get out of here," he said.

They got back on the interstate and sped down the road. According to the radar, conditions were ripe for the formation of wall clouds, hail, and all that came with them—including microbursts and tornadoes.

Lightning struck the horizon before them like thin, crooked fingers of light.

Van loved it. "You see that?"

"Yeah," she said. "Thank God that's not where we're headed."

"Actually, it is."

"What do you mean?" she asked, whipping her head around.

"I mean, before we ease on down the road to Atlanta, I need to call this in, take some readings, get pictures and video."

"You're not serious."

"Of course I am. Look, I know it's a detour, but—"

"Detour? It's not a detour, it's crazy thinking. You really believe it's cool to chase this storm now?"

"Actually, storm 'chasing' is a misnomer. What you really want is to stay ahead of the storm and relay updates and changes to a station or weather center. Out here in the boonies, there probably aren't many storm spotters. Since I'm here, I'm obligated to do my part to help people be safe." His voice sounded a little more animated than he'd intended, but it was to be expected. Chasing was in his blood.

"At the risk of your own safety, and mine?"

"Morgan . . . it's who I am. It's what I do."

"Then you need a new line of work," she said, and crossed her arms against her chest.

"It won't take that long."

"Van, baby," she said, voice laced with sarcasm, "you see that dress in the backseat? My sole mission in life in the past two weeks has been to get that dress to my sister."

"Except when you wanted to take a singing detour," he shot back.

Morgan recoiled. "I did that to get us the money we're using right now for gas!"

"Is it that you think I'm stupid or that you really are in denial? We could have made it to Frankfort to get a wire transfer even if I had to use the twenty dollars Harley slipped me to do it. But if we'd done that, you wouldn't have been able to show off—correction—perform."

"You're nuts."

"No, but you are if you think I don't recognize when a too-hot-to-trot woman like you is using what she's got to get a man. I've been a player in the game much too long for that."

The moment he said the last sentence, he wanted to pull it back into his mouth and swallow it down hard.

Her eyes narrowed to furious slits, but she remained silent.

The storm outside grew in intensity as if to match the storm inside the car. It was nine-thirty at night. Van had turned on the headlights to see now. The wind shoved and nudged the car like a giant giving them the elbow.

As long as no one was harmed, this was Van's kind of weather.

"I put up with your delay, but you can't put up with mine?"

"There you go again, Mr. Wrong. I've been putting up with your delays from mile one."

She fixed her face—he guessed to resemble his—and continued. "Let's take the two-lane highway instead of a major interstate; yes, Mr. Robber, whatever you want; staying with the Hineses is a good idea; and don't let me talk about how weird it is to find out you've got all those pictures of me in your luggage."

Van glanced in the rearview mirror. Mother Nature was truly flexing her muscles. The clouds rolled in like an angry mob prepared to go to war with the world.

They were running out of time.

He pulled over. "Look, Morgan, you see that off the road over there?" He pointed toward a dirt road that led to a vacant barn. "I can set up shop right over there, phone the weather service, upload photos and video into my laptop, and transmit. The storm is coming this way. I have a chance to help some people."

"You could help me by getting this bucket on the road and getting the heck outta here."

He scanned her face. She was too upset. "It's not the storm you want to get away from, is it?"

"Va—"

"No. You've been acting funky since you won that contest."

Her eyes shot daggers at him. "In what way?"

"How about the way you poured yourself into me behind Bear Diggers? I'll bet that scared you so bad you can't wait to get away from me—or rather, yourself and the way you feel about me. You can't move through your fear for one minute. It would be the greatest adventure you—we—have ever experienced."

"Your whole life is an adventure!" she blurted, throwing up her hands.

"What's wrong with that!"

"Nothing, for you. But for the people who end up being your excursion for a day, it's not so cool. I'm not going to waste time with someone who's not serious about creating a real, lasting relationship."

"And One-Eight-Seven is?"

Morgan shot him a look.

"Whatever the heck his name is! Murder One? Clyde. I'll bet the only things he's serious about are wearing platinum necklaces and finding the next chicken head—there's one for old Harley—to suck him dry."

"Then pay up now, Mr. Wrong. Clyde is the sweetest, most unassuming, respectful man I've ever met—unlike some people in recent company who continue to prove beyond a shadow of a doubt how pigheaded they are!"

Van blew out a breath of exasperation. "This is not about me. It's about you. What's the matter? Can't run the ball in the red zone?"

"Look, I know I don't owe you any explanations, but here's one. Let me put it on repeat for you: Clyde and I are just friends. Just friends. Does that ring a bell? It should because I told you that at the beginning of this foolhardy road trip. And now I'm telling you at the end. The next truck stop, rest area, hick-ass town you come to, let me out. You go chase your storm. I'm going home."

Van gripped the steering wheel so tightly, his knuckles turned white. "I've been preparing my entire life to fall in love with you. When I do, you turn me away like plain-label clothes."

"Oh, so now the great Van McNeil, lover extra-ordinaire—"

"Thank you!"

"—thinks he's in love and suddenly the world is supposed to stop and take notice."

"Not the world, Morgan, just you."

She rolled her eyes and shook her head. She knew Van was not used to losing. But neither was she. And the last thing she wanted to lose was her heart to someone who was incapable of settling down, even during a life-and-death situation.

"Woman, don't you know I was prepared to love you through the mustache years of menopause?"

Morgan turned away. She couldn't hear any more of his silly bravado. She picked up his cell phone and dialed a number stuck in her head.

"What are you doing? Who are you calling?"

"None of your business."

"You couldn't do it, could you? You had to bring your sisters into this just like I thought. Well . . ." His voice had lost some of its thunder. ". . . call them and have them send the Williams' private jet for you. You'll be home in time for bed."

"Hey, it's Morgan. Yeah. Where are you? Really? Well, I'm on Interstate Seventy-Five South. Coming up on the Lexington exit. Can you come and get me? Yes. Okay, thanks. I really appreciate it."

Van did as she asked and they took the next exit into Lexington. Sure enough, there was a truck stop, and by gosh it was busy. They pulled into an empty car slot and Van cut the motor.

"This storm is going to get real bad real fast. Your brother-in-law won't be able to land anywhere near here."

"I don't want to talk about it anymore, Van."

Weather updates droned on through the scanner. Van turned it down, but did not turn it off.

"I think you just need some time to cool off. Why don't we just sit here for a few minutes. We can talk or not talk. But any minute you're going to get a call from someone telling you they can't make the trip due to weather conditions. What will you do then?"

If he only knew, she thought. "Van, let's not make

this ugly. We've had a good time. We just have different goals. Let's leave it at that."

"See, I don't think we have different goals at all. We have the same goal. And that scares the hell out of you. Because no matter what, we are more alike than you want to admit. And you can talk about wanting to settle down, but when it comes right down to it, you're more threatened by the idea than I am. And something else . . . the fact that your smart, independent, full of potential, beautiful black ass fell for a Killer Joe like me, irks the heck out of you, doesn't it?"

"You don't know everything, Van."

"You may be right about that, but I'll tell you what: after thirty years, I sure as hell know *you*."

They sat in silence for twenty-five excruciating minutes. In the background, hard rain and the constant hurry of cars, motorcycles, and semis rushed past. People who knew exactly where they were going. Morgan realized that at this point in the day, and in her life, she didn't have a clue.

When a semi parked in the truck space behind them, Van said her name and gave her a long, searching look.

Her heart nearly disintegrated from the pain she saw in his eyes, but the cards had already been dealt for Morgan and Van before they'd even started playing the game. She couldn't stop the forward progress even if she wanted to.

Brax was smart. He stayed in the truck and waited for her.

"Van," she began, without a thought in her head as to what she was going to say. The storm was starting to build. Van's eyes darkened like the thunderclouds above them.

He pounded his fist on the dashboard. "Get out of my car," he said.

His words came out hard and sharp, each one a precise blow to her psyche.

His eyes went liquid with emotion when she opened the door. She could have sworn she heard "Good-bye, Mahogany" through the raindrops.

The moment she stepped out of Van's car with her luggage, she knew she'd made the wrong decision. Inside, her conscience called her an idiot and demanded she tell him how right he was and apologize.

But the big ball had been set free and it was rolling behind them now. She turned toward Brax's truck, but something in her resolve stopped her feet. She was about to turn back when Van took away her options. He sped off as though leaving the scene of a crime.

And, in a way—the only way that mattered—he was.

The rain soaked right through her top and two-hundred-dollar jeans. She walked faster, pulling her luggage and cradling Ashley's dress. Her poor masterpiece had been through a lot.

Once inside the truck, she closed the door and apologized for dripping all over Brax's interior.

He said nothing, just nodded, put the semi in drive, and headed toward the freeway ramp.

It was a long time before either of them said anything. She just watched the skies grow darker and darker and listened to the big sound of the diesel engine.

Brax kept his eyes on the road and his hands on that large round wheel. Jean jacket, black t-shirt, Levi jeans. He looked at home.

"You sure about this?" he asked.

She stared out the passenger's side window. "I'm not sure about anything right about now."

"You wanna talk?"

"No."

"Good. I would hate to hear how you're all torn up about the brother in the Ford. Not when I came to"— he glanced over for a moment—"rescue you."

Van was right—the storm was gaining intensity by the

second. In less than five minutes, it was nearly pitch black and the wind pushed the semi around like it was a Tonka truck.

"I gotta pull this puppy over. It's too risky to travel through this. We'll have to wait until the storm blows through before we get back on the road."

Her shoulders sank. She hadn't made any progress at all. Only a few miles down the road and they were already pulling over. It must have been God's way of telling her the grass wasn't always greener. The more important message was that she had made a mistake by leaving Van.

"I really *am* Mahogany," she said aloud.

"What's that?" Brax asked, taking an exit marked VIS-ITOR'S CENTER.

"Nothing," she whispered.

They weren't the only ones who had decided to get off the road. Numerous cars and trucks packed the small center's parking lot.

Brax took the closest spot to the front door and they made mad dashes for the entrance.

Someone from inside was watching and held the door open for them. Their feet hit the linoleum with loud, wet smacks. They'd managed to avoid a soaking.

Not so with some of the other people taking shelter. A few of them must have walked to the building, including the guy who held the door open.

Morgan paced around a bit and shook off a few raindrops. She ignored the sound of things crashing in the background.

They exchanged hellos with many of the storm refugees. There were about thirty in all. Several families, several truckers, and a few men and women who appeared to be lone travelers—all seemed irritated by the storm delay.

Morgan was irritated by something else—her behavior. Brax leaned against the wall and crossed his long, thick legs at the ankles, watching her, examining. Probably trying to decipher her intentions. Well, more power to him and good luck. She surely hadn't been able to do it.

Staring out the window, she paced back and forth and watched as a great thunder and lightning show transitioned into darkness, wind, and hail.

Van was back there, doing what he was born to do, and she hadn't been there for him. No, all she could think about was getting home and getting the dress to her sister, but, most of all, getting away from the man who had caused such a turmoil in her soul, she didn't recognize herself.

The storm moved fast, very fast. She hoped—no, prayed—it would be over soon so she could do what her soul was telling her to do . . . go back.

When the train drove over the roof of the building— or at least that's what it sounded like—Brax was still staring at her, studying her, trying to figure her out. She thought she should apologize. Tell him she was sorry for using him to take her all of three miles down the road, but she was going back to the brother in the Ford, and from that point on, she was never looking back.

When two large glass windows exploded, a few women screamed. Most people just ran away from the windows and scrambled toward the interior of the one-story building.

Brax grabbed Morgan and ushered her along with the others. He covered her with his body just as glass from the front door shattered. Seconds later, there was chaos, people shrieking, and wind and rain rushing in through the hole in the door.

Brax hugged her close in his big, solid, truck-driver arms, but she didn't feel safe. And she wouldn't feel safe until the arms that held her from now until the end of time belonged to Van McNeil.

* * *

"Are you sure this is what you want?"

"For the first time in my life, I think I finally know where I'm going."

"Then why don't you let me drive you? It's dangerous for a woman walking alone on the interstate."

"It's only, what, three miles did you say? The storm is over. The sky is clearing. I've got to go back."

"What if he's not there?"

"He's there. Mr. Wrong never does anything half-assed. He's still collecting readings or something. Especially since there's no pressure from me to get back to Atlanta."

Brax nodded.

"If nothing else, he'll see me on the interstate." She just hoped that, after everything, he would stop to pick her up.

With dress and suitcase in hand, Morgan left the visitor's center along with so many others. But she was the only one on foot. She watched Brax take off and head down the road, then started the trek back. She had her comfortable heels on and hoped that by the time she made it back to Van, she would still think they were comfortable.

"Rich, it's McNeil. I'm in Nowhere, Kentucky, and there's a supercell here the size of Massachusetts! I don't have a crew with me so I can't transmit to the station. If I e-mail you video and photos, can you get them to NWS?"

"Sure thing!"

"Great. I don't see any spotters or chasers around, so the service will probably want this information right away."

"Gotcha, chief! Say . . . you out there all alone?"

"Yeah."

"Watch your backside, buddy!"

"Will do, Rich."

Van ended the call and placed his cell phone next to his scanner. The back hatch of his Explorer was open and a big black wall of clouds was headed in his direction. He struggled to keep his footing while the wind and rain whipped him around like paper.

He grabbed his digital camera and snapped enough pictures to fill the memory. Then he downloaded the pictures and e-mailed them to Rich. Next he took his video camera and walked toward the fast-moving front. The video was spectacular. He saw the clouds amassing like a regimen of soldiers gathering for final battle. He moved out farther to get better footage.

Van felt as though he were standing in a river. The windbreaker he'd put on wasn't much help against the onslaught of rain. When the sky hurled down hail the size of a small fist, Van knew it was time to get out of there.

He headed back to the car, fighting the wind as he went. For a moment, it was as if he were standing still, unable to push forward against the massive stopping hand of gale-force winds.

The hatch of his SUV blew shut and the video camera was yanked out of his hand as though God himself had snatched it.

He knew he was in trouble even before he saw the funnel cloud dip from the sky. Half a second afterward, he ran like hell.

Even with the heart of the storm bearing down on him, his thoughts were consumed with the missed opportunity of filming the event of a meteorologist's life—and his most important missed opportunity: Morgan. Would he live to see her again?

Hoping his car survived the weather, he headed straight for the barn in the distance.

Unfortunately he could tell by the hail beating down on him and the fact that the wind was pushing him off course that he wasn't going to make it.

Mother Nature stopped flexing her muscles and delivered a one-two punch. Hail pelted Van and the land he scrambled to run across. The cold-hot wind whipping across his body sounded like an angry freight train.

He saw a glimmer of hope a few yards away and he gasped for air in the midst of it all, praying that his feet stayed on the ground long enough for him to get to safety.

Chapter Eighteen

The closer Morgan got to the spot where she believed Van was working, the more debris she encountered. At first there was just wet concrete and muddy grass. She stayed away from the grass and pulled her luggage behind her on the shoulder, cradling the wedding dress in her arms as she went. Her shoes clicked softly against the pavement and she counted her steps silently in her mind.

Five hundred sixty-seven, five hundred sixty-eight. Her feet were tired already and she'd only walked about a mile.

By the time she noticed the scattering of tree limbs, scattered paper, and other trash strewn across the road and in the grass, she noticed something else as well.

She was being followed.

It was Brax. His flashing hazard lights blinked his slow progress. It was a dangerous thing he was doing, driving so slowly on the road. Even when he pulled over to the shoulder and followed her from there, she still felt badly. But she'd made a good friend. Feeling her sister's intuition about things, she knew Brax was a good man. Morgan wished him well and hoped that on his numerous travels, he would find the love of his life one day.

She stepped over McDonald's hamburger cartons, wet paper bags, small tree limbs, and dirty diapers washed clean by the storm.

Somehow the atmosphere felt as though it had just taken a deep breath, released, and relaxed. Completely chilled out. From the fury and gusts of the wind to the clear, cool calm, it seemed to Morgan like two different days had passed within an hour. She remembered her first date with Van. He'd talked about barometric pressure. She hadn't understood it then, but she did now. As the storm rushed on behind her, the horizon before her looked like a clear evening.

The smell of rain and humidity that had hung so heavily in the air before had dissipated, leaving only a moist memory behind. She walked on, determined to make sure that what she had experienced with Van during the past few days wasn't just a memory, that it meant something—something that lasted forever.

"Whew," she said to no one. Cars whizzed by. Now and then she would catch someone looking at her through the rearview mirror. Two people actually stopped and asked if she needed help. The first was a man, the second a woman. She said no and pointed at the truck behind her, assuring them that he was making sure she got to her destination safely.

By the time she saw Van's car on the side of the road in the distance, she was dog tired. Her feet ached and her arm was tired from holding a dress that got heavier with each step.

I should have taken Brax up on his offer, she thought. But it was too late now. A few more yards and she would be there.

She signaled Brax. He pulled up alongside her.

"You are a strong, determined woman, Morgan. Just the kind of woman a man could make a life with."

The sincerity of his compliment warmed her heart in the cold aftermath of the storm. "Thanks for everything, Brax."

"Don't mention it."

An awkward silence passed between them. Morgan glanced at Van's SUV and then back at Brax's rig.

"You gonna be all right with that heartbreaker?"

If he only knew. Van was the only man in the world who could heal her heart.

"Yes," she said. "I'm going to be fine."

Brax nodded and steered toward the interstate. She watched as his hazard lights stopped blinking and he picked up speed and headed down the road.

She took a deep breath and, with renewed determination, continued on toward the car.

"Van!" she called out.

No response.

As she approached, she noticed how the SUV was parked askew. The tracks in the mud suggested that the vehicle had slid to the side . . . or been pushed.

She checked inside. He wasn't there. She left the wedding dress and her suitcase in the back and realized Van's equipment appeared to have been tossed awkwardly onto the back floor.

Her breath quickened and her heart fluttered in her chest. "Van!" she called out again.

Morgan looked around, panic rising hotly in her throat. The more she looked around, the more devastation she saw. The farther away from the road she got, the more cracked tree branches and trash she came across. She picked up the pace, heading toward the old barn where she hoped Van went for shelter, and ran smack dab into a tree. It was lying on its side as if it had suddenly decided to take a nap and didn't want to be disturbed from its slumber. If it wasn't for the roots protruding from the end, shredded and exposed, the whole scene would have been peaceful and serene.

A sickening wave of fear rose up from the pit of her stomach.

"Van!" she screamed. Her voice sounded frantic and shrill and carried in the wind left behind by the storm.

She ran toward the barn. She didn't know why she was running. Her legs just started pumping on their own. Again, she called out for the man she loved one more time and thought she heard something. Morgan paused briefly to listen.

"Over here!" the voice said.

"Van?"

"Yes! I'm over here!"

She didn't see a thing but grass, trees, and debris, but she followed the voice.

"Keep talking!" she shouted.

"I would," his voice said, "but I can't think of a damn thing to say except . . . get me out of here!"

"Oh, my God," she said when she saw the well. "Please, Lord don't let Van be—"

"Are you a sight for sore eyes!" he said, looking up from a dark, narrow hole in the ground.

Morgan peered down into the darkness. "How on earth?"

"I jumped in when the weather went south. How do you think I got down here?"

"I don't know. Maybe you were blown in or something."

"Well, I tell you one thing, it's going to take more than a strong breeze to get me out of here."

"You ain't kidding."

"I'm not far from the top. Do you think you can reach in and pull me out?"

"I'll try," she said. She braced herself against the stone rim of the well, leaned forward, and extended her arms.

Van reached up. There was still about three feet between the tips of her fingers and his.

"No good," she said, straightening.

"I've got jumper cables and a towrope in the toolbox in the car."

"I'll be right back!"

Morgan hurried to the car, flung open the back doors, and unlatched the storage box. She rummaged inside but was disgusted by what she found. An empty fifth of Popov Vodka, a half dozen Budweiser beer cans, and the dress the woman from the robbery had been wearing, along with a matching pair of underwear—both dirty.

"Uh!" she said, and slammed the top down. When she and Van had gotten the car back, they'd been so focused on checking to see if the contents of their luggage was there, they hadn't bothered with the storage box. Everything in it was gone. First aid kit, flashlight, flares, jumper cables, towrope. Everything. What the heck had the thieves done with that stuff?

Desperate, she was breathing frantically, searching the car for anything long enough to lower into the well that she could use to pull Van out. She couldn't find anything.

She tried breaking off a branch from the fallen tree. Then she realized that any branch she could break off would probably snap in two against the strain of Van's weight.

Her pulse roared in her ears as she searched frantically, yet came up empty-handed.

For a moment Morgan thought she could tie together a few articles of clothing and get him out, but her common sense and knowledge of fabric told her that only worked in the movies. What she needed was a piece of fabric or material, like a coat or something—one unit long enough to reach to Van and give him leverage to climb out.

When she realized Van's only hope, she slumped against the car. Morgan closed her eyes, but the orange solution flashed in her mind like a neon sign.

* * *

"Morgan! Morgan!"

"Yeah," she answered.

"Where are you?"

"I'm right here," she said. She had walked back to the well, Ashley's wedding dress in hand, and stood for she didn't know how long, thinking about what she had to do.

"What are you doing?"

"I'm thinking," she said.

"Thinking! Lower the cables so I can get out of here. You can think later!"

"The cables are gone," she said dryly. "The towrope, too."

A hurricane of expletives echoed from inside the well. "You'll have to go for help. I'll toss up the keys. Now hurry. I'm up to my knees in water and who knows what kind of bacteria and organisms are in it."

"I've got something that will get you out of there," she said with a thin sigh. She stared at the well and every emotion she had marched right out of her body.

"Then let's go, Allgood!"

She moved closer to the well. He could see her now. She held the dress close to her breast.

"Yes," he said. "That will work. Now hurry. There's something swimming in this water."

She didn't move. She just stroked the dress that contained parts of her soul and blessings for her sister's future happiness.

"Morgan! Throw down the damn dress!"

"Shut up!" she said. "You had no business jumping in there!"

"Morgan," Van said. His voice was calm and resolute.

She had to do it. She had to risk ruining the very thing that had defined her life for the past two weeks.

She took a deep breath and tossed the top of the dress into the abyss.

"Got it!" Van called. "Now step back and hold it tightly so I can get some leverage against these slick rocks."

She did as he asked. Van grunted and huffed. The seams of the dress strained with his weight. When she heard the first few stitches rip, she bit her lip, but held on. More ripping. *Rip, rip, rip!* She felt each one inside her heart. Just when she thought the top of the gown was going to tear away, Van's left hand reached up and grabbed the top of the well. Morgan rushed over and helped him out the rest of the way.

When he was free, they both heaved as if they'd spent hours doing heavy labor.

"Thank you," he said through hard breaths.

"Don't mention it. As a matter of fact, don't mention anything. Can we just get in the car and drive straight to Atlanta? Nonstop. Do not pass *go*. Do not collect two hundred dollars. Do not talk."

She'd just pulled him from a well. She thought he'd be grateful in some way, but instead he eyed her with fresh contempt.

"No problem," he said.

On the day before his road dog's wedding, Van McNeil sat in his own living room and he still couldn't believe Gordon was going to go through with it. Knowing the pain women were capable of causing, he wondered what man in his right mind would willingly volunteer to be tethered to one for the rest of his life.

In the same instant, Morgan's image filled his mind—a beautiful sun-drenched memory—and he wished like a crazy man that she could see the truth that was right in front of her. More importantly, the man who was standing beside her.

Oh, well, he thought. *You win some, you lose some.* But one thing was certain, he wanted nothing more to do with the Killer Joe routine. Mr. Wrong was about to be *somebody's* Mr. Right. Life was too short to go through women like rain through a sieve. And it had taken him way too long to realize that the reason he'd never fallen in love with any of the women he'd dated, was because he was saving his love for Morgan. One day, soon he thought, he would put his feet up with someone and settle down; he now knew he was capable of it.

The phone rang, reminding him there was a real world to deal with. He picked up the receiver.

"McNeil."

"Van! Buddy! How's it going!"

He pulled the phone away from his ear. "Hanging in, Rich. Hanging in. What's up?"

"I was calling to say congrats on the photos! I saw them on the Internet! I guess AOL picked up a few, too!"

"Yeah. But the important thing was the warning. It got out in time so that the NWS had live data to back up the Doppler."

"Yeah, buddy! You are doin' the darn thing!"

Van nodded, wishing he was as excited as his friend. He was proud, no doubt. But excited . . .

"Think about next year's conference. Your photos would make a good session: 'Spotting on your day off!' "

Van laughed. Rich was crazy.

"Well, I gotta go, home dude! You take care and don't be a stranger!"

He smiled at the phone he held two inches from his ear. "I won't."

No sooner had he hung up from Rich when his phone rang again.

"McNeil," he said.

"What up, dog?" Gordon Steele's voice came energetically through the phone.

"You got it," he replied.

"Man, I'm downstairs. Come take a ride with me."

"Why? What's up?"

Gordon hesitated. "I just need to talk about a few things."

Now Van hesitated. "All right, man. I'll be down in a second."

Sounded to him like his homeboy was having second thoughts or was just a little nervous about the wedding. Well, if he wanted to talk, Van had an ear to listen. He grabbed his wallet, cell phone, and keys and headed out the door.

He got into Gordon's sports car and they sped off into traffic. They made small talk until they hit the interstate. Then Gordon clammed up tight and fidgeted like a man guilty of something.

"So where are we going?" Van asked.

"Kenyon's crib."

"Kenyon?" he asked, wondering what Gordon's future brother-in-law had to do with anything.

"Yeah, he said I could hang out there and . . . talk."

Suddenly Van didn't trust him. "You better not be taking me to see Morgan. You're my dog, but I'll break your jaw if you're taking me to see her."

"Calm down, man. I'm not taking you to Morgan." Gordon slid him a sideways glance. "What happened with you two anyway? I thought you were hanging tough in Chicago."

The sisters, Van thought. Like crystal balls. They know all, see all, tell all.

"Nah, man. We just drove back together, that's all."

Gordon leaned over. "And you didn't hit that?"

Van's jaw tightened in anger. "I thought I was riding to hear about your issues."

"Me? I don't have any issues. Are you kidding? I'm getting married to my soul mate tomorrow. I'm the happiest man in the universe."

"Then what's with the 'I need to talk' speech?"

"I do need to talk. And we're going to the mansion to do it. That's all."

"Mm-hmm," Van said, not believing a word from his friend's mouth. They had been friends too long. Something was up. All he knew was Morgan Allgood better not be involved in this "talk" or Gordon would have to get himself another best man.

When they finally pulled up into the block-long Williams' driveway, his body stiffened with disbelief. A line of three cars was parked in the round near the front door. He recognized them immediately and eyed Gordon with contempt.

Gordon recoiled as though Van had actually punched him. "Look, man, if you don't want to go in, just say the word. I'll take you back to your apartment."

Van shook his head in consternation. "I'll go inside. See what they have to say. But if it gets ugly, I'm out. Got it?"

"Got it," he said and escorted him inside.

The sight of the men in the library made Van pensive. This was it. If he could survive this, he could survive anything.

"What's up, fellas?" he said.

Kenyon Williams, Xavier Allgood, Ross Hayward, and Cleon Fairchild sat in large expensive chairs. Waiting. They were the significant others of the Allgood sisters.

"What's up?" they responded. Their gazes darted one to the other. They were just as hesitant as he was. He and Gordon took their seats and then it dawned on him.

"Oh, I know what's up," Van said. "Your women have closed down conjugal operations until this thing between me and Morgan is fixed, right?" They couldn't fool the kid. He knew whupped men when he saw them, and these brothers looked like they knew a thing or two about giving in to women.

Ross snorted like a horse. "Man, please. Amara's switch *stays* on."

Laughter and retorts of "Lucky dog!" came from the group.

"You all don't know this, but Ashley and I are making love right this very moment, spiritually. I feel her vibe, she feels mine. We *never* stop making love."

All the men stared at Gordon as if he'd just grown seven arms.

"Man, shut up!" Xavier said.

"Is he for real?" came Haughton Storm's voice from the speakerphone.

Kenyon shook his head. "Despite your efforts to ruin all our reputations, no, brother Van, they are not holding out on us."

"And we don't want them to!" came the truth finally from Cleon Fairchild. "So we've planned this little . . . intervention. And for the record," he said, turning to Ross, "keep that information about my daughter Amara to yourself, please."

Van had heard enough. The Allgood women had these brothers brainwashed. It was sad. He felt sorry for them.

"Look, fellas, this is really—"

"Important?" Xavier finished.

"No. I was about to say none of your business and not that deep."

That must have bothered Cleon. He stood up and approached Van like he knew him.

"Van, look around. We wouldn't be here if it wasn't that deep. Now have you ever seen the movie *Soul Food?*"

"Yeah, I've seen it."

"Remember any of it?"

"Sure."

"Well, this family functions the same way as the family in the movie. We're all for one, like the Musketeers. Now, I'm not trying to say we're lovey-dovey all the time, that we always get along, or that we like each other twenty-four-seven. But one thing we are all the time is family. And to us that means that no matter what or how long it takes, we work through our own."

"What's all that got to do with me? I'm not in your family."

"But according to the sisters, you should be," Gordon said.

"So that means you all just go out, grab a brother, and hem him up until he gives in?" Van asked.

First laughter, then quiet, then the men's synchronized answer, "Yes."

Van had seen enough, heard enough. If he wanted to forgive Morgan, he would do it in his time and on his terms. He refused to be blackmailed, bullied, or strongly suggested into something akin to a shotgun wedding. "Gordon, are you going to give me a ride back or do I have to walk?"

The crash of thunder outside pissed Van off. *They say when it rains it pours.* Why was it happening to him literally? A thought struck him like the lightning outside. "You all planned this, didn't you? You picked this storm so that walking would be a bad option, didn't you?"

"Guilty," Gordon admitted. He laughed. "Playas don't like to get wet."

When everyone laughed, he couldn't help but laugh, too. Yet there was only a small amount of truth in that statement for him. The reality was, he loved weather. Loved to be in the middle of it. It was unpredictable and everchanging, unlike most people, whose minds he could almost read. Truth be told, he liked being wrong. Loved it when Mother Nature fooled him and the most sophisticated weather prediction equipment on the planet. One could never really have a relationship with the weather. The closest you could come was a distant friend who settled down every now and then, long enough for you to see her smile or cry and then dance off again.

He had a challenge going with Mother Nature. A long-standing wager. Of course, she won most of the time. The odds were always in favor of the house, but with the gamble came the chance of beating the odds. Victories like that came sweet, but paled in comparison to the sweet victory he would have had loved to have had with Morgan.

"Just what is it you think needs intervening?" he asked, ready to repel any response they gave. Why was this so important to them?

"We just wanted to give you a few pointers. 'Cause from what we've heard, you're going about this all the wrong way."

"Well, if that's what this is about, then get ready for a surprise. It's not my fault. I'm not in the wrong."

Gordon shook his head. "I hate to ground your cloud, dog, but this just in: when it comes to women, we are *always* wrong."

The men in the room laughed.

"Yep. Best thing you can do is apologize and move on," Ross added.

"Move on? Would you move on if you were having a fight with your woman and she used your cell phone to call another man to come and get her?"

All the men in the room drew in an audible breath.

"Morgan did that?" Xavier, her brother, asked.

"Morgan did that," Van answered flatly.

Cleon took his seat and rubbed his temples. "You sure it wasn't because of something you did to her?"

"I'm positive."

Gordon blew out a breath. "Damn, man. I didn't know. None of us did."

"Yeah, man, sorry. That's on her then," Haughton said on the phone.

"Then you know what that means . . ." Kenyon said.

"What?"

"It means the sisters will have a meeting and get her straight."

Van could only hope.

"If they do and she apologizes, will you forgive her?" Gordon asked.

Van thought about it. After all he and Morgan had experienced on their trip, for her to turn to another man, even for transportation, was a hard slap in his face, a brutal insult and the kind of behavior that made him question her sincerity.

He glanced at each man in the room, then settled his gaze on his close friend. "I don't know, Gordon. I just don't know."

Chapter Nineteen

"Morgan, the dress is fine!"

"Not yet, but it will be," Morgan said. She checked the dress again for the eighth or ninth time that day. After repairing the rips and sending the dress to one-hour emergency dry-cleaning, she still fussed over the dress like a mother hen over her chicks. She'd only had to make a few alterations—her sister's hips were spreading even though she wouldn't admit it—and it had fit perfectly. But she wanted to make sure there were no leftover traces from the ordeal the dress had suffered to get to Ashley. None.

"Are you sure you want to wear it? I told you everything that happened to it. I wouldn't blame you if—"

"Morgan, stop!" Ashley insisted, placing her hand on Morgan's shoulder. Ashley stood behind her while Morgan sat at her sewing machine in her sewing room, double, triple, quadruple checking all the seams to make sure they were intact, and scanning every inch of the orange star-burst fabric to make sure there were no smudges or imperfections of any kind.

"Don't you get it? I want to wear it *because* of everything it's been through. Because of everything *you've* been through. It's the most special gift I could ever receive—besides Gordon."

Morgan nodded her understanding. On the most special day of her life, Ashley would wear the dress she had made. The tradition would not be broken. The Allgood women all became wives in a Morgan original gown.

Maybe there was something to this dressmaking thing after all. She might actually give Connie's offer of going into business some serious thought. Especially since ESPN had called to tell her she didn't get the job. The representative didn't say it, but Morgan heard the words "too old" and "not enough broadcasting experience" in her voice.

"What are you thinking about?" Ashley asked.

"My future," she said honestly.

"Wonderful," Ashley said, beaming. "Your future with Van?"

There it was. She had wondered when Ashley was going to bring that up. She'd held out for almost an entire day—an Allgood record.

"Van made it very clear during the drive home that he didn't want anything to do with a future with me."

Ashley fumbled awkwardly inside the purse-pouch Morgan had made her, placed it on a side table between them, and sat down. "Why? What happened?"

It was going to come out sooner or later. She might as well make it sooner. Morgan was just glad Ash had respected her wishes and had not brought the entire family with her when she'd come over today. That encounter would have been way too stressful.

She took a deep breath and recounted all the foolish things she had done and said to Van. When she told Ashley about leaving with Brax during the storm, and her hesitation to use the dress to get Van out of the well, Ashley's face grew sad with concern. When she finished her tale, they sat in silence, but Morgan could have sworn she heard voices in the room.

"Don't you have a potion I could use to fix this?" Morgan asked, thinking of her sister's propensity for mysticism.

"Sorry," she said. Her voice came out quiet, remorseful. Not at all like her typical bubbly self.

"No?" Morgan said, irritation raising her voice an octave. "My sister, who can read palms, tarot cards, tea leaves, and auras, doesn't have some kind of spiritual mojo she can lay on me so I can get my man back? What kind of world are we living in?" Morgan choked back the sobs threatening to break through her resolve.

"My sister, you have to understand, your love for Van is the most powerful potion in the universe. Nothing is stronger. If you want him back, you'll have to use your own personal magic and cast your own spell."

Morgan just stared inwardly at all the places within herself that missed Van terribly.

"What did you say?" Morgan asked.

"Nothing," Ashley said, smiling strangely.

"Ash?" she said. Morgan felt something weird was going on. "Did you conjure some spirits or something?" she joked.

"No, heifer! It's us! And we think you should go get your man!"

Morgan looked around. Where was that coming from? "Roxy?" she said. "Where are you?"

When Ash's eyes darted from Morgan to her purse and back again, Morgan understood.

"You've got me on speaker?" she said, trying to strangle her sister with her eyes.

"Sorry, sister. It was either that or bring them with me. And you said—"

Morgan got up from the chair. Paced in the small room. "I guess what I said doesn't matter."

Ashley pulled her cell phone from her purse and placed it on the table.

"Aunt Morgan," Amara, her niece, began, "I think you owe Van an apology."

"Not the baby," Morgan said. "You didn't bring the baby in on this, too."

"Uh, Aunt Morgan, I'm not a baby anymore. I'm married with children and you should be, too."

"As a matter of fact," her sister Yolanda cut in, "*my baby* is going to have a baby. See what you've been missing gallivanting around with that weatherman?"

Morgan's heart leaped. Her niece had married a man who already had three children. But to have one of her own . . . "Amara?"

"Yep, I'm two months pregnant. Aunt Ashley says it's a boy!"

"Well, she would know," Morgan said, happy for her niece.

"She knows something else, too," Marti added. "She knows you have to be woman enough to go after the man you love. You're going through a trouble spot right now, but it will pass. You have to believe that. You have to create that future for yourself."

If anyone knew about rough patches, it was Morgan's sister Marti. She and her husband had made it through a big rough patch before they got married. And today they were doing fine.

Morgan sighed. "I doubt if Van will welcome me back with open arms."

"You'll never know until you try," Ashley said with hope in her eyes.

"Okay," Morgan said, "tonight, after the rehearsal dinner I'll pull Van aside. I'll talk to him and apologize."

"Good!"

"Excellent!"

"All right!"

"The universe is on your side, my sister."

Morgan hoped Ashley was right. Because if she wasn't, she didn't know how she could live with the pain of going on without Van McNeil in her life.

By the time Morgan went to bed that night, she'd discovered that the universe might have been on her side, but Mr. Wrong wasn't. During the rehearsal, Van made it quite clear he wouldn't forgive her, apology or not. When he spoke to her, he used clipped tones, one-word sentences. He made sure they weren't in the same room for any significant length of time. When he looked at her, the disdain she saw living there pricked her heart like a splinter.

In bed, she closed her eyes but knew she would not be able to sleep.

True to form, Ashley's wedding was as unique as she was. As a woman who rejected tradition in favor of her own creative impulses, she had none of the standard trappings of a traditional wedding on her special day.

First, all her family and friends gathered in a country garden. There were chairs at long tables for everyone. Instead of gifts and cards, guests were invited to bring a covered dish for a community feast. The bride and groom were escorted into the garden by two dancers, a man and a woman, their choreography expressing the union of two people joined together by God. After the dance, any who wanted to stood and gave a testimony as to why Ashley and Gordon were soul mates and why their community of friends supported their union. The final testimonies were given by Van and Morgan, as best man and maid of honor.

With the crowd's blessing, Ashley and Gordon then recited the vows they had written. A minister then pronounced them man and wife, and Gordon laid a kiss on Morgan's sister to end all kisses. The crowed cheered and clapped enthusiastically.

Morgan had never seen her sister look more beautiful. The orange silk dress with all the mementos and blessings of the Allgood family gave no hint of the ordeal it had survived; the dress only served to help make her sister the most radiant bride Morgan had ever seen. Morgan wiped tears from her eyes, feeling more pride than she'd ever known for the most wonderful garment she'd ever made and for her sister Ashley Allgood-Steele for having the courage and intelligence to marry the man of her dreams.

The happy newlyweds turned to the guests with grins a mile wide. "Let's eat!" Gordon shouted.

Yolanda had cooked enough food for an army. She was the best cook in the family, and usually Morgan would knock somebody down to get to her mac and cheese. Yolanda had even made her favorite, peanut butter pie. But Morgan couldn't eat.

While Xavier sang love songs for the guests, Morgan went through the motions of filling up her plate. But it was no use. Her appetite was on the tip of Van McNeil's tongue. If only he would find it in his heart to say he forgave her. Until then, she would be miserable and no good for anything.

She stared at him all through dinner. A couple of times her sisters came over and asked her if she was all right. She said yes and continued to hope she would catch his eye. Morgan prayed for a signal that meant he might be willing to talk to her. Either that, or she would just go over anyway. Make him listen to her.

When he finished a second helping of tofu spaghetti, their eyes caught and held. His gaze was more relaxed this time. Less venomous. She grew hopeful until the moment he got up and she heard the words "good-bye" and "catch you later" flow from his lips.

The bottom dropped out of her stomach and she knew she couldn't let him leave. Not without telling him how wrong she she'd been. She had to do it in a way in which he understood. She didn't know where she was going for a while, or even what she wanted, but now she was sure. She was sure she wanted him, and she never wanted to look back.

Morgan hurried to catch up with him. The blood pounded so loudly in her ears, she couldn't hear anything else. Van shook hands with Gordon, kissed Ashley on the cheek, and said his good-byes. Ashley's eyes found Morgan in the crowd. *Do something,* they said.

Morgan's breaths came so fast and ragged, she felt like she was having a panic attack. Her thoughts spun wildly, but she knew she had to think of something, say something. Shout, scream, holler *stop*!

"I'm a widow from the south side! My ol' man left me with back rent and six kids!" she shouted at the top of her lungs, knowing that she had completely lost her mind. "Van!" she said.

He stopped. Turned toward her, his face still and unreadable.

Morgan slammed her hands on her hips and hoped she looked good in the off-white dress she wore. "I said my ol' man left me with back rent and six kids! What you gonna do about that?"

The buzz of the guests had stopped. Even her sister-in-law Destiny, who had been happily snapping pictures the whole time, lowered her camera and stared. All eyes were on the two of them. Morgan took a step closer.

Anguish washed freshly over Van's face. "What are you talking about, Morgan?"

The pain in his eyes was acute. It matched the pain she'd felt being without him. It was time for the pain to end. She knew it. And she wanted Van to know she knew it.

Morgan stuck her hip out, determined to play the role to the hilt. She had only seen the movie once, so she hoped she was remembering the scene correctly. In any case, she was going for it. She was going for her man!

Van's features relaxed. He looked sad and tired. And just when she thought he was about to let her in, he turned and started to walk away.

Tears streamed down her face. She knew her sisters would never let her live this down, but she didn't care. She would not give up.

"Van, please. I know I was wrong and you were right. I was scared. And stupid. I love you and I know you love me. Oh, baby, please. . . ." She was shaking and sure her tears were ruining her makeup. But it didn't matter. Nothing mattered until the man that she loved returned to her life.

She reached out. "Van," she said, anguish taking her voice. "I know now that you're not Mr. Wrong. You're so right for me, it hurts. It hurts to be alone in this world without you. And for the first time in my life, I'm surrounded by my family, but I still feel alone."

He stopped and again turned slowly toward her. Concern played on his face as though he was considering something monumental. And then a miracle happened—Van's eyes sparkled and the sun came out in Morgan's life.

"Do you want me to help you with your back rent, Lady Mahogany?"

Happiness burst open in her soul. She took a deep breath and shouted, "Hell, no! I want you to help me get my ol' man back!"

The slightest hint of a smile broke across Van's face. Someone in the crowd yelled, "All right, now!"

"What are you prepared to do to get him back?" he asked, taking a step toward her.

She could barely breathe or think, but she had to answer him. "Anything," Morgan whispered.

Van took another step toward her. Smiled a little

more. "Then, madame, if you really want your ol' man back, are you prepared to stand by him when the going gets rough?"

"Yes," she said, taking a step toward him.

"Madame, are you prepared to be by his side through sunshine?

Morgan smiled through her tears. "Yes."

"Cloudy days?"

"Yes!" she shouted.

"Rain?"

Her joy was so great, she thought her heart would burst. "Yes! Yes!"

"Bright skies?"

"Yes! Baby, yes!"

"Then, madame, if you are willing to do all that . . . I *guarantee* you I'll get you your ol' man back."

The wedding guests cheered. Morgan and Van rushed toward each other and swept each other into a soul-wrenching embrace. Morgan tried to speak to tell Van just how much she loved him, to assure him she would never hurt him again. Tears choked her words. Van held her tightly, stroked her hair, and said, "I know, baby. I know."

Chapter Twenty

Van McNeil stared down at the angel in his arms and could barely believe his eyes. Morgan Allgood was not only in his arms, but in his heart. They'd been together at his place for eight days and she hadn't left yet. Even when her agent called to say he had go-sees for her, she'd let him know she was taking time off from modeling and would contact him in a week or two. Van had also gotten a few extra days away from the station and he and Morgan had spent most of their quality time pleasuring each other beyond words and exploring the meaning of their newfound love.

He tried not to disturb her sleep, but he couldn't stop touching her, couldn't stop kissing her, and would never stop loving her. She'd stolen something from him he never wanted back . . . his heart.

For the tenth, or probably hundredth, time that morning, Van bent to kiss Morgan's delicious mouth. This time her lips came alive and pressed softly back against his.

"I didn't mean to wake you," he said.

"Um," she moaned, snuggling closer. "That's okay. What time is it?"

"I have no idea," he said. And it was true. He didn't

care what time it was. He only cared about being with Morgan and keeping her happy. His heart swelled with contentment when her smile reminded him that he never again had to look at her picture and hope the woman he loved was okay. For that blessing he was willing to endure her well-meaning sisters and their husbands.

The lips he'd seen in dozens of magazines, smiling or pursed next to products like Temperton's Soft Wave and Brown Glow Magic, the mouth he'd watched and studied that uttered phrases like, "This way, please," and, "I love it!" called to him silently only inches away. He'd already taken these lips, a queen's lips, Morgan's lips, gently like he was nursing a pomegranate or a plum, deftly sucking sweet juices that cooled and refreshed him. And her response was always the same—a long, soft breath of surrender floating into his own parted mouth and warming his very soul. He wanted her lips and all that came with them until eternity reset itself and started again.

She opened her eyes. They looked drunk and sleepy. "What are you thinking about?" she asked. She reached up, stroked his hair. He kissed the back of her hand.

"There's something I want to tell you," he said.

She smiled lazily. "Yes?"

He leaned closer to her. The scent of powder and Morgan's perfume made him crazy. "I have to whisper it," he said.

"Ooh!" she gasped, staring up at him.

He lowered his head and took a deep breath. "I love you, Morgan Allgood. I love you more than any man has ever loved a woman. I want you in my life now . . . and forever. And I want to give you all the things you need to make you happy. If you want to swim, I'll be the water. If you want to eat, I'll be your nourishment. When you wake up, I want to put the sun in the sky for you. And if you ever need it, I want to be the soft place where you fall. I will never leave you, Morgan, and if you stay with me, I promise long, satisfying nights, and if you ever asked me, I would bring you the world on a plate.

"Stay with me, Morgan . . . forever."

Tears stung the corners of her eyes. Morgan stared into the face of the man she loved more than her own life. To her, he was precious—dipped in gold. It only took her a moment to know that she loved him, days to trust that love, and now that she did, she never wanted to be without it.

"Van, baby, I love you. And I have to tell you what's in my heart. I will never, ever leave you and I promise to love you with my entire heart and soul for the rest of my life."

The sun's rays glowed warm and golden on Van's gorgeous skin. Her reflection shone in his eyes. She had never felt more beautiful. In his arms, Morgan felt infinite peace and satisfaction. Now that she was in his life, she knew, without one ounce of doubt, *exactly* where she was going.

She couldn't wait for the journey to begin!

Dear Readers,

Thank you for joining Morgan and Van on their road trip to love. I knew the only thing that would get these two together was if they were forced to face each other until they realized they were staring at their true love. I hope you enjoyed the journey. Some of you may recognize Morgan from my Allgood Series. Please check my Web site if you would like more information about the books on the Allgood family.

My main goal for *With Open Arms* was to make you smile. Drop me a line if you get a chance and let me know if I succeeded.

I wish you safe journeys that lead to love and blessings!

Until next time,

Kim Louise

P.O. Box 31554
Omaha, NE 68131
MsKimLouise@aol.com
www.kimlouise.com

About the Author

Kim Louise believes it is her life's purpose and joy to put pen to paper, create stories, and literally entertain. Writing since she was a teenager, Kim is a hopeful romantic who has been blessed beyond measure by having her poems, novels, and other writings published and available to readers all over the U.S. She is a national bestselling author, the recipient of the University of Nebraska 2005 Women of Color Award, a sought-after speaker/presenter, and a B-movie buff. In her spare time, Kim reads, creates scrapbooks, makes greeting cards, and plays hide and seek with her 2-year-old grandson Zay.

Shane
773 220 — 8148

More Arabesque Romances by
Donna Hill

__TEMPTATION	0-7860-0070-8	$4.99US/$5.99CAN
__A PRIVATE AFFAIR	1-58314-158-8	$5.99US/$7.99CAN
__CHARADE	0-7860-0545-9	$4.99US/$6.50CAN
__INTIMATE BETRAYAL	0-7860-0396-0	$4.99US/$6.50CAN
__PIECES OF DREAMS	1-58314-183-9	$5.99US/$7.99CAN
__CHANCES ARE	1-58314-197-9	$5.99US/$7.99CAN
__A SCANDALOUS AFFAIR	1-58314-118-9	$5.99US/$7.99CAN
__SCANDALOUS	1-58314-248-7	$5.99US/$7.99CAN
__THROUGH THE FIRE	1-58314-130-8	$5.99US/$7.99CAN

Available Wherever Books Are Sold!

Check out our website at www.BET.com.